HIDDEN THINGS

HARPER Voyager

An Imprint of HarperCollins*Publishers*

```
H A S E T I O J M D I L N L H B I V I
N I O C E U R E R D E A X D O T F B T
C Y M E S E G Z M C R G R S F D C M S
Y P H I D D E N C N P P J B P D H R E
L J I A D S O Q I N Y H R C Y L D C G
D B S E E M Y A Y R H Y M E S E G Y Z
S P Z M C R G R S F F D C M N I O L M
E D C E U R E R d E A X D O T F B D C
E H T H A S E T i o J M D I L N L S R
M I H B I V I R S T y N I P H R I E G
Y A I T O L G C Z E A c E L M O N E R
A D N L R J D X W B T U e V Y C S M S
Y S G Q Y R E H A R L E Q U I N I Y F
R O S X T E G L O I F R I E N D S A F
H Q D R A G O N L O G U I D E O K Y D
Y I M W S R M J M Y D E S J X E E R C
M N T L Q E D F t e s t e r m a n H M
E Y H T P T M W F P G J C L O W N Y N
S Y M E S E G Z M C R G R S F D C M I
O C E U R E R D E A X D O T F B T H A
S E T I O J M D I L N L H B I V I R S
```

HIDDEN THINGS. Copyright © 2012 by Doyce Testerman. All rights reserved. Printed in the United States of America. No part of this book may be used or reproduced in any manner whatsoever without written permission except in the case of brief quotations embodied in critical articles and reviews. For information address HarperCollins Publishers, 10 East 53rd Street, New York, NY 10022.

HarperCollins books may be purchased for educational, business, or sales promotional use. For information please write: Special Markets Department, HarperCollins Publishers, 10 East 53rd Street, New York, NY 10022.

FIRST EDITION

Designed by Shannon Plunkett

Library of Congress Cataloging-in-Publication Data has been applied for.

ISBN 978-0-06-210811-1

12 13 14 15 16   OV/RRD   10 9 8 7 6 5 4 3 2 1

For Russel Testerman, who showed us the joy to
be found in telling a good story

But when, Calliope, thy loud harp rang—
In Epic grandeur rose the lofty strain;
The clash of arms, the trumpet's awful clang
Mixed with the roar of conflict on the plain;
The ardent warrior bade his coursers wheel,
Trampling in dust the feeble and the brave,
Destruction flashed upon his glittering steel,
While round his brow encrimsoned laurels waved,
And o'er him shrilly shrieked the demon of the grave.

From "An Ode to Music," by James G. Percival

HIDDEN THINGS

1

A **RINGING PHONE** jerked Calliope Jenkins out of a sound sleep. She fumbled for the source of the noise, startled and trying to blink her eyes into focus. The blocky red alarm clock LED hovered in the darkness like a bad memory, reading 1:43˙.

On the third ring, she managed to find the handset and roll it off the cradle into her palm. "H'lo?"

"Calli," said the voice on the other end of the line. "It's me."

She smiled and pushed herself farther underneath the comforter. "*Hey.* I thought you'd be home and asleep by now."

The strange, hiccuped silence of an interrupted cellular connection broke through the call for a moment. "A few things came up; I'm still out on the road, actually."

"Cripes, really? When—" A murmur drifted from the opposite side of the bed. Calliope half glanced in that direction and lowered her voice. "Hang on a sec." She got up and padded toward the door to the bedroom, snagging her robe as she stepped into the hallway. "When do you think you're going to get back?"

"I don't . . . Everything's pretty complicated."

"Complicated how?" Yawning, Calliope shuffled into the kitchen and pulled open the refrigerator door.

"Can't. Too late to get into any of it, anyway. You going to be all right?"

She shrugged, still staring blankly into the refrigerator. "I'm fine, except it's two in the morning."

She could hear him smile on the other end of the line. "Cranky. You should take a shower and wake up."

She pushed hair out of her face. "See, this's your main confusion. I don't *want* to wake up. I wasn't actually lying in bed thinking, 'Oh, I wish someone would call and give me a reason to get up.' I wasn't thinking anything. I was *asleep*. I was enjoying it. I'd like to get back to it sometime tonight."

"So . . ." She could hear the smile broaden in his voice. "No shower?"

She smiled. "Freak."

"Hardly."

"We could use that for the new ads: 'Joshua White: where mind and gutter meet.' You'd be very popular."

"Wrong kind of clientele."

"Because our current client base is so normal." She frowned at the open refrigerator. "What *are* you working on right now?"

"It's a new one, kind of. I shouldn't have taken it."

"Obviously."

Another pause on the other end of the line. "Yeah. Say, I was hoping you could . . . I know it would be a huge hassle for you, but I was wondering if you could talk to Lauren for me and explain what's going on."

Calliope's eyebrows drew together; she pushed the refrigerator door shut. "You can't call her?"

"It's really all I could manage to call you."

"Whatever. They only allow you one call before they put you back in with—"

"Seriously."

She nudged at the raised edge between the dining room carpet and kitchen tile with her toe. "Can we go back to talking about me in the shower?"

"It's all right if you don't want to. I'll understand."

"You're going to owe me."

She felt the relief on the other end of the line. "I'm going to owe you huge, Calli. Huge."

"Yeah . . ." She wrapped an arm across her midsection, pulling the robe close. "That all you needed to wake me up at two in the morning for?"

"That and the shower thing. You're the best, Cal, I swear. Go back to sleep. Tell your guy I'm sorry about the call."

"'Kay." She glanced out the kitchen window at the pale streetlights. "Just be safe."

"Don't worry about me. I'm fine."

"Sure."

"Safe as houses. Go to bed. Watch out for the hidden things."

Her attention came back to the phone. "The hidden things what?"

The line was already dead. Calliope turned her gaze back to the window, the phone forgotten in her hand. Seconds passed before she shivered inside the folds of the robe, set the phone down on the counter, and headed back to the bedroom. The red LED of the clock read 1:48˙.

═⌒

The clawed thing took the phone from Joshua. "She sounds . . . nice."

Joshua snorted; his eyelids, glossy and dark, sagged. "Sure."

The thing fidgeted, picking at the scraps of clothing clinging to its body. "I'm glad you decided to stay."

"For now." Joshua was looking at him, but his eyes were unfocused, watching something far in the past; something better. The wind outside pushed at the walls, tested the windows and roof while the creature watched the man. Shadows and memories and hidden things scrabbled through the darkness, taunting both and filling the space between them. "Long enough to get this straightened out."

"You mean fix it." The thing's face twisted; the damaged side a sneer, the other—the one Josh knew—a sad smile.

"I suppose." Josh settled his shoulders, ignoring his exhaustion. "I made a promise, didn't I?"

"And you always keep your promises."

He turned back to the window of the empty room. "I try."

"You try." The thing's voice was bitter. "Not when you won't—"

"Shut . . ." Joshua's voice was soft. His chin dropped toward his chest. "Just . . . shut up. I'm going to try. *We* will." He half turned, really looking at the creature for the first time, then looking away. "Maybe we can't. *If* we can't, I'll head home and try to figure something else out."

"Head home?" The thing's face twisted, caught between anger and a kind of grief that was older and much, much worse. "You *are* home, Josh." It took a step toward him. "I thought you knew that." Around it, the snickering, skittering, scraping things grew louder and louder, like locusts in the summer. The sound shook Joshua from his reverie; he looked from shadow to shadow, trying to track the source of the growing noise, his eyes going wide.

"Mikey?"

Thirteen seconds later, Joshua White was dead.

J B P D H I A D S O Q I N Y C Y L
H R C Y L D S E E M Y A Y R D S E
H Y M E S E G Z M C R G R S E M Y
F F D C M N I O C E U R E R A Y R
D E A X D O T F B T H A S E H Y M
T I O J M D I L N L H B I V E S E
I R S T Y N I P H R I I T O G Z M
L G C Z E A C E L M O N N L C R G
R J D X W B T U E V Y C S G R S F
Q Y R   F D C
S X T   M N I
S D R   O C E

STAGE ONE

O K M W S R M J M Y D E S J U R E
X E E T L Q E D F T E S T E R D E
R M A N H T P T M W F P G J A X D
C L O H R U G E O G P H E T O T F
E A C E L M O N N L R J D X B T H
W B T U E V Y C S G Q Y R E A S E
H A R L E Q U I N I S X T E T I O
G L O I F R I E N D S D R A J M D
G O N L O G U I D E O K M W I L N
S R M J M Y D E S J X E E T L H B
L Q E D F T E S T E R M A N I V I
H T P T M W F P G J C L O W R S T
N E G I O H D T U L O H F D Y N I
B O J N M V R W Z O Y W Q J P H R
W R H Y V S I L P J N F C W O K S

2

THERE WAS COFFEE waiting by the time Calliope made it to the kitchen the next morning. Not a good sign. Tom's way of starting any kind of touchy conversation involved a preemptive peace offering.

She filled up a cup and took a drink, keeping her eyes on the mug. "Thanks."

"No problem." Tom picked at his acoustic guitar while his own coffee cooled in front of him.

The guitar was another bad sign; he expected a fight. He'd unconsciously pick up the instrument whenever things got tense, as though using the rigid body as a shield.

"You didn't have to get up—"

"It's no problem," he interrupted. He turned his attention to the guitar strings. "I was already awake anyway."

It was a simple enough comment, but gave Calliope all the context she needed. "Yeah. I'm sorry about the phone call last night."

Tom's eyes, barely visible behind lowered lashes, flicked over her clothes. "I assume Josh made it back into town all right?"

Calliope shook her head. "No, he—" She paused, processing what she'd seen. "Wait, what?" She scowled. "What's wrong with my clothes?"

"Nothing." His eyes were blue and steady and beautiful and, at that exact moment, annoyed her. He reached for his coffee and took a drink, looking at nothing in particular over the rim of the cup. "You look nice."

Calliope glanced down at the skirt she had on beneath her usual leather jacket. "You—" She cut herself off. He hated it when she analyzed him. "I've got a meeting with Lauren."

He dropped his hands and his attention to the guitar strings. "Ah. Lauren."

Calliope set her own cup down, hard. "What?"

"Nothing." He tuned a string. "Josh's wife, right?"

Calliope's face and chest were hot, her hands cold. "Yes."

Tom strummed a test chord. "I'm . . . sure that will be tough." He glanced up and caught her expression—raised a hand in a gesture of surrender. "Hey, it's none of my business."

"You're—"

"I don't have any right to comment on late-night phone calls with old boyfriends."

"We *work*—"

"Yeah," he said. "I know."

The tone in his voice—tired the way DMV workers and court bailiffs were tired—stopped her, drained the heat out of her chest. It was the sound of someone who had stopped listening, simply to protect himself.

And Calliope felt exactly the same way.

The kitchen was quiet, except for a few tuneless chords.

"I'm sorry, Tom."

He searched her face, looking for the anger that usually

accompanied this particular dance. His shoulders relaxed. "Hey, don't worry about it; it's a bad morning. I get—"

"I should never have asked you to move in." She walked out of the kitchen, her voice echoing strangely back at her. "Pack your stuff. Get out of my house. I've got to go. I'm late."

The house was quiet as she pulled the door shut behind her.

⟜⟝

The air around the corner of Bush and Taylor changed when Vikous arrived.

It was a distinctly unmagical place—everything from the streets to the sidewalks to the head-down pedestrians colored in various shades of gray—but for a moment, the air changed: filled with a hush stolen from a magician's audience, thick with the sound of a daydreaming crowd.

A bus roared past a double-parked garbage truck, clouding the air with diesel smoke and timetables, and then he was there—hands jammed into his pockets, leaning against the cheap, painted façade of a three-story building as though he had been there all along—maybe he *had* been there all along, unnoticed. Pedestrians blinked, wondering what they'd been thinking about just then. A few checked their wallets as they walked by.

He was bundled in several layers of clothing under a threadbare trench coat, a hooded sweatshirt pulled up to cover his head and most of his face. Black eyes, shining like coat buttons, watched the building across from him. Watched the Jeep pull up outside. Watched a scowling Calliope Jenkins get out, unlock the door beneath a sign that read WHITE INVESTIGATIONS, and go inside.

By contrast, no one was watching Vikous. Passersby failed

to acknowledge his presence even when forced to step around his (unusually large) feet. He didn't bother making apologies; did not in fact seem to see the other people on the street any more than they saw him. He watched the door Calliope had entered and for several minutes—almost a quarter of an hour—that was all he did. At 8:42, he pushed himself away from the building façade, shifted his shoulders underneath his coat, muttered something that might have been "time to get to work," and started across the street.

He'd made it four steps past the curb when a police car pulled up in front of the White Investigations office. Two uniformed officers got out and went inside. Two minutes later they emerged, Calliope (looking even more grim) walking between them, got back into the car, and drove off.

"Great." Vikous watched them go; it might be accurate to say he stared. "Just . . . great."

⌒

Thirty-five minutes later, Calliope walked into Lauren Hollis-White's private office, under escort. Two men standing off to the side turned toward the door at her arrival. She ignored them and walked directly up to the woman's desk.

"Lauren." Calliope's jaw was tight, her eyes bright. Lauren herself looked drawn and pale, but unsurprised by Calliope's entrance.

She extended her hand without standing. "Calliope." Her eyes flickered. "I like that skirt."

"Thanks," Calliope said. "What the fuck's up with the cops?"

Lauren blinked, her arm still extended up and out at an awkward angle. She withdrew her hand and sat back. "It wasn't my idea." She looked over to the two men who'd been watching the exchange. Her voice was clipped and tense.

The younger of the two stepped forward. His dark, curly hair was trimmed neatly and his face was friendly in a sad sort of way. "We apologize for bringing you down here this way, Ms. Jenkins. I'm Detective Darryl Johnson and this is Special Agent Walker." He indicated the lanky, spare-framed man behind him. "We understand that you left a message with Mrs. Hollis-White's office this morning indicating you had information regarding her husband?"

Calliope nodded. She'd called early, during her drive to the office, knowing she'd get Lauren's answering service. "Is there a problem? I was supposed to—" She stopped. Lauren, staring out the window, had let out a strangled sound somewhere between a gasp and a sob. Her eyes were wide and damp. Calli turned back to the detective. "What's—"

Agent Walker moved forward. "Miss Jenkins, Joshua White's body was found at approximately six A.M. this morning, just outside the city limits of Harper's Ferry, Iowa. Foul play was involved." The corners of his mouth tugged down, as though he'd bitten into something that had gone foul. "No offense, but we were wondering what you knew about it."

~

Calliope dropped into the chair behind her desk and sighed. Afternoon sunlight forced its way in through the dirty window across the room and lit up dust motes floating in its path before it fell, exhausted, across the worn carpet. She glared at the patch of light, then at her skirt. She had no idea why she'd worn it; she'd had no illusions that it would help when she

met with Lauren, even before everything she found out this
morning.

> *"Josh wanted me to tell Lauren that he was hung up on a job and
> wouldn't be back when he expected. He definitely didn't sound like
> he was in any kind of trouble."*
>
> *"You and Mr. White both work in the same private investigation
> agency, Ms. Jenkins?"*
>
> *"We are the agency."*
>
> *"I see. And do you know the nature of this new contract?"*
>
> *"No. Josh handled it. I only knew he was headed out of town and
> when he thought he'd get back, which was last night. I can check
> the office for records but I think he had everything with him—it
> was very short notice. Are you absolutely sure—"*
>
> *"Don't you have family in that area of the country, Miss
> Jenkins?"*
>
> *" . . . What?"*
>
> *"You're familiar with the area Mr. White was found in."*
>
> *"What? Harper's Ferry? Not really. It's hours from my family's
> place, and I haven't been back there in ten years."*
>
> *"Was Mr. White? Had he been in the region before?"*
>
> *"Yeah. He grew up around there. We drove there, once, a few
> years ago."*
>
> *"What was the nature of that visit?"*

Calliope stared at her desk and the stack of envelopes
she'd dumped across it when she'd opened the office that
morning—bills and junk mail. There was only one message
on the machine. Calliope hit the playback.

"Calli, it's Josh."

The connection was abysmal, even worse than it had been
last night. "Listen, things have gotten a lot more complicated.

It'd probably be better if you didn't tell Lauren about what's going on, at least until I figure everything out."

Calliope stared at the machine. The next few seconds on the message were choked with static and nearly inaudible to her, smothered under the too-loud sound of her own breathing and the thump of her pulse. She started to lean closer, turning her head and lowering her ear toward the speaker to pick out anything she could, but the static suddenly cleared, leaving the recording so clear she could make out the rasp of Josh's stubble against the mouthpiece. " . . . get hold of him and he'll be able to explain most of this to you. I'll see you soon."

3

DETECTIVE JOHNSON SAT back in the chair across the desk from Calliope, a single vertical crease between his brows. "I don't know what I'm supposed to be hearing, Ms. Jenkins, but if you'll let us borrow the machine, we can take it back and see if the lab boys can work anything out of the static."

Calliope reached over and hit a button on the digital answering machine she'd badgered Josh into buying. An artificial female voice announced "Message left at . . . five . . . oh four . . . ay em . . . Wednesday . . . October . . . thirtieth."

She waited. The two men across the desk from her said nothing. Unwilling to waste any more time on the conversation, she said, "This thing stamps the call according to its own time zone, *Detectives*."

For a few seconds the two men said nothing, then Special Agent Walker's eyes widened and he stood up. "Oh, you have got to be kidding me! We drove down here for this?"

Johnson jerked a look back at the other man. "Agent Walker?"

Walker split his scorn between Calliope and his companion. "There's a two-hour time difference between here and the victim's location, Johnson. If that thing's right, the call would have had to have been made an hour after the body was found, probably two to five hours after he was killed." He jerked his pointed chin toward Calliope. "She thinks she's got a message from behind the grave."

"Beyond." Calliope interrupted Johnson's reply. "The phrase is beyond the grave, and no, I don't." She waited until both men had turned back to her. "I think it's obvious that the man you found wasn't Josh. He might have had his ID, but Josh must still be alive."

Detective Johnson shook his head, his already sorrowful expression growing graver. "Ms. Jenkins, there was a positive ID: fingerprints, driver's license photo, and we could get dental if we wanted it. I didn't bring along the crime scene photos earlier out of respect for Mrs. Hollis–White but let me assure you: it *was* Joshua White that they found, and he was not about to get up and make a phone call."

Calliope motioned to the machine on the corner of her desk. "Then explain that."

"I can't." Johnson ignored the dismissive expulsion of breath from the man pacing behind him. "I'd like to have our boys look at it."

Calliope made a welcoming gesture with both hands. "Go ahead. I'd love to know what's going on. I'm sure Lauren would as well."

Detective Johnson's dark brown eyes came back to her. "Ms. Jenkins, I must ask you not to set any false expectations with the family of the deceased regarding this phone call. It would be premature and unkind."

Calliope started to reply, but the detective's formal tone and serious expression stopped her retort. She didn't say anything as Detective Johnson gathered up the answering machine and left with Special Agent Walker in tow. The federal agent's narrow face seemed even sharper in the late afternoon light; bitter, like that of a man who'd been told he would have won a grand prize, if only he were taller. Unlike Detective Johnson, he did not wish Calliope a good evening.

Vikous watched the men leave. He scanned the pair—even from across the street, even amid the growing gloom of dusk. Johnson: build like a football player, face like a marriage counselor. Vikous's attention lingered on him for only a few seconds. Walker: looked as though something large had grabbed him by the skull and pulled him through a hole two inches too small for him, as though he'd been stripped of—

Vikous pushed his hood halfway back, letting the remains of the daylight fall across his too-pale skin and too-red mouth. His nostrils flared; he sniffed at the evening air like a hunting dog and, like a dog, he growled.

The men got into Detective Johnson's car and pulled into the street. Vikous watched them, shiny black eyes never blinking, until they were almost out of sight. Just as the brake lights of the car flared in the distance, then pulsed to signal a turn, he took three steps, ducked past a pedestrian, stepped around a lamppost, and was gone.

By six o'clock, Calliope knew that Tom wasn't going to call—he had a gig, and he liked to warm up early. She watched the sky fade away to the reddish brown that was the closest it ever got to night in the city. When the first streetlight began to brighten outside, she made a wish, ordered pizza, and got to work.

His office was just the same.

Josh's files had always been an amateur shrine to disorganization. Calliope had tried to get him to invest in a computerized system for most of the last two years, but he'd resisted with the same smile he'd used to get her to take the job in the first place. Calliope stood at the threshold of his office, taking in the stack of folders on the corner of his desk and the overstuffed file cabinets along both walls.

They'd always interviewed clients in Calliope's office.

When the pizza arrived, Calliope was still standing in the doorway. She paid the driver, took a deep breath, and marched into the room, flipping on the light as she went. She balanced the box on the windowsill, pulled out a slice, and dropped into Josh's office chair with the first folder from the stack on the desk, looking for something that mentioned Iowa.

The notes in each of the folders were handwritten, tiny snippets of her partner's voice captured on paper.

Have informed family that Desiree is fine. Got impression they were looking for 'your daughter's not dead, just dating a drummer' discount. Stnd. fee.

Mr. Vaughn has moved to Seattle—needed to "get away". Mrs. Vaughn did not understand. Has apparently never met herself.

Collected fee for Cal's skip trace, minus cost of her kicking target Amy Whellan through motel door. Need to talk to Cal about calming down. Not while standing in front of a door.

Calli smiled as she read. Josh knew she always reviewed her case files, and he'd always used the notes to let her know how she'd handled the job. Reading them now was like talking to him again.

Like the answering machine.

She wiped the sleep from her eyes and ignored the dampness on her fingers. She hadn't cried—wouldn't—at Lauren's uptown law office; she hadn't while she waited for the cops to come to her own office to hear Josh's message; she wasn't going to cry now, when finding out about his latest job was so important to figuring out what was going on.

She'd worked through the stack on his desk by eleven and leaned back in the chair, rubbing her neck. There hadn't been anything of use in any of the files. Most were closed cases.

She looked at the desk drawers. Notes in a file were one thing, but Josh had always respected Calliope's privacy and she had returned the favor. It would feel like going through his wallet, but it was worse to not know. Sliding forward in the chair, she moved the last folder back to its stack on the desk and reached for the top drawer on the left.

Someone knocked on the glass front door of the office.

For three seconds, Calliope didn't breathe.

"The bad guys don't usually knock, Cal." She stood, moving around the desk with the sort of stride she hoped was a good mix of Confident Woman and who–could–be–knocking–so–late caution. When she stepped through the office door into the waiting room and saw who was on the other side of the glass, her breath caught again. She kept walking to the door simply to keep from freezing in place, flipped the lock, and stood back.

Lauren Hollis–White shoved her way in behind a gust of cold air, a spot of high color on each cheek. She glared at Calliope.

"What the hell are you doing here?" Lauren asked.

Calliope blinked. She was fairly sure that she'd never heard Lauren swear before, and she was absolutely certain she'd never seen her in the office. Before that moment, she would have been willing to bet the woman didn't know where the office was.

"I'm . . ." Calliope shook her head. "What are *you* doing here?"

Lauren had already turned away from Calliope and was looking in at Josh's desk. "This is his office? Jesus, it's just like at home. Why is the light on?" Without waiting for an answer, she stepped through the doorway.

Calliope followed her. Lauren's eyes moved over surfaces Calliope doubted her hands would ever touch. She ended her visual tour with the old leather couch in the corner of the office, where Josh would occasionally catch an afternoon nap when things were slow. Staring at it, her expression shifted from distaste to outright anger.

"What are you doing here?" she asked Calliope again, her voice gone hard.

"I'm . . ." Calliope moved to the desk to distract herself from the look on Lauren's face. "Johnson and Walker came by here earlier this afternoon. They wanted to know if there was anything in Josh's files that might tell them what he was working on in Iowa, but they got one look at this"—she gestured at the desk—"and asked me to do the digging for them." Calliope's knack for tweaking the truth had always bordered on the mythic.

"You just decided to help them out?"

"I wanted something to do and I knew this would keep me busy."

"Why not go home and leave it for tomorrow?" Lauren asked.

Calliope watched the other woman's face. "I kicked my guitarist boyfriend out of my house this morning and I want to give him time to move his stuff out."

Lauren snorted, another first in Calliope's experience. "Figures," she muttered to herself as she dropped into a chair beside the desk.

Something clicked as Calliope watched her guest brush a strand of hair from her face. "You're drunk." She couldn't keep surprise out of her voice.

Another snort. "Hardly." There was a short pause. "I have been *drinking*, but I am certainly not *drunk*."

"There wasn't enough alcohol in the house," Calliope said. Lauren didn't reply. "You figured that since Josh was living out his Sam Spade fantasy down here in the slums he'd have a bottle of . . . what? Rye? . . . stashed in a filing cabinet?"

Lauren sat very still, her expression sullen. Calliope watched her for a few seconds, then walked across the room, pulled open a drawer, and withdrew a bottle. She set it down with a thump on the edge of Josh's desk nearest her guest.

"Johnnie Walker, actually."

Lauren stared at the bottle, her eyes slightly damp but unreadable. "Do you have any clean glasses?" she asked without looking up.

⌇

"Cold pizza and whiskey," Lauren commented from the couch. "It reminds me of college." She glanced at Calliope, sitting in the padded chair behind the desk with her feet up. "I suppose it reminds you of last week."

Calliope ignored the barb. "I'd have to go back at least a

couple years for something like this." She took another bite of pizza. "Probably while I was still in the band."

"Oh yes . . ." Lauren dropped her chin to her chest and raised her glass in mock salute. "The *band*."

Calliope frowned. "You know, you knock it, but you don't know anything about it. It was . . ." She gestured with her glass. "It was good."

The other woman shook her head, possibly more vehemently than she would have an hour ago. "What *you* don't understand is *me*." She struggled to the edge of the couch. "I don't like bands."

"Oh," Calliope said. "I know."

Lauren scowled. "What I *mean* is, I don't like bands, or band members, or backstage passes, or any . . ." She shook her head, her hands pressed together in her lap, her lips trembling. "I liked *Josh*. Just Josh. It didn't have anything to do with what he did, or how much effort he'd put into something that had never gone anywhere—I liked him *despite* that."

It was Calliope's turn to snort her derision. "You didn't exactly have to deal with it for very *long*, though, did you?"

Lauren's eyes snapped back to her. "I never asked him to stop."

Calliope's mouth gave a wry, bitter twist. "And yet."

"He gave that up on his own—I think you knew about it before *I* did." Lauren glared at Calliope's unchanged expression. "Do you honestly think"—she gestured around the room as she pushed herself upright—"that I would have tried to get him to become *this*? He's brilliant . . . was brilliant. He could have done anything. This . . . private detective fantasy had nothing to do with me." Her eyes went to Calliope, then the desk, then seemed to lose focus in a very particular way, her expression neutral. "I don't even know why he did it."

Calliope watched her face. "You don't look like you don't know why."

"I don't." Lauren shook her head and took another drink, but didn't meet Calliope's gaze. "I don't know why he started this business, I don't know why he kept at it for two years while it lost money—a lot of money—and I *really* don't know why I helped him pay the bills."

"And you don't know why he hired his ex-girlfriend to work with him." Calliope's voice was quiet.

"No." Lauren shook her head, her mouth in a grim line. She took another drink. "No, I don't know that, either."

"It wasn't—" Calliope began.

"But you know," Lauren cut in, turning back to the desk where Calliope sat, "that's not what bothers me." She pursed her lips, her jaw moving as though she had bitten into something that tasted awful, but which she was too polite to spit out. She moved the tumbler in a slow, flat circle through the air, speeding up the motion as she went, as though she were building up enough momentum to force the words out. "What *bothers* me . . . is that I don't know why he ever broke up with you." She spoke carefully, her voice lower than normal, in that particular way of someone who is trying to speak calmly about something that makes them very angry.

Calliope didn't speak. The silence built up into a tangible thing that seemed to take on a physical presence in the room, forcing the two women to look at each other. Eventually. Calliope opened her mouth to give Lauren an answer—any answer—not even sure what she'd say, but Lauren shot to her feet and turned away, wandering barefoot around the room, her eyes looking beyond the paneled walls. "So . . . he was in a band, and I loved him anyway; and then he did this, and I loved him anyway; and now he's dead." She trailed off, staring at her empty glass. "I need another drink."

Calliope picked up the dwindling bottle and poured, steadier than Lauren only by virtue of the fact that she was sitting. She pondered what Detective Johnson had said to her about Josh's message and debated telling Lauren about what she suspected. He was probably right; it wouldn't do her any good to hear if nothing came of it. She might be a bitch but—

"Whoa. Enough. Calli, shit, *whoa.*" Lauren pulled the glass away just as Calliope pulled the bottle back, splashing some of the brown liquor across the blotter.

"Sorry." She shook her head. "Distracted."

"Yeah." Lauren took a drink from her brimming glass, grimaced, and licked a few drops from the back of her hand. "I can't feel my tongue anymore," she muttered as she turned back toward the couch. She took a few halting steps before coming to a stop.

At her sharp intake of breath, Calliope looked up. They both stared at the figure standing in the doorway. Somewhere in the back of her mind a calm, sarcastic voice was telling Calliope that whoever it was had been standing there awhile and that she was a big drunk idiot who was probably about to die.

"You left the front door unlocked, before." The voice coming out of the shadowed hood sounded like the owner had gargled a shovelful of gravel and washed it down with tequila. "Shouldn't do that. It's not safe."

Next to him, on the wall, the clock read 1:43 A.M.

4

"EXCUSE ME?" LAUREN'S voice was sharp and hard. "Who are you?" She turned toward Calliope. "Do you know this—"

The figure in the doorway turned his head toward her. He spoke one guttural word that bounced off the dark paneling of the office; Lauren dropped to the ground like a puppet that had just had its strings cut. Her glass hit the floor with a thump and jumped sideways, spilling its contents over the thin carpet. The room filled with the stink of whiskey.

Calliope was standing before she realized it, and a wave of alcohol dizziness swept over her.

"The *hell* did you just—"

"You can't take her with you." The vagabond in the doorway stepped forward into the room, closer to Calliope. "You can't."

For a moment all Calliope could do was stare at the shadowed recess of the man's hood, then she shook her head. "Okay, you're obviously a little bit *completely* out of your mind, and I always try to be nice to the insane, but *what the hell did you just do to her?*" She made a sharp gesture with her hand as the stranger started to move again. "Stay there or I will kick your chest through your backbone. What did you do to her?"

The man made a dismissive motion with one gloved hand. "She's fine. I wanted to talk to you. Didn't want her around. She's not part of this. You can't—"

"Yeah, take her with me. I heard. I'm not planning to take her anywhere, dumbass, and you really need to get out of my office."

"You don't understand." He took a step closer.

"Warned you," she muttered under her breath. She vaulted over the desk and snapped the heel of her foot at the intruder's chest.

Under normal circumstances, the kick might have missed. Calliope had been drinking and was, Josh's frequent comments to the contrary, generally out of practice with such maneuvers. But she was also very angry and not a little frightened, and those two things together helped her succeed where she might have failed.

The kick landed square, the shock of impact riding up into her body. She landed in defensive stance, her skirt swirling around her legs.

Solid, she thought, *he's solid.*

But not immovable. Caught by surprise, the vagrant tumbled backward through the doorway of the office. Rather than sprawling flat with the sort of sounds that Calliope found most satisfying in such situations, he rolled away and sprang up to his feet in a move that was both acrobatic and somehow comical. She caught a glimpse of pale skin beneath the hood and noticed, incongruously, that his shoes were unusually if not ridiculously long, which added to the odd pratfall feel of his recovery.

"I made a mistake here," her visitor said from the outer office.

"Damn straight," she said.

The hood seemed to nod toward her, and he was gone, the outer door easing closed behind him.

Calliope walked to the door, locked it, checked the street through the glass, and headed back into the office. About halfway there, the room began to spin.

Joshua White stops on the frozen gravel driveway. It is afternoon, and the sun is nearly done for the day—he can barely make out the outline of the porch and railing ahead. He looks down at his feet where the cracked cement of the front walk meets the driveway gravel. Crude chalk drawings, more bestial than childish, cover the concrete. He studies them for a moment, thinking of a rhyme from his childhood, then peers back up at the dark windows of the house.

"All right." He steps onto the walk, and up to the door. "Ready or not, here I come . . ."

He will be dead in two days.

Pain pressed at the inside of her skull like an inflating balloon.

One of the reasons Calliope had chosen her office over Joshua's when they'd first found the space was that its window faced west. Joshua's faced east and was also larger. He'd joked on more than one occasion that the window meant he could work uninterrupted until noon, since Calliope tended to avoid natural light.

The end of the couch that Calliope was curled up on was the first part of Josh's office the sun reached.

Groaning, she shoved herself into a half–sitting position away from the glare. In doing so, she came to rest on the feet of the couch's other occupant. Remembering the blank stare on Lauren's face the night before and her own struggle to arrange the woman comfortably before dizziness overcame her, Calliope slid toward that end of the couch.

The thick smell of spilled whiskey rising from the carpet made her head feel worse, but she saw that Lauren's eyes were closed and that she was breathing normally, even snoring slightly. Shoving her way to her feet, she contemplated curling up in her own office chair away from the growing light of dawn—uncomfortable, but darker.

Someone knocked on the front door.

Calliope blinked for several seconds before checking the clock. Six thirty-eight. Shrugging, she shuffled toward the outer office. As an afterthought, she pulled Joshua's door closed behind her.

The light coming in through the front door was a physical, painful thing. It was several seconds before she managed to relax her squinting eyes to the point where she could see. What she saw should have surprised her.

But then a crazy homeless man who can knock people out by speaking magical Hungarian attacked me, Calliope thought. *It's a bright new day.*

She unlocked the door, opened it a crack, and said, "Our normal office hours are from nine A.M. to six P.M. Please call back."

"Ms. Jenkins," Detective Johnson said. "Have you been here all night?"

Calliope could only stare at the dark-skinned detective and the federal agent behind him. "Have I . . . ?" She shook her head. "Jesus, we *both* need some coffee, I guess. Come in." She turned away and headed for the cabinet with the coffee-making equipment that Joshua had bought a few weeks after they'd opened their doors.

"Have a seat," she spoke over her shoulder.

"Ms. Jenkins." Detective Johnson showed no signs of irritation at repeating himself. "*Have* you been here all night?"

Calliope turned back to the men. Both were still standing. Johnson looked serious; Walker looked suspicious. "Yes, Detective, I have been here all night. I do not normally get to work this early in the morning, and on the rare times it does happen, I don't look like *this*. Are there any other blindingly obvious questions you'd like answered?"

Johnson's expression remained stern. "You'll have to forgive me for asking, Ms. Jenkins, but Mrs. Hollis–White was reported missing this morning and we are checking out all her known acquaintances."

"That's smart," Calliope said. "She's in there," she added, nodding at the closed office door and turning back to the coffee machine. "Do you want sugar?"

The silence that greeted her announcement was almost worth being awake so early.

"Don't wake her up," she added when she heard one of the two men head for the closed door. "She had a hard night."

She heard the door open; a few seconds later, Johnson let out a sharp exhalation. "Pretty much drank it all, didn't you?" he commented. Calliope turned back to him, leaned against the cabinet, and said nothing.

The detective looked over the room as best he could from the doorway, then pulled the door shut and turned back to her. "The two of you didn't exactly strike me as drinking buddies."

"We're not."

"Then this looks a little curious."

Calliope met his gaze, ignoring the throbbing in her temples. "You want to tell a woman how to mourn her husband, Detective?"

Johnson raised his hands. "No arguments, Ms. Jenkins. It's really none of our business."

Calliope turned to fill three mismatched cups. "Have you found out anything about the answering machine message?" She turned back to the men with a cup in either hand. "I didn't tell her anything," she said in response to the question in Johnson's expression.

The detective nodded as he took the proffered cup. "Thank you. Nothing yet on the recording; they told me they might have something by lunch."

She nodded. "I should be back here by then."

"You're going back to your residence?"

"That's the plan." She reached back for her own coffee. "I take it you checked for me there first?"

Johnson rubbed at his jawline. "Your neighbors didn't think you'd been home."

Calliope's lips pressed together, but she raised her cup to the detective. "That's why they pay you guys the big bucks. Did you need anything else?"

Johnson glanced at his companion, who remained silent and hadn't touched the coffee cooling in his hand. "No, I think that's it. Everything here has been all right?"

Calliope tipped her head. "I looked through our files for something about Iowa, but didn't find anything. Like I said, he must have taken everything with him." She motioned toward Josh's office. "I didn't get a chance to check everything since Lauren showed up around eleven and we had to chase off a homeless guy around two A.M." Johnson nodded, but Walker's face grew taut.

"Homeless man? Does that happen often in this neighborhood?"

Calliope already regretted mentioning the visitor. "Not really, but I told him to leave and he did."

"Did you get a look at his face?" Walker asked.

Calliope kept her expression neutral and masked her annoyance at sidetracking the conversation. "I didn't. It's pretty dark at two in the morning. Is this"—she glanced at each man in turn—"important in some way that I'm not understanding?"

It was Walker who answered; Johnson seemed as puzzled as Calliope. "An unidentified individual, possibly transient, was seen around the area where your partner was killed, Miss Jenkins."

Calliope blinked. "And you see a connection? You couldn't possibly drive from Iowa to here in twenty-four hours, and I'm pretty sure this guy didn't have a car to begin with . . . or a plane ticket."

Walker stared at her, his eyes hard and unreadable. Finally, he shook his head and attempted a smile that seemed to stretch his face in uncomfortable directions. "You're right, of course. I apologize."

Calliope didn't reply. Detective Johnson stepped forward and set his cup down on the unused front desk. "We're sorry to have bothered you so early, Ms. Jenkins. Thank you for the coffee. We'll let you know what we find out from the answering machine."

Calliope nodded acknowledgment, watching as the two men left.

As soon as the outer door closed, Josh's opened. Lauren stood framed in the doorway, her face wan and her arms hugged tightly around her.

She glared at Calliope. "What answering machine message?"

* * *

Dammit.

Calliope resigned herself to an endless cycle of uncomfortable conversations with people she didn't particularly like. She poured another cup of coffee and took it over to Lauren. "Josh left a message here a few hours after he called my place. Mostly static. They're checking to see if they can get anything out of it."

Lauren looked down at her coffee. "What . . . what did he say, that you could make out?"

Calliope felt a twinge of sympathy. "He mostly talked about you, actually. He said he was going to find a way to tell you what was going on."

Lauren flinched.

"I'm sorry," Calliope said. "I thought you should—"

"Could you get my jacket for me?" Lauren asked, walking past Calliope toward the front window of the office. "If I go back in there again, I'll throw up."

Calliope half nodded, half shook her head at her guest's back. "Sure."

The miasma of greasy pizza and spilled whiskey was stronger now, thickened and warmed by the morning sunlight. Calliope held her breath as she retrieved her and Lauren's shoes, both jackets, and Lauren's purse.

"Thanks," Lauren murmured as Calliope held them out to her.

"No problem." Calliope sat down and picked up her coffee. "You're right about that room; it smells a little Sam Spade in there."

"It smells like Sam Spade's ass," Lauren said. Calliope laughed out loud, and the other woman turned to her. "What?"

"Oh . . . nothing. You're just a little out of character today."
She raised a hand at Lauren's expression. "No complaints.
You're more than entitled."

Lauren turned back to the window and knelt, working her
shoes on. "Thank you, incidentally, for telling them off on my
behalf. But why did you lie?"

Calliope raised an eyebrow. "Excuse me, Counselor?"

Lauren straightened, shaking her hair back into a semblance
of order. "The vagrant. I don't remember much about that, but I
didn't get the impression he was going to leave simply because
you asked him to."

"Okay, I kicked him in the chest and *then* I told him to leave
and he left." Calliope waved her hand. "Details."

"They're the police."

"They're *people*. That's it. People doing a job, which right now
is finding out what happened to Josh. Our visitor didn't have
anything to do with that."

"Agent Walker—"

"Admitted that a teleporting hobo is an unlikely suspect."
She eyed Lauren. "Let's say I tell them everything and they
think it might be a clue. So they waste two days on bullshit instead of working on the real case. Hell with that. It happened.
I handled it. It's done. None of their business."

"But they're the *police*. How—" Lauren pursed her lips and cut
herself off. "I need to get home. My parents probably called
them in the first place."

"Sounds reasonable." Calliope's words hung in the air like a
judgment.

Lauren ducked her chin rather than reply and walked out
the front door. Calliope watched her cross the street to her car
and swore to herself in the quiet of the empty office. After a

few moments, she locked up and headed back to her house, replaying the morning's conversations, the surreal exchange with the vagrant the night before, and finally the evening talk with Lauren.

"I don't know why *he broke up with you."*

In the middle of the drive home she pulled off onto the shoulder, crying too hard to see.

5

"Calli?"

Slowly, the room comes into focus. Calliope smiles up from her hospital bed.

"Hey . . ." She manages a smile. "How are you?"

Josh's eyebrows rise. "How am I? That's funny, considering I'm not the one in ICU. How are you?"

She shrugs. Regrets it. "Did the cops find the guy?"

Joshua nods, his lips tight. "Yep."

Calliope traces the lines of tension on his face with her eyes. Her fingers shift on the coverlet. "I'm okay."

"I know."

"It was just a precaution."

"I know. You just . . ." He looks out the window. "Can't keep putting yourself in situations like this. You're the only pseudo-family I've got."

She raises an eyebrow. "Think you're forgetting your wife."

He makes a face. "That's not what I mean. You can't pick fights with three-hundred-pound guys no matter how many self-defense courses you've taken." He shifts forward. "I should have gone with you."

"So you . . . wanted to make it up to me by bringing me his head?"

"Hmm?" He glances down at the large paper bag in his hand. "Oh. I brought you . . . stuff." His eyes flicker in a way with which Calliope is quite familiar. She smiles.

"Stuff?"

"There were balloons, but they wouldn't let me bring them in here—said they'd mess up the monitors."

"Screw the balloons, what's in the bag?"

He glances inside. "Flowers, candy, a bear from the gift shop, and a few toys."

She waggles her eyebrows. "I like toys." Her grin grows when he reaches into his jacket pocket instead of the bag and places a narrow, six-inch cylinder of black metal in her hand. "Is this the thing you were talking about?"

Josh retrieves the cylinder and gives it a strong flick with his hand—the tube telescopes out to eighteen inches.

"They wouldn't let you bring in balloons, but this was okay."

"It never really came up."

"Cool." She holds out her hand, looking up at his face when he doesn't hand the baton over. "What?"

"Did you think about the other thing?"

"I'm not quitting."

"It's not—"

"I. Am not. Quitting." She reaches her hand out farther, grimacing. "Now, gimme the damn thing."

"Do you have a permit for that?" asks a half-familiar voice from the doorway.

"Who—"

⌐

A ringing phone jerked Calliope out of a sound sleep. Fumbling, she ripped the receiver off its cradle. "Josh?"

There was a moment of silence on the other end of the line. "Ms. Jenkins, I'm sorry. I didn't mean to wake you." Detective Johnson's voice was apologetic. "Again."

Calliope jerked her head off her pillow, checking the windows and clock. Afternoon. Three.

"Sorry, Detective. I laid down for a second—"

"Completely understandable, Ms. Jenkins."

Calliope lay back, frowning at the ceiling. "I was supposed to be at the office. You were going to—did you, what did you find out about the answering machine?" She sat up on the edge of the bed and pushed her hair out of her face.

"We got some more of the recording, although the techs say some of it simply isn't there to be recovered." There was a pause and Calliope could hear the rustle of papers over the line. "Do you know . . . someone called the fat man?"

Calliope paused, wondering if she's misheard.

This is the part where I realize I'm dreaming.

"Ms. Jenkins?"

Calliope shook the thought away. "I'm sorry; I heard you ask if I know 'the fat man'? Please be joking."

The papers shuffled again. "I'm definitely not joking, Ms. Jenkins. The last portion of the recording seems to be 'the fat man knows what's going on, so just get hold of him and he'll be able to explain most of this to you.'"

"I'll see you soon," Calliope murmured.

"Excuse me?"

"'I'll see you soon'," she repeated. "That was the very last part of the message."

"Yes," the detective replied after a moment. He didn't say

anything else, and the silence stretched to the point of being awkward.

Calliope cleared her throat. "The fat man."

"Exactly."

"I have no damn idea what he's talking about, Detective. I'm sorry."

There was a pause. "You're sure?"

"I am," Calliope said.

"Would you mind if we had an officer check over Mr. White's files for some reference to this?"

"Oh, who do you hate that much?" Calliope whispered.

"I'm sorry?"

"Nothing. Thinking out loud." Calliope pulled herself up-right. "Yes, Detective, that would be fine; you're welcome to it." When he didn't respond, she added. "Detective?"

"I'm sorry, Ms. Jenkins. Thank you. Could we meet at your office in an hour?"

"I'll be there."

It was well over two hours later when Calliope finally pulled up at the office in her Jeep. Two cars—unmarked, but unmistakably law enforcement—waited outside. A younger agent climbed out of one as she pulled up, followed by Johnson in the other.

"Sorry for making you wait. The traffic was terrible." Calliope could hear the tension in her voice; she'd never minded being late, but it irritated her when the delay wasn't her doing.

Johnson shook his head to deflect the apology. "Not at all, Ms. Jenkins. This is Agent Hyde. He works with Special Agent Walker." The younger man offered his hand in greeting. Calliope filled it with a spare office key. "Door you want's on the right, coffee's in the cabinet. Feel free to pull files into the front room to get away from the smell." The younger officer hesitated, then nodded in a way that felt like a salute and headed inside.

Calliope watched the young man walk away. "Junior agent?"

"When I was a rookie in homicide they made me categorize the dog feces samples taken from a crime scene at a county animal shelter," Johnson deadpanned. "Walker's letting him off easy."

Calliope smirked. "If that's everything, Detective?"

He scanned her face. *He's got police eyes,* she thought. *Sad, and nice, but still police eyes.*

"Everything regarding this," Johnson replied. "But can I ask an unrelated question?"

Calliope crossed her arms against the evening chill. "Sure."

"Don't be offended, but I was expecting you to ask for a warrant."

Calliope studied his face in turn. "This should be done right, Detective." She looked at the front window of the office, through which she could see the young agent carrying a stack of the desktop files she'd gone through the night before into the front office. "I don't want to look back on this and think I might have been part of the problem."

Johnson said nothing.

Waiting. She glanced at him, then back at the window. *Police waiting. Goes with the eyes.* "And . . . I can't think of anything else to try."

Johnson rested his hands on his hips, letting his eyes drift to the front of the office. "I don't think that'll last," he said, glancing at her sidelong, the corner of his mouth quirked upward.

Calliope gave him a curious squint. "I'm sorry?"

He raised one hand and let the hint of a smile grow into something open and comfortable. "Please don't take offense, Miss—" He shook his head. "May I call you Calliope?" He extended his hand. "I'm Darryl."

She looked at his hand for only a second before taking it. "Sure . . ."

"Thank you." He released her hand, now somehow awkward in a way that made Calliope return his smile. "Anyway, what I was saying; you don't strike me as the sort of person who goes very long without any ideas. If you *do* think of something else to try, I'd just . . . appreciate it if you let me know."

"Ahh . . ." Calliope shook her head, bemused. "Sure. Absolutely." She smiled; small, but genuine. "Darryl."

"Thank you, Calliope. Have a good night. Happy Halloween." He turned back to his car.

"Happy . . ." Calliope's voice trailed off. "Oh. Huh. That explains the traffic."

"Glad I could help." The detective smiled as he opened the door. "I'd better get home. Trick-or-treaters." He climbed behind the wheel.

"Sure," Calliope said, though his door had already closed. "Happy Halloween."

Johnson raised his hand in a final mute farewell and pulled away. Calliope watched the car roll down the street.

"The police won't be able to help," said a rough, almost familiar voice.

Calliope's head snapped around. "What the—"

The vagrant from the night before was standing next to the old Jeep's dented rear bumper. His hands were jammed deep inside his coat pockets. His hood moved a fraction of an inch as he spoke. "What I don't understand is, the message on the answering machine told you to talk to someone who'd have answers." The strange cadence of his speech made him sound like a mystic oracle born and raised in New Jersey. "But *you* just said you've got nothing else to try. That . . . that confuses me."

Calliope pointed at the lighted office window, her eyes locked on her stalker. "There is an armed federal agent sitting right in there." Her heart hammered at her chest. "You might want to call him for help."

Calliope slipped Josh's gift baton out of her jacket pocket and flicked it open with the very satisfying and noticeable *snick* that always got people's attention. She could see the vagrant's attention shift. It was one of the reasons she liked the thing— between that sound and the resulting eighteen inches of black metal jutting from her fist, most people never noticed anything else.

When the spray from the can in her off hand went into the depths of his hood, the transient's head jerked back so violently it bounced off the side of Calliope's Jeep. She was walking up to him by the time he hit the ground.

"Seventeen percent oleoresin capsicum," she commented, her voice conversational despite the violent writhing of her victim. "I went for the optional identifying dye mix." She held the can at an angle to the light shining from her office, pretending to read the label that she'd long since memorized. "They say the loss of sight is temporary, and they *seem* to be right about stopping 'even the most aggressive assailant', so I wouldn't worry." She paused about five feet from the growling, mewling form curled in a fetal ball before her. "This is the riot–control–rated version the police use, so I *could* have hit you from about twenty feet away. You should probably remember that from now on." She watched his gloved hands clutching at his face inside the hood. "Yeah. It'll be about thirty minutes before you stop wanting to rip your own eyes out. It'll seem longer."

She walked toward the front of the Jeep, tucking her things away. "I was going to hit you a couple times with the baton, but I think it's important for you to remember that I didn't *have* to." She opened the door to the vehicle. "Leave. Me. Alone."

Calliope climbed into her Jeep and backed into the street, leaving the stranger lying on the pavement behind her.

Traffic had broken up somewhat by the time Calliope made it to the highway and headed back to her house. The difficulties she'd had during the drive over now made sense. What didn't was the fact that she'd forgotten the date, one of her favorite times of year. She wasn't really in the mood to go out, but as she pulled into her driveway and parked, she realized she wanted to spend all night alone and indoors even less; the thought of potential trick-or-treaters made her grimace. She sat in the Jeep, staring at the front door of her house for over a minute.

"I'm sorry."

"Hey—"

She walked out of the kitchen. "Pack your things. I've got to go.

I'm late."

Calliope's jaw firmed and her lips drew together. "All right," she muttered as she opened the door and climbed out. "Let's get a costume."

It had been two years.

The wall of sound vibrated in Calliope's chest like an ultra-sound turned up too high. She'd debated her outfit for over an hour, and it was well into the evening before she'd gotten to the club. The bouncer at the door looked her over, already moving aside the rope on the doorway. "You some kind of gangster?" he asked, looking at the gray, tailored suit she'd bought for rare court appearances on behalf of White Investigations, mismatched with a broad, striped tie of the cheapest polyester and topped with a broad-brimmed fedora.

"I'm Sam Spade, baby," she replied, walking into the club.

The music vibrated up through the ground even outside the building. Inside, it was a physical object that pulled at different portions of her body like an animal that was mildly curious about how you would taste. A member of the staff was handing out earplugs just inside the entrance. Calliope had put in her own pair as she'd parked the Jeep.

Looking over the dance floor and catwalk-like levels that surrounded it, Calliope realized that she'd forgotten what Halloween could be like. The stage provided an anchor point at one end of the lowest level, a heaving mass of costumed dancers surrounding it. Angels, devils, vampires, ghouls, teddy bears, prostitutes, flappers, Egyptian queens, cheerleaders, and at least three Valkyries surged across the dance floor or leaned over railings on the levels above. Calliope felt the familiar buzz of sound and people merge into a sort of electric frisson that she always got in places like this. It was one thing she missed from what she thought of now as the "old days", something that she'd avoided for the last two years.

The band's set was finishing up when Calliope arrived. She was both relieved and unaccountably nervous when she realized that the burly staffer blocking the backstage door was familiar.

"Toby, hi," Calliope began. "I need to see Tom."

The ebony-black man had arms the size of Calliope's legs, folded across his chest—the requisite staff costume of two small devil's horns on his smooth forehead seemed utterly redundant. The first expression to cross his face at Calliope's greeting was one of amused surprise. "No one is allowed backstage, miss."

Calliope waited, silent, until the bouncer took a closer look. Slowly, annoyance and suspicion turned into surprise. "Calli Jenkins?"

Privately pleased at being recognized so quickly, Calliope tipped her head, covering a grin. "Yup."

"*Hey*, I haven't seen you around here in forever," Toby said as he engulfed Calliope's hand in his. "Are you singing tonight?" The hopeful expression on his face—weirdly at odds with his normal demeanor—filled Calliope with another wash of embarrassed pleasure.

"Umm . . . no, actually. I'm just here to see Tom."

"Oh, right." Toby hesitated. "You know I can't let anyone back there during sets."

"I know."

Toby looked as conflicted as anyone who could tear a phone book in half could probably look.

"How about you ask him if it's all right?"

The big man looked relieved. "Sure. Go ahead and wait at the bar over there. I'll be right back."

Calliope moved as directed. The club was relatively quiet compared to when the band was playing, but the sound system and unrelenting dance crowd still meant she had to repeat herself three times to the bartender before she was understood. While she waited for either her drink or Toby to arrive, she watched one of the Valkyries order and collect a platterful of mojitos for her other Nordic warrior friends giggling in a booth.

"Penny for your thoughts."

Calliope glanced away from the women. A man costumed as a rather unsavory circus clown was leaning against the bar on the other side of the space recently occupied by the departing Valkyrie.

"Excuse me?"

"You had a pretty interesting expression on your face just then, so . . ." He gestured with his glass. "Penny for your thoughts."

"I was just wondering if it was possible to roll your mind's eye." Calliope nodded toward the booth.

The clown glanced over his shoulder. "I know what you mean. I've never understood the idea of heavy-duty costumes."

"Really?" Calliope made a show of looking over the spikes of green hair jutting from the man's head, the pale white face, and the odd distended-mouth illusion that his makeup gave him.

He seemed to realize what he'd said and gestured to his face. "Oh, yeah . . . this is—"

Someone tapped Calliope's shoulder. She turned to face Toby. His expression told her what she needed to know. She raised a hand before he had to say it.

"It's okay, Toby. I'll just talk to him later." She smiled and patted him on the shoulder. "I guessed he might be too busy. It's no problem."

Calliope was a very good liar. Toby smiled in response to her easy tone. "Great to see you again, Calli. Come back and sing sometime."

Calliope winked and turned back to her drink. Toby hesitated, then walked back to his post.

"So . . . you sing."

Calliope managed a half smile with no feeling behind it, but didn't look up at the clown-faced man. "I used to. Not tonight, though."

"That's all right," the man replied, taking a slow drink. He set down his glass and turned it slowly counterclockwise on the bar, as though it were a dial. The sounds of the club around them seemed to fade, allowing his quiet words to carry. "You should probably be working on that whole Joshua White problem anyway."

Hearing it clearly for the first time, Calliope realized why the man's voice had seemed familiar. "You don't learn very fast, do you?" she asked. She turned back to her drink, her face blank.

"I usually do all right."

"Right. How are your eyes feeling right now?"

Out of the corner of her eye, she could see him shrug, his hand still on the glass. "Nobody's perfect."

"Especially homeless stalker nut jobs wearing face paint."

"It's Halloween. Everyone's in costume."

"I was thinking 'man clutching himself and crying' might be a better look for you."

"You know . . ." The clown pivoted on his stool and glared at Calliope, his hand still on his glass. "You've kicked me in the chest and teargassed me. I may have startled you, but the only thing I've actually done is tell you I can help you. If I'm being persistent, then I'm either crazy for going anywhere near you, or it's really *important*. You don't lose a thing by listening to me."

"I'd waste time," Calliope said.

He sneered, his oddly painted mouth moving more than it should. "Yeah, sitting at a bar drinking black and tans—my mistake; you're hot on the trail, I'll just get out of your way."

"Son of a bitch," Calliope said through clenched teeth.

"I *dare* you." His eyes were bright and wide. To Calliope they seemed like a doll's eyes; she couldn't see any whites, though she would have sworn she had only a few seconds ago. "I dare you to prove me wrong."

Calliope filled her voice with the sneer she didn't bother to put on her face. "You're pathetic."

His expression held, somewhere between triumph and anger. "You're afraid. Of me. Of what I know."

She leaned in close enough to smell the stink of the street on him. "I will never—"

"Prove it," he growled.

She searched his face through narrowed eyes and didn't like one thing she saw. Reaching back, she grabbed her drink and finished it off. "Right or wrong, I'm gonna kick your ass again before this is over. Pay the man."

He stood, lifting his glass from the bar. The sound of the club flooded back around them as he drained the glass. Calliope walked past him toward the exit.

Calliope stood next to her Jeep as he approached. "Thanks for waiting," he said.

"You've been following me for two days. I figured you could find the parking lot."

"Yeah. We going to go or flirt on your back bumper all night?"

"Two questions," Calliope said. "Or you can go to hell."

He snorted. "Sure, whatever you want."

"Name."

"Vikous. Doesn't stand for anything."

Calliope ignored that. "What did you do to Lauren last night?"

"Knocked her out."

"How?"

"That's three questions."

Her eyes narrowed and she turned to unlock the Jeep. "I'd advise you against trying that crap on me."

He moved around to the passenger side. "That's cute coming from someone who suckered me with a can of tear gas."

She yanked open her door and glared through the car at him. "You were expecting me to give up a hundred pounds and a foot of height and reach and fight fair?"

He blinked his black, shining eyes and grunted, regarding her through the passenger window. "Good point, I guess." He pointed at the door lock. Calliope frowned and flipped it up. He climbed in. She didn't. Without turning, he said, "It's easier to make the car go if you're inside."

"Did you kill Josh?"

He turned his head then, his ridiculous face solemn. "No."

She watched him for a few seconds, then got in. "Where are we going?"

He slid the seat back. "White left you a message, told you to talk to somebody. Who was it?"

"No," Calliope snapped and turned in her seat, suddenly angry again. "How do you *know* that?"

Vikous rolled his colorless eyes. "What difference does it make? I know things. I don't know everything. That's the way it is."

"That's . . ." Calliope squinted as though he'd gone out of focus. "'That's the way it is'? That's your explanation? You're out of your goddamned mind if you think—"

"Listen," Vikous said. Calliope started to speak again, and he rubbed at his eyes, pinching the bridge of his nose in exasperation. "*Listen.*" He waited to see if the silence would hold, then took a breath. "What's going on right now—this thing you're caught up in—it's happened before."

Calliope tilted her head, as if she'd misheard him. "When?"

"Lots of times." His expression was grim beneath the makeup. "Point is, it always happens the same way. Always."

Calliope's face felt cold, colder than it should be, even at night in late October. Josh and she had, through sheer dumb luck, never worked on a missing person case that had turned out to be anything more than a rebellious teen, parole jumper, or inconstant spouse, but the potential had always been there. "And you know about how it—about what to do?"

"As much as anyone living," he said. The low rasp had dropped out of his voice, leaving behind a sincerity Calliope found herself wanting to believe, despite herself.

"You can help?"

"I can try," he replied. "Doesn't always work out. Sometimes it does. Best I can promise."

Calliope tried to meet his gaze, but his eyes were lost in the shadows of the harshly lit parking lot. She turned back to the steering wheel. "He said I should see the fat man."

Vikous let his head fall back against the seat. "Lovely."

She glanced at him. "What?"

"I know him."

"And?"

"You're not going to like it." He motioned to the street. "We should go."

STAGE TWO

6

COLD AIR WHIPPED through the cab of Calliope's Jeep as they drove along the freeway, headed for downtown. Vikous glanced over, his face expressionless. "What's with the open window?"

"You smell like a beach full of dead birds."

"Not a lot of bathing opportunities in my simple life." He pulled out a mangled but mostly intact cigar from an inner pocket and pointed at a passing road sign. "Turn here. Mind if I smoke, since we're gonna die of pneumonia anyway?"

"Could you just shoot yourself in the chest instead?" She took the exit he'd indicated. "I can tear out your trachea with my bare hands and rub asphalt on your tongue afterward if that would help you get the buzz. Maybe I could leave your body lying on a pile of burning tires."

He stared, then tucked the cigar away. "Most folks just say no when I ask. You've got some confrontation issues. You know this?"

"It's been mentioned," she replied, her expression sour. "Where am I going?"

Vikous pointed down the street. "Park down there. We'll have to walk the rest of the way."

"Where are we going?"

"You haven't been there."

"How do you—" She stopped at his closed expression, her own face tight. At the next block, she pulled the Jeep over and parked. They were downtown, but nowhere near the more popular clubs; the street was quiet and mostly abandoned.

"What should we—" she began as she climbed out of the vehicle, but Vikous was already walking away down the street, lighting the cigar as he went. Calliope watched him, her face carefully blank.

"My foot," she muttered to herself. "My foot, kicking your ass, very soon, I swear." She checked her jacket pockets once and went to meet the fat man.

Their route took them east three streets, over a glass-enclosed pedestrian overpass and, inexplicably, through a construction site. Vikous shuffled along in his ridiculous, oversized shoes, passing through the automatic doors of a glass-fronted executive high-rise. At the security desk he paused, his hands jammed in his coat pockets, the cigar leaking a thin line of smoke into the air from the corner of his mouth. The guard eyed them both suspiciously.

"Business?" he asked.

"Top floor. The party." Vikous looked bored.

"Invitation." The guard leaned forward, hand extended. Vikous just looked at him. The guard settled back in his seat, his eyes hooded. "How do you know there's a party if you don't have an invitation?"

Vikous watched the guard, black eyes shining under the

fluorescents. Like a great cat lowering itself to the ground before pouncing, he pulled his gloved right hand out of his pocket, laid it on the counter, and leaned toward the guard. "Well, there would have to be a party, wouldn't there?"

Calliope couldn't see Vikous's face clearly from that angle, but something in the guard's face seemed to give way for just a moment, leaving his eyes showing white all the way around as he looked at Vikous.

"Second elevator on the right." His voice was barely audible. Vikous pushed himself upright and turned to the elevator banks without another glance at the guard. After pressing the call button, he put his hand back in his pocket and watched the LED display on the wall descend to 01.

Once the doors had opened and closed behind them, Calliope spoke. "Was that like the thing with Lauren?"

Vikous was watching the display above the doors climb. Neither he nor Calliope had touched any of the buttons inside the car. "What?" he said without looking at her.

"With the guard. What did you do to him?"

He looked at her, his painted face expressionless. "I suppose you could say I scared the devil out of him."

"How?"

He glanced at her sidelong for a moment, one eyebrow raised, then turned back to the opening elevator doors. "I guess clowns scare some people."

Noise flooded the elevator as the doors opened. Calliope followed Vikous out of the car and into a room that looked like a private club, almost a miniaturized version of the one where Tom had been playing, although Calliope had to admit that the costumes here were much better. Succubi and dark-suited G-men with gray skin circled pale, silk-clad vampires and cat people on the dance floor. There were definitely no angels or middle-management Valkyries. A young, androgynous man in a sleek suit—his face shaped by what had to be movie-studio-level makeup and prosthetics into something that looked like a cross between Legolas and an insect—moved to meet them, arms positioned in a way that, to Calliope, said "security" rather than "host".

"Here to see himself," Vikous said.

Without shifting his gaze, the guard seemed to indicate Calliope.

"She's clear," Vikous said.

The guard's glistening eyes flickered over her for moment, appraising, before he turned to lead them across the club.

The office they entered was spacious and utterly soundproof once the doors had been pulled shut. The fat man glided across the thick plush carpet to greet them.

His was not the firm sort of fat found in those who are forced to be active against the trend of their predilections. Parts of him—his cheeks, chins, limbs—shook as he moved, jiggled with each step despite the apparent ease of his gait. His torso was a broad, taut teardrop that extended to his knees; his arms, also quivering, were flat wide sacks that swung ineffectually at his sides in counterpoint to his move-ments. Puffed lips pouted beneath bright eyes that had been forced into a permanent squint by the flesh that pressed in from above and below. He was dressed in a garish Ori-ental silk gown that only emphasized the rolling motions beneath. His black hair had been slicked back on his head and was possibly the only portion of his anatomy that didn't constantly move.

"Vikous, it's quite a surprise to see you." His voice, although cultured and calm, seemed to be coming from the throat of a man drowning in butter. He turned to Calliope. "And you've brought a guest. Charmed, my dear. Quite charmed." His face seemed to be making an attempt at a smile as he extended a fleshy pink starfish of a hand. Calliope left her hands in her pockets.

Vikous's glance flickered back to her for a moment; he moved past their host and farther into the room. "You know her, Gluen."

The hand seemed to falter and with it, the smile. Gluen's eyes flickered over Calliope; they were the only part of him that seemed to move quickly. "I do? I think I would remember meeting such an"—his lips twitched—"enchanting creature." He inclined his head to Calliope, giving himself three additional chins in the process.

Vikous turned away from the windows that overlooked the city. "I didn't say met. I said you know her. This is Joshua White's friend." His smile was confident and encouraging if it wasn't examined too closely. "He told her to come see you."

The fat man frowned, shaking his head and by extension the flesh of his neck and upper torso. "Joshua White? That doesn't sound like one of my clients, I'm afraid." He gave Calliope another smothered smile. "I'd love to help you, my dear, but my hands are tied."

"That'd be some rope." Calliope's voice and eyes were flat.

Gluen's smile vanished beneath the sea of pulpy flesh. "I'm sorry?"

"Obviously." Calliope turned to Vikous. "You said he'd heard something. I can't even see his ears. I'm leaving."

The bulbous man's eyes narrowed to nothing but shadowed slits in his face. "You question my ability to gather information?"

Calliope looked back at him as though she'd forgotten he was still there. "Honestly, I'm surprised you're not on display somewhere, washing yourself with a rag on a stick."

His eyes widened a fraction, and he pivoted toward Vikous in accusation.

The shabby vagrant laid a gloved hand across his chest and chewed the stub of his cigar to the corner of his mouth. "I just brought her, Gluen; you let her in." His black eyes locked with Gluen's pig-eyed glare.

Calliope waited, smothering the instinctive repulsion that had driven her initial exchange with the fat man only because Vikous had said Gluen might know something about Josh. Something about Gluen made part of her—a primitive core with deeper memories but fewer words—want to crawl away and hide, mewling, in an abandoned corner. Perversely, her more conscious mind responded to that fear with aggression. It was a classic cockroach reaction: *crush* and *cringe* surging in equally powerful waves.

Gluen stare-squinted, smiled, and clapped his hands together. His arms rippled within their sleeves. "Well, I suppose I must prove my worth." He inclined his head to Calliope. "Shall we discuss payment?"

Before she could reply, Vikous said, "You've already been paid, Gluen, and now you're wasting *my* time."

Now the fat man truly did smile, pushing deep crevices into his wreathed cheeks and revealing small sharp teeth. "I have been paid to deliver a message only, my dear Vikous." He swept a heavy arm toward Calliope. "This one wants information as well; for that I have not been recompensed, and I shall be." He raised his eyebrows at Calliope, deep wrinkles furrowing his brow. "Miss?"

Calliope pushed her fedora back and shoved her hands into her jacket pockets. "How much?"

Gluen smiled without showing teeth. "I require only an exchange of information, my dear."

"I don't know anything about what's going on."

He shook his head. "Nothing like that. I want you to tell me something about . . . food."

Calliope hesitated, sure that somehow, in the stillness of the office, she'd heard him wrong.

Gluen turned away from her and moved smoothly back toward the center of the room. "We are, all of us, tied to the idea of consumption. It is the heart and soul of everything we are, everything we do. It is, really, not just how we live but *why* we live. I want to know something interesting about you and that which you have consumed."

Calliope stared at him. "And then you tell me everything I want to know."

He bowed his head graciously, his neck folding in loose rolls. "That's it?"

"My needs are simple." He smiled.

She looked at Vikous, who gave her no hints. "I don't have any . . . stories like that."

Gluen shook his head again, even that small motion sending echoes throughout his body. "Let's not be coy, my dear. In my experience, everyone has 'stories like that', as you say."

She stared at his broad back as he stood at the window. "I . . . choked on a chicken bone once, when I was a little kid."

Gluen's broad smile was a dim reflection in the floor to ceiling windows. "Ahh . . . go on."

Calliope frowned. "There isn't much more to say. I was sitting at the table with my family—we all had a specific seat where we'd sit—my dad was on the right of me where he could see into the living room and to the TV. Mom was on the left where she could get to the stove and the refrigerator, and my sister was across from me. I sat against the wall of the kitchen and I could look out of the kitchen window into the branches of the cotton-wood tree outside of our house." Calliope shifted her stance, but fought the urge to pace. "Dad farmed and Mom kept chickens, for meat. We raised cattle, but we ate chicken a hundred fifty times a year."

"Why do you mention such a particular number?" Calliope couldn't be sure, but it seemed that, in the window's reflection, she caught the tiny pink point of Gluen's tongue dragging across his lips as he spoke.

"That's . . ." She blinked as her memory filled in the answer. "That's how many chicks she got each year. A batch of broilers, she called them."

She shook her head and continued. "Anyway, one weekend—it must have been a weekend because it was during the middle of the day but we were all there—one weekend I started choking on a bone or something. I didn't know what was happening. My dad picked me up—lifted me right over the table and carried me to the sink that was right under the window I always looked out of, bent me over it, and pounded on my back until I coughed the bone out."

"Were you frightened?" Gluen turned back toward her, but his eyes were glistening and far away. "Frightened you might die?"

Calliope shook her head. "It was over too fast to really get scared. I was more scared by my dad pounding on my back. Mostly"—she frowned—"mostly I just remembered that while I was choking, I'd been the center of attention. Everyone was paying attention to me and nothing else. That didn't happen very often."

There was silence in the room for a moment.

"What happened after that?" Gluen seemed on the cusp of some sort of revelation; his face was turned toward the ceiling rather than Calliope, his eyes half closed, his mouth partly open.

Calliope narrowed her eyes at the fat man and looked away. "For the next few weeks I pretended to choke on bones every time we ate chicken."

"Why?"

Calliope's face was a mask. "I wanted them to pay attention to me like that again."

Gluen's eyes closed fully, and his mouth opened farther in something like a perverse rapture. "Thank you, my dear. Thank you very much."

The look on Gluen's face made Calliope feel as though she had shared a much more familiar intimacy with him. Confusion and resentment flared in her chest, along with something close to self-disgust. She had no idea why she had told that story—she hadn't thought about it or anything about her old life for years. Some compulsion had almost seemed to draw it out of her.

"Consumption," Gluen said, his breath a bare rasp of pleasure. "Not just of food, certainly, for you have built a culture of consumption, gluttony." His eyes slowly focused and shifted to Calliope. "We all crave more than what we currently have, do we not, my dear? Force another bite down, angle for more time with a loved one, squeeze yourself into the spotlight just one more time: that is the nature of . . . things." He blinked sleepily, in an almost postcoital languor. Again, his sharp pink tongue, far too dexterous for the rest of his body, flitted over his lips.

Calliope shuddered, but concealed it within the folds of the oversized wool suit; she had no desire to let Gluen realize how deeply disturbing she found the turn in the conversation. "Really glad you're getting your rocks off, but you told me I'd get information; the only thing I've found out so far is that you're a creepy fuck."

Gluen blinked away the last of his glassy-eyed stare and turned away from Calliope. "She is a crude young woman," he said to Vikous.

Vikous chewed slowly on the end of his cigar, shaking flakes of ash onto the lush carpet. "Pay some attention to who you're complaining to if you want any sympathy, fat man."

Gluen scowled for a moment, his face an obese parody of a cherub. "Indeed." He turned and moved toward his desk. "Indeed." With great care, he maneuvered himself into his chair.

"Tomorrow," he said. He raised his arm and motioned to an attendant, flesh swaying on his arm like a damp towel. The man approached with a tray covered with appetizers and candy—both in a number of unlikely colors.

"What?" Calliope looked at Gluen, then the slim attendant, then turned back to the fat man. "What the hell?"

"You already took payment, Gluen," Vikous murmured, taking a half step forward. His hands were buried in his pockets, but the smoldering cigar jutted at an unfriendly angle.

"Technically, I took payment several weeks ago, my dear Vikous." Gluen's pig-eyes flickered to Calliope, the motion mirrored by the darting pink tip of his tongue. "This little exchange was a . . ." He paused, a smirk pushing at the mass of his cheeks like fingers in wet dough. "A trick or treat."

"What the fuck—" Calliope began, her face growing hot, flushed with anger and something very much like shame.

"No business transactions," Gluen interrupted, "on this night." He clicked his tongue, his voice full of regret and admonishment. "*You* know that as well as anyone, Vikous; I'm surprised you bothered bringing the poor girl all this way. Wasted her time."

"Why—"

"Tomorrow," Gluen cut in again, his eyes back on Calliope, hard and black. "Night."

Silence dropped over the empty spaces of the room like loose stones.

"C'mon, Calli." Vikous turned to the door. "Fat man's got candy to eat." He stopped, angling his head back toward Calliope, who had not moved. He opened his mouth to say something, but before he could, she turned and left the room, hitting the doors with enough force to rattle the glass. Vikous watched her go, taking his time following.

"She's unpleasant, Vikous." Gluen spoke around a mouthful of sweets, sucking stickiness from his fingers and examining the tray held before him. "You should rein her in."

Vikous paused, as though he might say something in reply, then kept walking. Only the guard by the door noticed that his mouth was stretched in a smile, and on the whole, he wished he hadn't.

INTERLUDE

Whispers echoed through dusty rooms, making outrageous claims or revealing hurtful secrets. It was difficult to tell the one from the other.

The thing stood on the threshold of what had once been a family room.

"They said you managed to contact the girl again."

"Is that what they said?" Joshua White stood (after a fashion) at the front window, watching sleeting rain slide down the dirty glass. He did not turn to face the thing speaking.

"Yeah."

"Well"—Joshua leaned forward until his hand seemed to rest on the wall—"I suppose they're right. They seem to know about things like that."

"They do." The thing shifted in the doorway, for all the world like a child afraid to approach an angry parent. "They also say you sent a message to Gluen." One bright eye glimmered in the gloom. "How did you do that?"

Joshua almost turned. His head moved a few inches toward his shoulder and the thing standing in the doorway. "They don't just talk to you." His eyes flickered. "Not anymore."

The thing blinked. "I'm . . . sorry about that. That's not why I—"

"She didn't like Vikous, did she?" There was a hint of a smile in Joshua's voice. His eyes were distant and far away.

Again, the thing blinked. "No." It straightened, its arm scraping like a rasp on the door frame. "No, she didn't."

"I didn't figure she would." This time, it was clear Joshua was smiling, and the room was silent for so long that he thought the thing had gone. "That'll change."

"Do you want to—"

"No." Joshua's smile faded. His voice, if it could be called that anymore, went flat. "I don't."

The thing didn't seem to know how to reply. Silence filled up the room like cold water. "This isn't—I thought this would be different," it finally said.

"I wouldn't know about that."

It took a short step into the room. "That's not true! You—" It stopped short, panting through an almost-normal mouth. "It doesn't matter how it starts with her, you know; it always starts different, but it always *ends* the same."

"Does it?" Joshua had turned back to his original position, but during the conversation, the rain had stopped, while the whispering in the corners had gotten stronger.

"It's a long way to have to go." The thing tried to sneer, but its lips trembled. "A very long way."

7

Calliope tried, and failed, to keep Josh from seeing she was crying. "Okay . . . okay, just . . . explain it to me again, please?" Josh gave her a look she knew well enough. She shook her head. "I'm not trying to be difficult; I'm just having trouble understanding, okay?"

"It's not complicated, Calli." Josh leaned forward in his chair, rested his elbows on his knees, and wove his fingers together. His eyes were on the carpet, though, not her, as though he were reading from a note card she couldn't see. "I don't think this—the band—is getting us where we thought we'd be, and honestly I'm too old to keep banging my head against the wall, hoping it'll eventually punch through."

"You're too old?" Calliope made a face. "You just turned thirty. Barely."

"And I pay my rent—barely—by playing bar gigs." His tone was that of someone who'd already said the exact same thing several times before—which Calliope realized he had. "I'm done, okay? I have to be done."

Fresh tears stung her eyes. She shoved at them with a fist, sniffing hard.

Josh's face was a mask. "I'm sorry this is hurting you so much."

She sniffed again, glancing up, then away. "Doesn't look like it."

"Well, it's hard, Calli, when—" He stopped himself and sat back in the chair, shaking his head, lips tight.

"What?" She saw his expression and looked away. "I can't read your mind, Josh." She looked back at him. "Please."

He didn't look away, but didn't answer, either. She waited; she wasn't as good at it as he was, but this time it was enough. He sighed through his nose, his lips still tight, and gave a small shake of his head. "I wasn't really expecting you to get that upset, I guess."

She stared at him. "Really."

He ignored the sarcasm. "It caught me off balance. I wasn't ready for it."

"You—" She stopped, looked down, and worked her jaw while she thought of a way to say what she was thinking that didn't end with her screaming. "I'm not sure how you'd think I was going to react."

"Not like this," he replied. His voice was a mixture of bemusement and anger. "Jesus Christ, Cal, you didn't so much as reach for a Kleenex when we broke up; why—"

"I knew that was coming!" She flung her hands away from her body, her fingers spread wide and aching from being clenched in her lap for so long. The motion left her feeling stupidly overdramatic, and she curled back in on herself, her eyes dropping to the floor.

The words hung, vibrating, in the air of her (once, their) apartment. Calliope imagined she could see them, glowing like a sign, waiting for someone to read them before they faded away.

"Well, that makes one of us." Josh's voice was quiet, soaking up and stealing away the energy of Calliope's shout. "But then, I was always stupid about things like that."

She frowned, still looking at the floor. "Is that what this is about?"

He closed his eyes, as though the question made him tired, and

shook his head. "No." His eyes met hers; he seemed to lean into
the gaze, as though he could push some kind of understanding
through the connection. "This is about me, leaving the band. Doing
something else." He dropped back into the chair and quirked a tiny,
self-effacing smile. "Growing up."

Calliope managed not to react to those last two words, for all
that they hurt the worst of anything he'd yet said; she could see he
hadn't meant it as an attack, and she was well and truly sick of
making him feel bad for every single thing he said.

"Okay," she said, wiping at her eyes with the heel of her hand.
"Okay."

Josh watched her, his face cautious. "Yeah?"

"Yeah."

"Hey."

Calliope opened her eyes only the bare minimum necessary
to get a hazy impression of her surroundings. Morning light was
stubbornly attempting to force its way into the room, but in the
gloom the figure sitting on the edge of her bed was little more
than a dim silhouette. She closed her eyes, letting out a deep sigh.

A moment later, her body tensed, and she jerked into a sitting
position, leaning back from the stranger in her room.

She blinked her eyes hard until the edges of objects and her
visitor came into focus. Another few seconds passed as she
stared through sleep-wrecked hair, then dropped back to the
pillow with another loud sigh that ended with "Hey."

She caught a small smile on Tom's face. "You always wake up
so gracefully." His voice was quiet and calm, pitched to wake
a person up gently.

"Mmm." She tried to inject a matching amusement into her

voice, but it sounded false even to her—like a different kind of emotion entirely. Bitter. Silence built up until the two of them being on the bed together felt awkward.

Tom unfolded the leg he'd tucked under himself and set both feet on the floor, turning away from Calliope. "They said you stopped by last night."

Calliope stared at his back until the words made sense. "Oh." She finger-combed her hair out of her face and nodded. "Yeah. The club. Yeah."

"I'm sorry I didn't have you come back." He glanced at her over his shoulder. "We had a bad first set and I couldn't really talk—trying to get my head on straight."

"It's fine," she said. The words came out precise and short, and Calliope could see Tom's shoulders tighten—she sounded angry, and couldn't seem to stop it.

"Okay. I just wanted to apologize." He stood up.

Calliope's chest tightened, and she said the first thing she could think of. "And . . . sneak into my house and watch me while I sleep."

Tom turned. "What?"

Shit. "Kidding. It just . . ."—she pushed herself up to the head of the bed and drew her legs up—"surprised me. I don't wake up very well, right?" Tom didn't immediately reply. In the shadowed room, she couldn't make out his eyes. "What—"

"I made you some coffee." He turned and walked out of the room.

Shit. "Wait. Tom . . ." Calliope shoved the covers out of the way and rolled across the bed and to her feet. She was still wearing everything but her shoes from the previous night— no surprise, since she only vaguely remembered getting home.

He was walking out of the kitchen and pulling on his jacket

when she walked into the front of the house. "I didn't mean to show up where I wasn't invited," he murmured, his eyes on anything but her. "You showed up at the club."

"I did," she agreed.

"I figured you wanted to talk," he continued as though she hadn't spoken.

"I *did*," she repeated. "I'm sorry, I just made a bad joke. I didn't mean anything by it. Please."

He glanced up at her, shoved his hands in his pockets, and leaned against the wall. Not great, but not leaving. She took what she could get.

"Thank you," she said, letting out a pent-up breath. "Do you want some of that coffee?"

He hesitated in the way he did when he didn't want to say what he was thinking; normally, Calliope found the habit irritating, but at the moment she was just as happy not knowing what was going through his head. "I'm good," he replied. "Already had too much today."

And now you give him a little smile and ask if he'll still be there in a minute if you go in the kitchen and get some for yourself. He'll like it.

But she didn't. A perverse part of her refused. Somehow, that was letting him win. Somehow, that was a bad thing.

The problem was it left her with nothing to say, even though she'd been the one to stop him, and the silence between them built up again.

Tom saved her. "Toby said you promised him you'd come back and sing sometime."

Calliope let out a short, surprised bark of a laugh. "Oh really?" She shook her head at the ceiling. "I think he might have been overstating my part of the conversation."

"He said you left pretty quick." Tom's eyes were still anywhere but on her. "With a friend?"

"It was just work."

He studied her in morning light coming in through the front window. His expression was carefully neutral. "Well, he wasn't totally wrong, then, if you were working on something with Joshua."

"I—" Calliope felt her eyes go wide as she turned and focused on him. "Oh. God. I didn't—"

"Didn't wh—"

"Josh is—"

dead

"missing." She heard her voice shake. "The police are still trying to figure out what happened."

Tom frowned, pushing away from the wall and moving a few steps toward her. "He called you—"

She nodded. "Last n—" She shook her head. "Two nights ago."

"Three," he murmured. At her look, his brow creased. He extended his index finger. "Last night, you were at the club." A second finger. "Night before, you didn't come home." A third finger. "Joshua called in the middle of the night." He turned his hand toward her, palm out, fingers still extended, and waggled them.

Calliope looked past the fingers at him. "I was at the office."

His eyes slid away from hers. "I didn't ask."

Heat bloomed in her face. "I was trying to help the cops with Josh—I was digging through files." She scowled in annoyance. "And how do you know I wasn't here?" Her voice sounded loud in her own ears.

"You told me to come by and pick up my stuff." Tom's voice

was calm and quiet. For Calliope, that was one of the most annoying things about arguing with him. "I waited about an hour past when you'd normally get home, then I took off." He stuck his hands in his back pockets. "I drove by after the show, but your Jeep was still gone. I went back to Sean's." His eyelids dropped, concealing his expression. "I wasn't stalking—just following orders."

Tom wasn't the easiest person to read, but that small signal was at least something Calliope understood. She sighed. "I'm really sorry I said that, okay? It was just a joke. A *bad* joke."

"It's okay." His mouth moved in an unexpected smirk. "It *is* a little stalkery when you list it off all at once, especially when you throw in the Cullenesque sleep–watching." He crossed his arms and faked a shudder. "Now I feel dirty."

Calliope laughed—a genuine, cleansing thing that felt like washing her face with cold water. Tom spread his arms, head tilted and eyebrows raised. Calliope nodded, took two steps to close the gap, and wrapped herself in him.

Above her, Tom murmured something unintelligible. "What?" she asked.

He lifted his head. "Did your all–nighter at the office help?"

"Maybe." She told him about the answering machine message and its impossible time stamp.

"Jesus, they think he's dead?" He squeezed her harder. "What kind of jobs are you two working on?"

She shook her head, her face still against his chest. "I don't know what this thing was—I never had anything to do with it."

"Good." Calliope tensed in his arms, and he could clearly feel it. "Sorry, I just mean it's kind of crazy, you know? Even if he's okay, the idea that he *could* be on a job that dangerous—"

"It's just work." She heard the defensiveness creep into her voice and hated it more than a little.

"You're not saving the world, Calli, you're tracking down skip traces." He gave her another hug, hard enough to squeeze the latent tension out of her. "There's a point where you have stop and say 'This is not worth my life.'"

"I know," she murmured.

"Does Joshua?" She pulled her head back and looked up at him, expression carefully neutral. "He's kind of a paladin, is all I'm saying."

She nodded and leaned against him again. "He knows. He's lectured me about it often enough."

"Mmm."

"Anyway," she said. "There's the phone call. He's not dead, even if he is in Iowa." Tom's low chuckle carried into Calliope's chest, easing her worry a fraction. "It's worse than that," she said, riding the momentum of Tom's amusement. "The only lead I've figured out might mean I have to go out there myself." She let the statement trail off into a small laugh, but stopped when there was no answering sound from Tom. Around her, his arms had gone unresponsive, dead weight holding her down rather than a comforting embrace.

"Go out to Iowa." It was a statement, not a question.

"Maybe?" The change in his mood left her off balance. "I'm not sure yet if it's even—"

"You told me once you'd never go back there," he said. "'Not for anyone.'"

Calliope's breath went cold inside her chest. She stepped back out of Tom's embrace; he let her go without a hint of reluctance. "That was something else entirely."

He nodded, moving slowly. "Well, it was me." He said the words the way someone might say *mostly cloudy*. "Not Joshua."

Her eyes narrowed. "He might be dead. Definitely in trouble."

"And you're running off to save him." Tom's mouth twisted, as though he'd just realized a new kind of pain. "Right into the same thing that he ran into. Blind."

"I don't—"

"No." He shook his head. "You can't do this."

She sighed. "Listen—"

"No." He leveled a long, calloused finger at her. "For once, you listen." Incredibly, even now, he wasn't raising his voice; Calliope wondered if he even knew how. "You—" His eyes came up to hers, and he stopped. For a few seconds, his finger continued pointing at her, then he lowered it. He took a breath as though he were about to say something, held it, shook his head, and let it out in a long exhalation. Calliope blinked when he turned to the door and opened it on the chilly morning.

"What . . ." She couldn't think of anything else to say, but it was enough to make him stop, at least for a second.

He turned just enough to look at her sidelong over his shoulder. "You've already decided you're going," he murmured. "I don't know if you know it yet, but you have." He turned back to the open door, straightened his shoulders from his subtle, perpetual stoop, and stretched. His next words were spoken to the open morning air. "And you're going for Joshua, pure and simple, and I don't know if you know that, either."

Her throat grew tight. "That's not fair."

"I love you," he said, as though she hadn't spoken. "I'm going to be crazy worried about you until you come back." He moved out onto the front step and turned back just enough to reach the door handle, without meeting her eyes. "So, please come back."

"Tom—"

"I love you. Be careful."

The door closed. The house might have been dead quiet, but Calliope couldn't tell over the pulse beating at her ears.

When the phone rang, Calliope—still standing in the entryway, staring at the door—jumped as though she'd been electrocuted.

She fumbled the phone out of the pocket of her jacket where it hung on the back of a chair. The screen displayed a number she already recognized, and she thumbed the answer button. "Good morning, Detective."

"Likewise, M—" He paused. "Calliope."

"Well done," she murmured, trying to inject some kind of amusement into her voice.

"Thank you," he deadpanned. "I practiced. How was your Halloween?"

"Eventful, but nothing worth reporting to precinct." Despite their conversation the previous evening, Calliope felt only the barest flicker of guilt at this evasion, remarkable only because it was there at all.

"Fair enough."

"How did your partner's boy do with the records down at the office?"

"My—" Calliope could hear a moment's hesitation in Johnson's voice.

"Walker."

"Ahh. Yes." Johnson took a breath. "Technically, Special

Agent Walker is not my partner—I am a liaison between his office and the department. I facilitate what I can, but he is directing an investigation in which I have no official role or jurisdiction."

Calliope could hear an overcareful precision in his tone and wording. She was willing to bet he was, at some level, vein-poppingly livid about something, but too good a cop to let it show. She'd also put a smaller bet on the source of his stress. "Things a bit tense down there?"

Johnson didn't respond immediately. "The agent didn't have much luck last night—or this morning, come to that."

Calliope winced. "Our filing system is a little arcane." She let her eyes drift to the front window, but Tom's car was long gone. "I could come down and help sort it out for him for a while, if you'd like."

"Special Agent Walker has assigned a second agent to the files," Johnson not-replied.

"I could still speed things up for them, even if there's nothing to find."

She heard Johnson exhale over the line and knew they'd gotten to the part she wouldn't like. "Special Agent Walker doesn't believe that your help will be necessary."

Calliope turned that over in her head. She chose each word as she went, moving through her reply as if each syllable were rigged to explode. "Would Special Agent Walker like me to stay clear of his agents while they work through the files?"

Another small exhalation she didn't imagine Johnson realized she could hear. "He would."

Calliope closed her eyes. "Has he filed any paperwork or given specific orders to that effect?"

"He has."

"He's keeping me out of our office."

"Yes." The detective cleared his throat. "The file system was very confusing."

"He thinks I'm obstructing." Her lips felt cold; numb. "Or he thinks I'm a suspect."

"No." Johnson's tone was adamant, but he hesitated after the denial. "Not a suspect," he finally added.

Not a murder suspect. That's a comfort.

"Do you think I'm obstructing, Detective Johnson?"

"I'm not heading up this investigation, Calliope," he replied, laying a soft emphasis on her first name.

"That's a pretty cheap sidestep, *Darryl*."

"I'm not even seconded onto it," he protested. His voice was even, but contained more than a little disgust. "I'm not exactly welcome around Walker either, now."

Realization came to Calliope, accompanied by widened eyes. "You went off on Walker?"

"If you need to reach me in the next few days," Johnson replied, "use my office number—I'll be at my desk."

"I'm sorry."

"Not at all." He cleared his throat. "As an upside, I can get home early and see my kids before bed this week."

"Congratulations," Calliope said.

"Thank you." Another pause. "I was hoping you might have thought of a more productive angle than the files in your office to work on, anyway."

It was Calliope's turn to deadpan. "I did say I'd tell you if anything came up."

"And I'd like to hold you to that," Johnson said. Calliope heard his chair creak and imagined him leaning forward over his desk, shielding the phone from the rest of his office.

"Though I have to warn you: given my new working arrange-
ments, it may take *quite* some time before I'm able to share any
new information with Walker."

Calliope laughed; after her talk with Tom, it was a relief. "I'll
take that under consideration, Detective."

"I'm glad to hear that," Johnson replied. There were a few
moments of silence. Calliope could smell the coffee Tom had
made, but couldn't bring herself to have any. Yet. She knew she
would, eventually, and that it would make her feel guilty, and
that *that* would make her angry; first at herself, then (mostly)
at Tom, even—

Detective Johnson cleared his throat. "*Is* there any new
information?"

"Sorry." Calliope shook the thoughts away. "I was just . . .
planning my day, I guess."

"You don't make it sound like it's going to be a very good day."

"Eh." She dropped onto her couch. "That's how it goes sometimes. Let's talk about the other thing."

Again, she heard a chair creak on his end of the line, and
her mental image showed him leaning back. "I'm going to take
a stab and guess it has something to do with the fat man that
Joshua mentioned in his message."

Calliope blinked. "You know you'd make a pretty good detective, Detective."

"Sometimes," Johnson replied. "Not so much in this case."

"How so?"

"Two reasons." Johnson shifted in his chair again, though not
so much as he had. Calliope didn't get the impression that he
was very used to sitting while he worked. "One, it was the only
thing that even vaguely resembled a lead, unless you were
withholding evidence, which I don't think you were."

"Thank you," Calliope said, and meant it.

"You're entirely welcome."

She got up and wandered away from the couch. "You said there were two reasons."

"I did." Calliope could hear him lean forward over his desk again. "The second reason is—yeah?" The last word came to Calliope slightly muffled, in a different tone of voice; Johnson had been interrupted at his desk by another officer. Guessing from the tone of his voice, Calliope didn't think it was a superior, but neither did she think it was anyone he particularly liked. Johnson's end of the line became completely muffled; Calliope could only make out that there were two men talking. She rummaged around the kitchen while she waited; first a cupboard for a mug, then a drawer for a spoon—pulling items out by absentminded habit. She was just setting the sugar back where it belonged when she heard Johnson's hand come away from his mouthpiece. "Sorry."

"No worries," she replied. "That's the job."

"That's the job today, yes." Johnson sounded annoyed. "But I can deal with that later—the second reason is something you should know about."

"Yeah?" Calliope sipped from the mug in her hands.

"Our . . . mutual acquaintance?"

Calliope's brow creased. "Walker?" she hazarded.

"Exactly. Our mutual friend has been very interested in the fat man reference as well." Johnson's voice lowered. "That's mostly what he has his boys looking for in your agency's files: some kind of record of him. Pretty obsessive."

"That," Calliope observed, "is something I am absolutely sure he's not going to find." She took another sip. "And not because I hid any files. It just doesn't exist." She reconsidered telling

Johnson about her whole weird evening, but decided against it. It felt too personal, like describing a vivid dream to a stranger. "I . . . know who it is now, but I can absolutely guarantee we never did any kind of work with the guy in the past."

"But you've spoken with him."

"Yeah."

"And he told you . . ."

"Nothing."

Silence on the other end of the line. "That doesn't sound like much of a lead."

"He was—"

Forbidden from conducting business on Halloween.

"—busy. Told me to come back later today."

"Doesn't sound very helpful," Johnson said. "Or safe."

"Helpful? No, he isn't. But safe? He's a downtown suit."

Kinda.

"He's not a threat," she said, trying to sound sure. She turned the mug in her hands. "And if he were, I could outrun him."

"Ahh," Johnson said. "The nickname's accurate, then?"

"You have no idea."

"Unfortunately, I don't." Johnson's voice shifted to Serious Cop. "This isn't my case, Calliope, and I told you to let me know if you found anything out, which you did. I have no reason to suspect you, and I don't . . ." He sighed. "With that said, this *isn't* my case, and you need to understand how your involvement would look to anyone else, and that none of it would break in your favor right now."

"I do." She considered what she'd told Tom. "I think it might mean I have to go out there."

"There?" Johnson turned that over in silence. Calliope let him work it out. "Iowa."

"Yeah." She tried to keep the tone of her voice neutral, but to her ears, it didn't seem as though it worked. "Maybe."

"You said your contact hadn't told you anything yet," Johnson countered. "What makes you think you need to go out to where your partner—" He caught himself. "Out there," he finished.

"I—" She paused, brought up short. Now that she thought about it, she'd had no reason to tell Tom that this morning. Somehow, her half-awake brain had munged all the stuff going on in the last few days into a half-sorted pile, and extracted—

> " . . . *you can't take her with you." The vagabond in the doorway stepped into the room. "You can't. She's not part of this. You can't—"*

"It's just a hunch," she said.

Detective Johnson didn't say anything for a few moments— long enough for Calliope to wonder if he was actually going to say anything, or simply wait for her to offer up something more compelling, less crazy. Finally: "Last year, I got put on a missing persons case."

Calliope frowned. "Oh-kay." She thought for a moment. "You're homicide."

"I am," he agreed. "It looked pretty bad." He paused. "It was a kid. A little girl."

"I'm sorry," Calliope said, still frowning. "I'm not sure—"

"The parents were very scared," Detective Johnson continued. "And a lot of us working on the case were parents. A lot of dads and moms trying to figure out what happened and how we could find the kid." He took a deep breath. "We had a lot of *hunches*. Hundreds."

Calliope bent her head. "But it turned out to be a homicide case all along."

"It did." Detective Johnson said. "I'm not saying anything about your partner—honestly, there's too much weird in this case to rule anything out—but make sure you know where your hunches are coming from. Make sure you know your reasons." Another voice spoke in the background on Johnson's end of the line. He muffled the phone again, said a few words, and then came back to her. "I need to go."

"Absolutely."

"Please contact me if you get any more information."

"I will," she said, her voice soft. "Promise."

"Good."

He hung up. Calliope stood, facing the counter for a few more seconds. Then she shook herself, set the phone down, and picked up the mug.

The mug filled with coffee.

Which she'd fixed without consciously realizing what she was doing.

It smelled really good.

She let out an explosive, wordless sound of annoyance, dumped the mug in the sink, and stalked out of the kitchen.

―――

Calliope stood in front of her mirror, wringing water out of her hair with a towel, her eyes tracking the dark water spots across the shoulders of the clean T-shirt she'd pulled on after her shower. Behind her, in the mirror, the bed was rumpled, the sheets twisted—proof enough of a bad night's sleep, even if she couldn't also feel it in her neck and back.

"You always wake up so gracefully."

She scowled and tossed the towel over the shower rack, then

started for the door of the bedroom. But she lost momentum and stopped after only a few steps. The crease across her brow deepened.

"Make sure you know your reasons."

Still facing the mirror, she turned her head, wincing at the pain in her neck, and checked the clock. Still morning. Early. Most of the day to kill, banned from the office.

"But those aren't the only old files to check," she murmured.

She finger-combed damp hair out of her face, blew out a long breath, and glared at the disheveled bed lurking behind her in the mirror.

Reaching behind her, she twisted her hair into a loose knot, turned, stepped up to the bed, and tugged the covers into an approximation of order. That done, she dropped into a crouch, reached underneath the bed and, after several half-voiced growls and curses, fished out two oversized, dust-coated shoe boxes, one labeled BAND STUFF; the other, NOT BAND STUFF.

She swiped at BAND STUFF with the edge of her hand and wiped the resulting film of dust on her jeans as she flipped the lid up.

Unlabeled demo CDs lay in a stack on top of several T-shirts folded with the rigid precision and sharp edges of an American flag presented to a soldier's widow. The other end of the box was a collection of flyers from clubs throughout Silverlake and Echo Park, bar coasters, clippings of reviews, and a small jumble of junk masquerading as mementos. All told, the box was two-thirds full, arranged like a memorial shrine for a distant relative.

Calliope riffled the edges of the CD cases, rolled her eyes at the ridiculously overenthusiastic headlines, and flipped the lid shut before pushing the box to the side.

Sitting back on her heels, she pulled the second box to her

and hooked her fingers under the rubber bands that held the bent, center-bulging lid of NOT BAND STUFF in place. The smooth outward tug pulled both rubber bands off simultaneously with a muffled *snap-pop*, and the lid immediately eased upward a half inch. Calliope lifted it and set it aside, scanning a heaped stack of paper and photos that—as far as organization went—had more in common with a clothes hamper than the BAND box that sat nearby.

The topmost slip of paper—a barely legible handwritten note—slid off the stack and onto the floor. Calliope picked it up, thumbed it open, and tipped her head to read the words she already knew.

Hiya!

I think I found an APARTMENT!
I know we said we were going to wait to look at an
APARTMENT.
But it's a good APARTMENT.
You should see this APARTMENT.
It's a good APARTMENT.
I love you, and will listen better next time.

—Josh

P.S. APARTMENT!

She refolded the note and set it back in place. Leaning forward, she picked up the overstuffed box, rose up, and dumped the contents onto the bed.

"I want a face to kiss."

Calliope, curled up in an overstuffed chair widely considered the ugliest and most comfortable in the city, speaks (loudly) to an empty room. Earbud headphones dangle from her neck; she holds a book half closed in her lap, one finger marking her place, and listens.

Several seconds later, a door opens and footsteps move in her direction—a steadily increasing drum roll cadence. Josh slides into view, tipping his weight at the last moment to lean against the room's door frame, his arms crossed. He raises his eyebrows, assuming the bored expression of a Bond villain, and says "Sorry?"

Calliope settles into the chair, a smirk poking dimples in her cheeks. "I . . . want a face to kiss."

He tips his head, brow furrowed. "I see. Well . . ." He glances over his shoulder and down the hall. "I can check the take-out menus— see if the Thai place has 'face'."

Calliope raises an eyebrow, fighting to control her expression. "I do not think you understand."

Joshua cocks his ear toward her. "I don't—"

"I." She points at her chest. "Face." She points at Josh, then swings her finger in a lopsided oval. "Kiss." Again, she points at herself; specifically, her mouth.

"Ohhhhh . . ." Josh exclaims. "Right." He rushes straight at her, building momentum and dropping to his knees halfway across the room to slide the rest of the way to the chair.

"Oh god," she says, lifting her book in front of her as a shield. The chair lurches and thuds against the wall. She lets out a small, much-delayed yelp and peeks from behind the book.

Josh waggles his eyebrows at her from a few inches away, still fighting for balance as he leans forward on one knee. "Hi."

"Hello," Calliope drawls, pulling her book slightly out of the way and tilting her face to the side. "Kees me."

He tips his head toward her, his lips a bare inch from hers. She feels his weight shift, catch, and shift again. "Crap," he comments, then crashes to the floor in front of the chair.

Her laughter rolls out of the open third-floor window, loud enough that several people on the street below look up at the sound.

"I want to go there." Calliope sits on the futon with her feet tucked under her. It's one of only three pieces of furniture in the apartment (not including the stool shared between the keyboards and drum set), and obviously the most used. She indicates the small television screen across the room with her spoon, then scoops up another bite of cereal. Outside the window, it's dark.

Josh glances up at the screen from where he sits at their keyboard, scratching at a score sheet and testing out chords. The set is muted, but the camera pans slowly over lush foliage and stone pyramids. "Belize?"

"Is that where that is?" Josh gives her an amused look and she whirls her spoon above her head. "Yes! Belize! My one and only dream! The place I have wanted to visit since . . ."

"Today?"

"Since years ago." She juts out her chin at him.

He grins. "Today?"

"Since before I could say the name." She takes another bite of cereal.

"Which"—he sets his pencil aside and pushes the rolling stool toward her, easing off it and onto the couch next to her—"was today, since you didn't know the name until about ten seconds ago."

She pulls the spoon out of her mouth. "Details," she enunciates, chewing.

"Mmm." He props his feet up on the rolling stool, watching the footage of Bermuda-shorts-decked tourists sweating their way up the side of a steep stone structure. "It looks pretty cool."

"I know, right?" She watches in silence, then returns to her bowl. "Someday," she murmurs.

"Someday," he repeats. They watch the images dissolve one into the other, the only sound the crunch of Calliope's cereal as she eats. Josh looks at her sidelong, then pushes himself into a sitting position, turned halfway toward her. "You know, we could get out of here for a while."

Calliope looks at him, swallows, and says, "You mean go on the road again?"

He shakes his head. "Nope."

"Good." She sips milk from the bowl. "Because the 'on the road' thing didn't work so well last time."

"Agreed." He scratches at his cheek stubble. "I meant just us going somewhere."

"The van's toast," she replies. "Twelve huunnnndred dollahs feex."

"Maggie said we could borrow her car anytime. She never drives it."

"True . . ." Calliope allows. "But we can't really afford to go anywhere."

"Unless we go somewhere we know people we can stay with."

She eyes him, making a skeptical face. "What, like Penny?" She softens her expression. "I mean . . . no, I'm sorry, she would totally let us crash, but it's been raining up in Portland for, like, forty-five days straight."

"Sure. Good point." He settles back into the futon and turns back to the screen. A few seconds later, he lifts his head and looks at her. "We could go somewhere it's not raining."

Bowl raised to her lips, she hesitates, then sets the bowl down, shakes her head, and starts to get up from the futon. "No."

"It's an easy drive." He leans forward again. "You told me you've done it lots of times."

She moves to the sink in the area just past the front door that had passed for a "kitchenette" in the rental ad. "Yeah, I did. I also said I didn't ever want to do the drive again." She sets the bowl in the sink, drops the spoon in, and runs water over the clatter. "Or go at all," she mutters. Over the sound of the water, she says, "We have to finish the new demo."

He pushes himself up and perches on the edge of the cushion. "We always have a demo to do," he counters. "And we don't have a job lined up until the nineteenth." He spreads his hands. "We save all our money for gas, sleep in the car, and we could stay out there for a couple weeks, no problem."

"A couple weeks?" She clenches her shoulders in a not-entirely-mock shudder. "I wouldn't last a couple days. No."

"You said you wanted to get away," Josh wheedles, smiling.

"I said I wanted to go someplace nice." She swirls soapy water around the bowl harder than necessary and blows drifting hair out of her eyes. "Someplace exotic." She looks sideways at him over her shoulder. "Driving to Bumfuck, Egypt, is not exotic."

He stands, sidling across the room toward her. "I bet someone out there is raising a camel."

"No."

". . . or a llama. That's exotic."

"No."

"Lllllllama." He slips his hands around her waist.

"No!"

. . . a ringing slap. Bright red handprint on her cheek. Surprised tears in wide eyes . . .

She shakes her head to banish the thought, yanks the faucet handle down, and jerks away from him, grabbing a dish towel. "I don't want to go back there. Ever. Jesus. Fucking listen." *She turns to walk away, stops, turns back toward him, stops, and finally turns back to the sink and grabs the bowl with a towel-shrouded hand.*

"Hey." His voice is soft. He starts to reach for her again, but she moves her shoulder away before she can stop herself. He stops, lets his hand drop. "Sorry," he murmurs, barely audible. She doesn't reply, and after a few awkward seconds, he walks around her and down the hall to their bedroom.

Calliope doesn't look up or watch him leave. Once the bowl and spoon are wiped down, she sets them in the drying rack, moving as though she is afraid they might break, or that she will. Once done, she hangs up the towel and leans on the sink.

The door to the bedroom closes, leaving her in silence, alone in the kitchen.

Just like before.

"Dammit." Her voice is a whisper.

Calliope jerked up from where she'd been curled on the bed, surrounded by old pictures and handwritten notes. For a moment, she didn't know what had woken her; then the knock came again—the kind of sharp, piercing rap that very few people could manage without using an actual knocker.

She didn't move, though, until the knock came a third time. When it did, she lurched to her knees, bounce-stepping across the mattress as carefully as she could to keep from bending photos. Papers drifted to the ground in her wake; she pulled the door to the bedroom closed as she left.

She checked the peephole, but saw no one and jerked the door open, stepping outside to call back whomever had knocked. She stopped after a single step forward.

"Hey," Vikous said, his face shadowed by the sweatshirt hood. He shoved his gloved hands into the pockets of his coat. "Ready to go?"

Calliope didn't reply. After a few seconds—during which she leaned forward far enough to check the street in both directions, as though hoping there might be someone else waiting—she stepped back and crossed her arms, leaning on the doorjamb.

Vikous sighed in a way that made his chest rumble. Unconsciously mirroring Calliope, he checked the street to either side as well. "Might not be such a great idea having a long conversation out in the open." He turned his attention back to Calliope, whose stony expression had not changed, and shrugged. "Just saying."

Calliope's eyelids lowered in annoyance and she looked away, her jaw working. Rummaging through her old life, sloppily jammed into a shoe box, had left her in a foul mood. It was everything she could do not to simply shut the door in Vikous's face, but she suspected she'd feel that way regardless of who was standing on her front step.

Finally, she turned and pulled the door open, motioning him inside with a twitch of her hand. Vikous seemed to accept this—wisely—as the best invitation he was likely to get and stepped inside, then moved out of the way as she swung the door shut and walked back into the house, dropping into an oversized chair in the corner of the living room. He sat down across from her.

She looked up and frowned. "You don't need the hood in here."

At this, he hesitated. After a few moments, he reached a gloved hand up and pushed away his hood, then sat back.

Calliope's eyebrow quirked. "That face paint has to be itching like hell by now."

Vikous's bead-black eyes stayed on hers, shining in the midst of the paste-white face and violently reddened mouth and lips of the clown's face that she'd first seen on him the night before. "Not really."

"How—" She cut herself off, fighting another spike of irritation. Any other time, curiosity would have pushed her further, but not today. "Never mind."

"Fine." He pushed himself forward and cleared his throat. "What—"

"Why are you here?" she interrupted.

"You have an appointment with Gluen." He folded his hands behind his head and leaned back in the chair. "Figured I'd tag along."

"That's tonight." She glanced at the cheap plastic clock hanging on the wall. Several hours later than she'd expected—she'd dozed off for longer than she'd thought—but still nowhere near nightfall.

"Yep," her visitor replied. Calliope waited, but he offered nothing further. Her eyes narrowed.

She stood up and walked toward the kitchen. "You want coffee?"

Vikous ignored the delaying tactic. "Coffee's fine. No sugar. Put yours in a travel mug, if you've got one."

The two didn't speak. There was no sound except the clink of cups being moved and filled, then Calliope returned and handed Vikous a cup. She sat down with hers—heavy, ceramic, and terrible for travel—held between both hands. "The cops called back this morning."

Vikous reached up, scratched at the corner of his mouth, nodding to himself as though confirming a suspicion. "You don't say." He took a long drink from the steaming cup and grimaced, his lips stretching back. "What did—" He interrupted himself, his face suddenly sharp. "Did you tell them about me?"

"Homeless stalker guy?" she said. "I mentioned you yesterday, but didn't say much." She took a drink herself, her mouth twisting. The coffee was still hot, but had been cooking down since early this morning, untouched. "Hot" was the only thing it had going for it. "I didn't want them worrying about something that didn't have anything to do with the case."

"Did they buy that?"

"Buy it? Hell, I believed it when I said it; there was nothing to buy."

"But they let it be?"

Calliope frowned, her head tilted. "Johnson did. Walker got a little squirrelly about it for a while."

"Which one's Walker?"

Calliope described the sharp V's of the federal agent's features. "Why?" she asked.

He shook his head and took another drink, swallowing forcefully. "Just wondering. Walker's an . . ." He shook his head. "Interesting name, at least."

His questions had reminded Calliope of something else. "Walker said that a homeless guy was seen around the place where Joshua was—" She looked down at her coffee cup, clenching her jaw. "Where they found the body."

Vikous looked at her over the rim of the cup. "Yeah?"

"Was there?"

He finished his drink and let his eyes slide away from hers into the empty cup. "Might have been."

"Was it you?"

He shook his head. "It's a very long way," he said in a different, softer tone of voice.

"I realize that. I'm purposely living about as far away from there as you can get without learning another language."

He looked up at that, then shook himself free of the quiet in the room. "So what did Detective Johnson and Special Agent Walker have to say?"

"It was just Johnson." She scowled. "They've gone over Josh's last message and can't get anything more out of it." She blew air between her teeth in disgust. "The official opinion is that the time stamp is a hardware malfunction."

"The one that says the call came in—"

"After he supposedly died."

"So they're giving up?"

"No." She told Vikous about being blocked from returning to her office while Walker's people searched the files.

"That's an awful lot of work to find something they heard about on a malfunctioning answering machine," Vikous observed.

"Kind of what I thought," Calliope replied. "But Walker and I didn't really hit it off; I figure it's just him pulling a dick move to amuse himself; mess up our files, leave them for me to straighten out. It's happened before."

"Sure." Vikous tipped his head to the side, as though mulling over possibilities. "Or they're actually trying to find out more about Gluen."

"Why would they? There's no real reason, from their point of view." She stood up. "They don't know half of what I do, and I don't know a goddamn thing." She looked at Vikous. "Do I?"

"I wouldn't put it that way," Vikous said, "but you're not

wrong." He stood up and handed her his empty cup. She'd barely touched hers. "You wanna fix that?"

Her brow furrowed. "How?"

"A little side trip before going to see Gluen." He made a show of looking out the front window of the house. "It's why I showed up early."

"Some cunning plan, like last night?" Calliope turned back to the kitchen and walked away. Vikous watched her back, then followed her as far as the archway. She looked up from the sink as she emptied her mug. "What if I say no?"

"Then you say no." He shrugged in a way that made his coat shift in unusual ways. "It's not a big deal—just something maybe-useful." He leaned against the archway. "If you want to hang out here for hours, pining for the moment you can go see Gluen again, that's your call."

Calliope turned back to the sink to rinse out the cup. "When you put it like that, not going along sounds pretty stupid."

"Only if you don't like Gluen."

"Which I don't."

"No one does," Vikous replied. "Even among his own kind, he's considered creepy."

"What's—" Calliope cut herself off with a shake of her head, pulling down a towel and drying her hands.

"What's his kind?" Vikous asked for her. "Short question. Long answer. Come with me and we can start working through it."

She turned back to Vikous, who returned her look with his impossible black eyes.

This time it was Calliope who gave in. "Where are we going?"

"*Kegeln*," Vikous replied.

Calliope looked from the sign above the building's entrance to Vikous, standing on the other side of her Jeep. "Bowling?"

"*Kegeln*," Vikous replied.

"Which means?"

"Bowling," he said, walking toward the entrance.

Calliope scowled at his back as he strolled across the mostly empty parking lot, then followed him.

Vikous was already at the cashier's counter (old; repainted so many times that the corners were rounded and each nick and chip looked like a bite taken out of a jawbreaker) when she entered. A young girl with half-lidded eyes and a face full of silver piercings asked him a question as she opened the till to make change. He turned to Calliope. "Do you need shoes?" Calliope raised an incredulous eyebrow. His face moved in a way that Calliope associated with rolled eyes—an expression somewhat wasted with him—and he turned back to the girl. "Yeah, she needs shoes."

"'Kay. Do you?"

"I'm not bowling."

The girl shrugged and reached under the counter, pulling out a pair of worn leather shoes that she pushed across the counter to Calliope.

Calliope eyed the shoes, turning them to check the size tattooed on the back. "Good guess."

The girl snorted and shook her head. "Whatever, man." She wandered down to the other end of the counter.

"Nice."

"Grab your shoes," Vikous said, heading for one of the lanes. He held a scoring sheet and half a pencil in one hand—the alley hadn't been updated with computerized scoring systems. Vikous settled into one of the orange, contoured fiberglass chairs at the lane's tiny, stained scoring tables; Calliope sat at the creaking players' bench across from him and set her shoes beside her.

She looked around. "This place is kind of a dump."

"Mmm." He pivoted away from her in his chair, cracked his knuckles, and hunched over the scoring sheet. "Keen eye for detail. You're up whenever you're ready."

Calliope stared at his back. "You seriously want me to bowl."

"Yup."

"Why?"

Vikous sighed, his head sagging over the score sheet. "I just do, all right? A little trust?"

Calliope snorted almost exactly the way the girl at the counter had, but reached for her shoes. Vikous said nothing. Once she'd pulled the shoes on, she rooted around the ball racks until she found one that seemed to suit her hand well enough and returned. "Now what?"

He looked up at her. "You don't know how to bowl?"

"Of course I know how to bowl," she replied. "I practically grew up in a bowling alley, watching my folks. I mean do you want me to throw it left–handed, or with my eyes closed, or keep track of which odd–numbered pins I knock down, or what?" Vikous looked at her as though she'd lapsed into another language. She returned his stare. "What?"

His mouth opened, then closed. Finally, he said, "I just. Want you. To bowl."

"Okay."

" . . . have to make it so complicated."

"Excuse me?"

"Just, please—"

"Perhaps," said a voice behind them both, "you'd like something to drink before you get started?"

Calliope turned. A man stood there, wearing the same tunic-style shirt as the girl behind the counter. He was older and almost certainly related—he had the same delicate, fine-boned facial features that the girl's piercings had largely occluded. Calliope couldn't decide if he was the girl's brother or father—he seemed too old for the former and too young for the latter. She settled on "brother" more out of optimism than any telltales.

She brushed her hair back. "Yeah," she agreed. "A drink would be good." She smiled. "Anything you can rec—"

"We're not staying that long," Vikous interrupted.

Calliope paused, gave a tight smile that didn't expose her teeth, and pivoted slowly on her heel to face Vikous. "I'm thirsty."

"No," replied Vikous. "You're not. Not here."

"What—"

"We're fine, thanks," Vikous said, leaning out in his chair to speak around her.

"The lady . . ." her pretty waiter protested.

"Is with me," Vikous growled. "And I know how long we'll be here for."

Tension hummed in the air around Calliope. "As you say," the man replied. Calliope could almost imagine an accompanying bow to go with his obsequious tone. Then he was gone; Calliope could feel him leave, as though a source of heat had been removed from behind her.

Vikous looked up at her from his chair, his black eyes unblinking. Calliope met his gaze until her eyes began to feel dry, then walked past him, approached the lane, threw her ball into the gutter, and stepped back to wait by the ball return.

"Twenty gutter balls in a row." Vikous led the way out of the bowling alley, pivoting on his heel to hold the door open for Calliope, who stalked by, the muscles in her jaw working. "That's a pretty impressive temper you've got." He let go of the door and rubbed at the side of his face. "I should have guessed that from the first time we met, but—"

"What the hell is your *problem*?" Calliope whirled on him, continuing to walk backward across the lot. "I've never—" She stopped, and stopped walking, a deep crease between her raised eyebrows.

Without turning her head, Calliope took in the bright lights illuminating the dark lot, still mostly deserted, and the garish neon that lit up the bowling alley's sign. Her eyes came back to Vikous. "What did you do?"

Vikous lifted a hand to his chest, fingers splayed, and struck an affronted pose. "Me?" His hood swayed back and forth in denial. "I didn't do anything."

"We got here at four in the afternoon." She pointed behind her, toward her Jeep, as though indicating proof of their arrival. "I bowled one game—"

"I dunno if you could really call that bowling," Vikous interjected.

"Shut up," Calliope barked. "It was daylight out, and now it's . . ." She looked up, waving her hand at the dark–but–never–starlit sky of the city.

"Probably around eight. Eight fifteen, maybe." Vikous's smile showed teeth, visible even within the shadows of his hood.

Calliope's eyes narrowed. "Explain."

He raised his eyebrows at her. "Really?"

"Explain."

He raised his hands in surrender, then dropped them into his pockets, watching her, his head slightly tilted within his hood. Finally, he asked, "You ever noticed that there's no windows in a bowling alley?" Calliope held her scowl and didn't reply. He nodded as though she had and strolled past her toward the Jeep. "There's a reason for that, sometimes, and it's not to cut down on sun glare." He turned once he reached the Jeep and rested his elbows on the hood, looking back at the bowling alley. Calliope had followed him, but at a distance, and stayed on the other side of the vehicle.

Still looking at the neon lights of the sign, Vikous said, "There are a lot of stories you tell each other that are almost–but–not–quite right, you know?"

He looked at Calliope, who gave her head a short shake and looked away. "No, I don't."

"Sure you do." He flipped his hand up, as though throwing trash into the air. "The three little pigs were the good guys. The bears forgave Goldilocks. Only one prince hooked up with Rapunzel. Sleeping Beauty was put in a hundred–year coma for *no reason.*"

Calliope shook the distractions away. "What's that got to do with this?"

He paused. "Once upon a time," he said, "there was a story about a guy who met some mountain elves while they were bowling, and the next thing he knew, twenty years had gone by."

Calliope's eyes narrowed in thought, then widened as she looked back at the alley. "He drank something of theirs."

"That definitely didn't help," Vikous allowed. "But mostly, I think it was the bowling."

She glared at him. "You knew this would happen."

"Of course I did. I was counting on it."

"You did it to me."

"I did it to *both* of us," he pointed out. "And I didn't *do* it."

"Bullshit."

He crossed his arms across his chest, a ghost of his former good humor still clinging to his features. "If I say 'let's go stand out in that big river', and we do that, and our shoes get wet, *I* didn't make our shoes wet: the water did. It's what water *does*."

"You knew it would *happen*," Calliope snapped. "And you didn't tell me. You *stole* from me."

"I *hid* us," Vikous growled. "I took us both *entirely* off the map until we needed to meet Gluen."

"Without explaining it or even asking me," Calliope countered. "Johnson could have called again. *Josh* could have called again."

"Oh, please." Vikous's face twisted in annoyance. "We both know *that's* not going to happen." His voice lost force as he spoke the last word. He looked at Calliope, who was staring down at the pavement, her jaw clenched.

Vikous cleared his throat. "Sorry."

"I'm going to the appointment," Calliope said. Her voice was tight and quiet. She walked to the Jeep, her boots rapping on the pavement, and unlocked the door.

"I should go with you," he said.

"Fuck off," she replied, in the same hard tone. "Walk." She swung into the vehicle, slammed the door, started the engine, and left.

The same security guard from the night before sat behind the lobby desk. "Hey," Calliope said, nodding at him with her chin and settling her arms on the counter in front of him. "I'm back."

The guard didn't rise from his chair. "I'm sorry, ma'am," he said. "There are no visitors allowed after seven."

She gestured at the elevators. "I was here way after that last night, and you sent me right up."

He looked up at her, narrowing his eyes as though he were trying to make out a small object at a distance. "I'm sorry, but I don't remember that."

"I was wearing a fedora and a gray suit coat for a costume?"

He thought for a moment and shook his head.

Calliope pursed her lips, unwilling to play her trump card, but finally relented with an annoyed sigh. "I was here with the clown."

"Oh." The man's eyes widened—not as much as they had the night before, but more than necessary. "*Oh.* The party."

"Yes." Calliope nodded like a teacher urging along one of her slower readers. "I was here for the party last night, and now I'm back."

The guard leaned out to look behind her, his brow creased. "Just you?"

"Just me," Calliope assured him, noting the flash of relief on his face, mixed with an awkward kind of discomfort.

"I'm sorry," he repeated, "but the party was a special occasion."

"But I have an appointment," Calliope persisted. "Same guy, same floor, same everything."

He made a show of checking his ledger, though even reading it upside down Calliope could see her name was not on the page. "No one mentioned it to us. I'm sorry."

Calliope's head sagged under the weight of the conversation. "Listen," she said. "Have you met this fat bastard I'm here to see?"

"Mr. Gluen?" Again, a brief look of panic skimmed his features. "I mean, not that he's . . . I didn't mean to say he's—" He cut himself off with a cleared throat. "No, I've never seen it. Met him, that is."

Calliope smirked. "But you've heard." She leaned forward a bit. "So, based on what you've heard, do you actually think you're doing me a favor by letting me go up there?" She shook her head, keeping her eyes on him. "It's the last thing in the world I want to do. I hate his guts and, believe me, that is a *lot* of hate."

He glanced down at the registry again, eyes darting over the blank lines, then back up to her. "I could call up."

"*Would* you?" Calliope settled back on her heels.

He picked up the handset and dialed. Calliope waited. Seconds continued to tick by, marked off by the nervous *takking* of the guard's fingernail against the desktop. After about thirty seconds, he covered the mouthpiece with his hand and said, "It doesn't seem like anyone's answering."

"Mmm." Calliope nodded, trying to keep her face from showing her growing anger. She was already at a slow boil after the fight with Vikous—getting stood up like this was going to permanently damage her mood.

"You know what?" she blurted out. "I can wait." She waved the guard's phone away. "Go ahead and hang up."

He pulled the phone away from his head, hesitating. "Are you sure?"

"As long as you don't mind me using one of those chairs over there." She indicated the lobby furniture nearby.

"Doesn't bother me, but . . ." He hung up the phone and leaned toward her on his elbows. "I'm on shift all night, so you won't be able to wait me out and get someone nicer." He smiled, and she returned it, letting him relax.

"I wouldn't dream of it," she assured him, turning toward the chairs but keeping her eyes on him, over her shoulder, as she walked. "I just want to sit down until my friend gets here." She dropped into an overstuffed leather armchair and let out a sigh that was entirely unfeigned.

The silence following that sigh stretched on for long enough Calliope began to wonder if the guard had caught her last words, but before she could figure out how to continue, his chair creaked and he stood, speaking to her over the tall counter. "Your friend?"

"Mmm," Calliope nodded, her head resting against the back of the chair. She closed her eyes and concealed a small smile. "He'll get everything straightened out."

"The c—" The guard paused. "Your friend from last night?" The tone of his voice—like a boy who found out Mommy was going to tell Daddy what he did—almost made Calliope relent.

Almost.

"Yup." She nodded, then chuckled. "The funny part is, he was supposed to be here with me right now, but I drove off without him."

"Really." The guard's tone had graduated to a deeper level of despair.

She sat up, as though eager to share the punch line. "Yeah, we got in this *huge* argument, and I got in my car and took off. I told him to walk." She laughed again, shaking her head. "He is going to be So. Pissed." She leaned back into the chair again.

More silence. The guard dropped back into his seat. Calliope began a slow count from one.

She'd gotten to four when he stood back up. "You know what?" he said. "Go on up."

She turned her head toward him, letting a confused yet hopeful look spread across her face. "Really?"

"Sure." The guard nodded, swallowing. "It'll be—" He paused, then nodded again, more emphatically, his eyes on the empty ledger. "I'm sure it will be fine."

Calliope leaned forward and stood. "I know it will be," she assured him, starting toward him and heading around his desk to the bank of elevators. "I can't thank you enough."

"It's no problem," he replied, as he pushed the secured elevator call button at his station. She gave him one more smile, and he added, "I'll send your friend up too, when he gets here."

"Excellent," she said, and stepped into the elevator. The door slid shut with a muffled, heavy thump.

"I'll send him right on through," the guard whispered, his eyes looking at nothing at all.

───

Calliope was expected.

Two guards, their features eerily similar to the staff at the bowling alley, motioned her out of the elevator when the doors opened. When they realized she was alone, they exchanged a look, but said nothing. One indicated she should follow him with a move of his head; the other fell in behind her as they walked to the office.

"My dear," Gluen murmured, "it's a pleasure to see you again."

"I kind of doubt that," she replied, her voice clipped.

Gluen settled his arms on his desk; the flesh around his elbows splayed out as though he'd set down two plastic bags full of pudding. He steepled his fingers before him. "Manners cost nothing. Where is our enigmatic Vikous this evening?"

"Walking," Calliope muttered.

"Excuse me?" Gluen's hairless eyebrow quirked.

"He had better things to do," she said, raising her voice to normal levels.

Gluen stared at her. As Calliope watched, the corner of his mouth quirked, pulling at his sagging jowls. Then, the other side moved a bit more and his lips parted. His sharp, shining eyes disappeared as his mouth opened farther, squeezing them shut—a thick, wheezing breath hissed into him, then out, then in again, deeper, as though he were about to explode.

In a way, he did.

Gluen laughed.

Anyone, if he is laughing hard enough, could be said to shake. With Gluen, laughter was something far worse. Watching as the fit of amusement overtook him, Calliope did not see shaking; she saw the sagging seam of a cheap garbage bag threatening to split and spill rotten food; she saw the swaying of an overfull colostomy bag being carried at a full sprint, she *saw* a visual representation of what vomiting *felt* like—her own gorge rising in response, the bile burning her throat and clawing at the root of her tongue. It was a nightmare worse than almost anything Calliope could imagine.

The fat man laughed harder.

She turned away and squeezed her eyes shut, thinking herself safe until she realized she could still hear him— not the laughter, but the actual swaying, sliding, sloshing movement the laughter caused. She clapped her hands over her ears, groaning through clenched teeth, wanting nothing in life at that moment but for the laughter to stop. She sank into a crouch, locked her fingers behind her head, and clamped her forearms over her ears, squeezing her head so tightly white spots flashed behind her eyelids as she rocked back and forth on her heels, her groan becoming a high, keening thing.

When Gluen's laughter did eventually subside, Calliope didn't know it. One of the lithe guards tapped her on the shoulder with two long fingers, then again when she didn't respond. She opened her eyes just enough to see his impassive, aquiline features, and, at his gesture, she stood and lowered her arms, moving like a gun-shy deer.

In the aftermath, the silence in the room was almost as much of a shock as the sound; Calliope could hear only Gluen's exhausted panting. Weirdly, with her back to him, he sounded like a much smaller person; each breath was a precise, frail thing that seemed entirely insufficient to the task.

She didn't want to turn around and see the expression on his face after being all but driven to her knees in front of him, but the only alternative was walking out the way she'd come, which meant going on without what she'd come for, and she'd already gone through too much for that.

She turned, braced for whatever mocking he might muster.

She had no reason to worry. Gluen sprawled in his chair, leaning back so far that he was nearly prone. His tiny gasps rushed into a mouth that gaped disproportionately wide, as though he were a fish trying desperately to suck life from the wrong medium. His face—in fact, every visible inch of him— was slick with sweat. His jowls slid over the folds of skin at his neck like mating eels; the printed silk of his shirt looked more like a full-body tattoo, it was so stuck to him.

Worse, his proportions were wrong. Before, he had been grotesquely obese; uncommon, but hardly unique—strange enough Calliope could never quite ignore it. Now, it was as if he had come undone. His abdomen on the left side sagged out and hung over the arm of his chair, apparently held in place by nothing except the clinging silk of his shirt. On the same side, his ear had grown twice the size of its counterpart, while his right eye sagged in its socket, lower than the other by at least a half an inch and looking for all the world as though it might fall out and roll down his cheek.

A low, impressed whistle wound through the room from the doorway. Calliope turned to see Vikous, his hands in his pockets, shaking his head slowly and clicking his tongue. "My goodness, Gluen," he drawled, his voice rough. He took a few easy steps, stopping just short of the desk. "You're really letting yourself go these days."

Still panting, Gluen could manage only a gesture in reply; his arm rose a bare inch from the chair, one quavering, nearly triangular finger indicating Calliope. Incredibly, his breath hitched and the corner of his gaping mouth quirked upward, as though his laughter might return. Despite her earlier resolve, Calliope tensed, ready to flee to the elevator.

Vikous looked over his shoulder at her, his eyebrows raised. "*You* did this?"

Calliope shook her head, at a loss. "No. He—" She swallowed against the burning in her throat and tried again. "He started laughing."

Vikous's eyes widened, more in astonishment than any kind of worry. "What did you *say*?" Before she could answer, he waved the question away. "Never mind. Go . . ." He gestured at the doorway to the office. "Go grab some water. I'll fix this."

Calliope's eyes slid back to Gluen; she didn't bother trying to hide her disbelief. "How?"

Vikous shook his head. "You couldn't handle the bowling alley," he murmured. "Trust me when I say you don't want to know about this." Calliope felt the urge to voice some kind of protest, but she let it go.

At the doorway, she turned, her mouth open to call something back, but Vikous was right there, his hand on the door. "Sorry," he said, his voice gruff, but not unkind.

"Me too," she murmured, hoping he understood.

He nodded and pulled the door shut.

The last thing Calliope saw was Gluen's eyes, filled with suspicion, watching her companion as Vikous turned away from her.

<hr/>

"Come on back in." Vikous stood in the doorway, silhouetted in profile.

Calliope stood. She'd been waiting outside the office for the better part of a half hour. In that time, she'd realized she'd lost more than that during Gluen's laughing fit. She didn't like to think about how far away she'd gone in her own mind to survive it, and she had no desire to go back into the office again.

"How bad is it?" she asked. "What happened?"

Vikous paused. "You want to know?" His voice was low, darkened by a shadow of irritation. He hadn't turned toward her. His head was lowered and cocked slightly to the side; he seemed to be watching her sidelong. "Because it doesn't seem like you really want to know about any of this."

Calliope worked her jaw. "I said I was sorry."

"Okay." He straightened, sniffed, and cleared his throat. "Everyone has to keep control over themselves, or bad things happen. That's just life." He jerked his head toward the office. "Sometimes those bad things are more obvious than others, and the way they lose control is a little weirder. That's what happened: you said something funny, and he lost it."

"I didn't say anything funny," Calliope replied. "He asked where you were and I said you had something better to do."

"Ahh," Vikous said.

Calliope waited, but he said nothing else. "What? That's not funny."

"It is if you're us." He motioned with one hand. "Come on." He turned away and returned to the office.

Reluctantly, she followed, keeping her eyes averted until she was close enough to Gluen's desk that there was simply nowhere else to look but at their host. When she did, her eyes widened. "Damn," she breathed.

Gluen glanced up from a stack of papers he was skimming. "And with that, both our lovely Miss Jenkins and her profanity reenter the scene." The corners of his mouth turned up in a per-functory socialite's smile that never reached his lips, let alone his eyes. "Lovely."

Calliope stared back, lips slightly parted, brow furrowed. Gluen returned her look with one of calm reserve. His clothing was the same, but immaculate and fresh. He not only showed no signs of the previous trauma, but was actually improved from when Calliope had first arrived. She looked at Vikous, at a loss for words.

"I am not, I assure you, unfamiliar with the wonder and astonishment my presence engenders in the fairer sex." Gluen picked up the stack and handed it, without looking, to one of his guards, leaving one sheet of paper on the blotter. "But I'm on something of a tight schedule for the rest of my evening, so you will excuse me if I move things along."

"How—" Calliope turned back to Gluen. "When we were talking before, and you asked me where Vikous was—"

"That's not a conversation I wish to revisit, Miss Jenkins." Gluen scratched lightly at the corner of his mouth with a fingertip. "I'm sure you understand."

"Not even a little bit."

"Yes, well." Gluen folded his hands on his desk. "That's not a problem with which I can help." His eyes flicked to Vikous. "I'm not convinced anyone can." He sniffed. "But a spark of curiosity, however dim, shows some promise. Perhaps you will find your Professor Higgins." Gluen leaned back, causing a now-familiar ripple beneath his clothes. "The goal of your quest lies, of course, within the Hidden Lands." His fingers played over the single paper on his desk. "Your lost young man—"

"He's not my man." Calliope muttered, defensively. "And what the hell are the Hidden Lands?"

Gluen shrugged. "Mr. White is something to you or you are something to him; in any case, you are tied to one another in such a way as makes your involvement requisite." He peered at her. "You . . . have a talent? You dance? Draw? Perhaps sing?"

Calliope frowned. "No." She glanced at Vikous. "Not anymore."

"You did."

She paused. "Yeah."

Gluen smiled. "The adoration of the crowd is truly a wondrous thing. One may almost become . . . hungry for it."

"The *point*," Vikous said. "Stay on it."

Gluen shot Vikous a look composed of equal parts frustration and annoyance. Vikous returned the look with nothing more than a raised eyebrow, and the fat man relented and returned his attention to Calliope. "As to your question, I will not waste my time or yours explaining something as elementary as the Hidden Lands." He indicated Vikous. "*That* is your guide, in case the two of you require introductions; it is your guide's responsibility to explain such rudimentary things."

Vikous grunted, but it didn't sound like dissent. Gluen continued, "White's death locale is significant. You will find his killer there. He is waiting."

Calliope shook her head. "Josh can't be dead. I got a call from him two hours *after* he was supposed to have been killed."

"Certainly. How else would you expect—" Gluen blinked once and turned to Vikous. Calliope felt her annoyance flare. "This hasn't been explained?" he asked.

Vikous didn't answer.

Gluen stared at him, then: "You are her guide." It seemed to be an admonishment. Vikous's eyes narrowed.

"Y'know what? This is crap." Calliope's voice sounded shrill even to her. "This information is nothing but made-up names and bullshit, so just give me his other message."

Gluen smiled, though there was no humor in it. "Very well," he said, his voice a quiet rasp. "Vikous, wait outside."

"I want to apologize, my dear," Gluen said.

"Sure." Calliope spat the word out as though it tasted bitter.

Gluen inclined his head a fraction, barely enough to add another roll of flesh to his neck. "We are not on the best of terms, you and I, but I want you to understand—truly—that I wish my role in this had been explained to you more fully before we reached this point."

"Whatever." Calliope closed her eyes, trying to keep her anger in check long enough to get what she came for. "Won't be the first time I don't understand what the hell's going on. Just give me the message."

Gluen watched her, his sagging face solemn. "I won't annoy you further by asking if you're sure, but once more, before we begin, I want to say that I am sorry for this."

"It's—" Calliope bit down on her reply, which she could feel growing into a shout. "It's fine," she continued in a more normal tone. "Could we just get this done? It's late."

"Of course." Gluen motioned with one sagging arm, and his assistant left the room, closing the door behind him. "If you'll give me a moment to recall things exactly," he said, then closed his eyes and lowered his chin in concentration.

Calliope looked away; in that position, Gluen's mouth was almost entirely concealed in the puffy expanse of his face. He could probably smother himself in his own flesh if he tried. After the laughing fit earlier, it was almost impossible to look at him without seeing his body misshapen and rear-ranged.

"Hi Calli."

Calliope jumped and whirled toward the door, but there was no one there.

"I'm over here, ya goof."

Calliope turned back to the desk, her mouth already opening to form the question, when she froze.

"Hey."

The voice—Josh's voice—came from Gluen's mouth, clear and unmuddled in the way the fat man's usually was. Worse, the doughy expanse of his face had changed; shifted and re-formed around his eyes and nose and mouth to look like the man whose voice she heard. Her own mouth opened again, then closed.

"This isn't how I was hoping to talk with you next," the voice—*Josh*—said, "but the phone was too . . . hard, and I wanted to make sure you got the message."

Calliope reached backward, searching desperately for the edge of a chair. Her fingers brushed its edge, and she gripped it so tightly the wood creaked. She shuffled sideways and lowered herself to the seat, her eyes never leaving the familiar features surrounded by doughy flesh.

"Josh?" Her voice was a whisper even she could barely hear.

"I don't have a lot of time," he said. "And I'm sorry. I'm really . . ."—his eyes closed—"really sorry, because you aren't going to like any of this."

His eyes opened again and met hers. They were the same blue she'd always remembered.

The street was quiet. By Vikous's reckoning, it was at least four hours past midnight.

They stood in the street itself, near the curb, directly in front of Calliope's Jeep. Vikous looked first at the front grille of the vehicle, then at Calliope. Calliope was looking only at the grille. Her eyes looked through and far past the vehicle with the same expression of blank apathy that they'd had since the two of them had left Gluen's office thirty minutes ago.

They'd been standing in front of the Jeep for a quarter of an hour.

"It's getting late," Vikous said for the third time. "We should get going." He watched his companion, gnawing on his cigar. "Calliope—"

She pulled her keys from the pocket of her jacket and held them out to him. She didn't look at him or give him time to react, and they fell from her hand to the pavement with a small clash of metal-on-metal-on-pavement. "Drive for me." She walked to the passenger side of the vehicle. Vikous followed her with his eyes. Finally, he bent and retrieved the keys, unlocked the doors, and started up the vehicle.

"Where to?" he asked once the motor was running.

"Home."

Calliope stared blankly through the front windshield as they drove, hunched slightly forward against a cold Vikous couldn't feel. A silent hour later, he pulled into Calliope's empty driveway. There were no other cars there, or on the street. He turned off the engine, relaxed into the seat, and waited. Calliope continued to stare into the distance far beyond the garage door they faced.

"I want to kill him," she finally said. Her voice was quiet, in the small cab of the vehicle at the darkest hour of the night.

"Gluen?" Vikous said. Calliope didn't respond but turned her head toward him and met his gaze. Vikous looked away first. "He's a messenger."

"Yeah," Calliope said. "And you're the guide."

Vikous became very still. After a few moments, Calliope reached over and retrieved her keys, then opened her door and got out, standing in the opening. "Get out of my car. Come back at noon."

He looked at her. "You blaming me for this?"

Her eyes finally focused on him, but instead of replying she turned and walked to the front door of her house.

"Fair enough," he said to himself once she had gone inside. He climbed out of the Jeep, pulled up the sweatshirt hood that concealed his face from the nearest streetlight, and walked away.

The light from the hallway fell across Calliope's bed, glistening on the old photographs scattered across the comforter, mixed with letters and notes and folded music scores. Numb with exhaustion and the meeting with Gluen, Calliope simply stood in the darkness of the room, staring at the scattered mess for several minutes, unable to process what to do next.

Finally, she shuffled to the side of the bed and pawed everything together as well as she could, lowered herself to her knees, and gathered the pile into both hands, turning and aligning the mass like someone straightening out a deck of oversized cards. It occurred to her that the reason the box had been such a disorganized mess when she'd opened it was because she'd done pretty much the same thing the last time she'd put it away, rather than sort things into any kind of order.

She managed to fit everything back into the box on the second attempt. This time, rather than the apartment note, the top item on the pile was a picture of Josh, driving. Afternoon sunlight lit up his face, shone on two days' worth of stubble on his cheeks. He was smiling.

Of course.

Calliope looked at the picture, her face as still and expressionless as it had been since she'd left Gluen's office. She reached for the lid, let her hand drop back to her lap, then reached out again and strapped it back in place, moving quickly. As soon as the box was closed, she shoved it and its companion under the bed in a rush, her eyes averted. The NOT BAND STUFF box hung up on the frame and she had to push it harder—almost punch it—trying to get it to move. Finally, she did punch it to get it to slide underneath—once, then again to finish the job. The frame left a gouge in the top of the lid.

She sat back on her heels, kneeling in the slice of light from the hallway, her eyes squeezed shut, her breath coming much harder than the effort had warranted.

"I think we ought to take a trip."

"Nnn . . ." The sound was half groan, half growl. Her fist lashed out, thumping into the side of the mattress, then again. Again. The strikes sped up, both fists flailing at the bed as a wordless, rage-filled scream built up behind grindingly clenched teeth, tears spilling down her face.

The attack came and went like a summer storm; first the flurry, then a sudden cessation punctuated with a few final strikes. Her hands dropped into her lap, their knuckles red and abraded.

Calliope looked down at them, squeezed her eyes shut, and let her head fall forward until it rested on the edge of the bed.

⌇

The keys scrape and rattle against the outside of the apartment door, accompanied by a muffled laugh and giggling. After several tries, the bolt finally opens and Josh stumbles through, off balance more because Calliope is trying to climb onto his back than because he is drunk.

Which isn't to say he's sober—far, far from it. It's been a good night.

He drops his keys on the floor, his legs spread wide to catch his balance. Calliope, still hanging from his shoulders, makes another lunge upward. The motion pushes him a half step forward, but he catches himself, then reaches around and hitches her higher, hooking his arms under her knees.

They freeze, in shock that they've finally achieved the position they've been attempting for two blocks and three flights of stairs, then Josh kicks backward at the door, knocking it closed and almost sending them both crashing to the floor. Calliope lets out an abrupt laugh and kisses his ear. "Strong work, White."

"Damn right," he mutters. He lifts his head for a moment, sights in on the futon, and begins a slow stagger across the room.

"Very. Talented. Group." He punctuates each step with a word as he crosses the room. "Label. Very. Interested." Calliope gives him a squeeze that threatens to cut off his air. He coughs and takes the last few steps. "Where's. Your. Demoooo . . ." He overbalances toward the futon, falling like a chopped tree with a shrieking squirrel on its back. Josh turns to face Calliope where she lies. "Hi."

"Hello." She waggles her eyebrows. "Kees me."

He does so. Calliope can feel him smiling against her lips. "It's a good night."

"It's a very good night," she agrees. Down deep, in a part of her that whispers about not getting hopes up, there is a bitter seed of doubt, but she squeezes it away, pushing it down as far as she can.

"You okay?" Josh asks. He pulls his head back, his face faintly shadowed. Calliope realizes she'd been shaking her head.

She smiles, nuzzling into his neck to hide her face.

He pulls back again, trying to catch her eyes. "Yeah?"

The fear wells up, coming at her from another angle. If he picks up on her mood, he might think she doubts everything that happened tonight, and it will be another fight about all the old things. That thought turns her fear into a self-disgusted kind of anger, and she looks up at him, her eyes bright with forced good cheer. "Yeah. You know what?"

He blinks at her mood shift, but his smile creeps back. "What?"

"I think we ought to take a trip."

He looks at her, searching her eyes, then tilts his head, as though *he hadn't heard her from all of two inches away. "You mean—"*

Calliope nods, biting her lower lip hard enough to make her eyes water. Josh misreads it as happy emotion.

"Yes!" He kisses her, hard, and leaps off the futon, swaying only slightly. "Tonight! We can leave tonight. I'll pack."

His puppy enthusiasm makes her laugh despite her misgivings. "How about in the morning, baby?"

He shakes his head. "I don't want to give you time to change your mind." A second later, his own words sink in and he stops. "I . . . just said that out loud, didn't I?"

Calliope pushes herself to a sitting position, and he kneels to meet her halfway. "It's okay." She cups the side of his neck and strokes his cheek with her thumb. "I'm not going to change my mind." She kisses him. "Promise."

"Okay." He leans into her. They stay that way as the cheap plastic clock on the wall ticks off second after long second. "But I'm still gonna pack," he whispers.

She laughs again, quieter this time. "Fiiine." She throws herself back on the futon. "Come take advantage of me when you're done."

He looks back at her from the doorway to the bedroom. "Yeah?" She rests her forearm over her eyes. "Oh yeah."

"I'll hurry," he murmurs, and leaves her smiling.

<hr/>

"Nice place."

Calliope starts awake. She is still on the futon. The bedroom doorway is dark. The apartment is cold.

A lean silhouette stands at the front door. "I'm sorry to wake you up, Calliope, but we need to talk."

Calliope sits up, scanning the room, trying to get her bearings; trying to remember what is going on, where she is, where—"Where's Josh?"

Special Agent Walker sucks air past his teeth, grimacing. "Bad question, Miss Jenkins. Not something you want to get into with me." He leans against the refrigerator. "Anyway, I'm really here to ask you things, not the other way around."

Calliope shakes her head, trying to clear it. "What—"

"Another question I'm not going to answer right now." Walker sucks at his teeth, popping his tongue against the roof of his mouth. "Let me try: where's the Fat Man?"

Calliope blinks, leaning back, her shoulders tense. "Excuse me?"

"Gluen, Miss Jenkins." Walker's voice grows rough. "The Fat Man. I'd like to have a talk with him."

"I don't—"

"How about this," Walker cuts in. "You tell me. I leave." A light comes on in the bedroom. "And you can get back to your regularly scheduled programming."

The light shifts, pushing back the cold in the room. Josh is—

Calliope squints at the light, trying to remember.

Josh is—

Calliope turns back to Walker, her eyes gone hard. "Josh is dead."

Walker's eyes go wide, and everything goes dark.

8

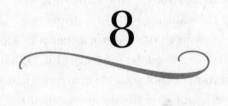

THE DOOR OPENED to Vikous's first knock. Calliope's face was wan, her eyes shadowed and bruised from lack of sleep. She said nothing, her hand still on the doorknob while those hard eyes took in his hooded form. She held her phone to her ear with her other hand.

"Darryl, this is Calliope. Sorry I missed you. Figure you're at lunch. Anyway, that thing we talked about is happening. I just wanted to let you know, because . . ." She walked away from the door, leaving it open behind her. Vikous stepped inside. "Well, because I said I would, I guess. I'll let you know if I figure anything out." She glanced at Vikous. "Don't tell—anyone. Okay? Thanks. Bye." She shut the phone and set it down, then slowly turned toward Vikous.

At her blank expression, he said, "You told me to come back here at noon. It's noon, I'm here."

She turned and headed toward the back of the house.

"What's the plan, boss?"

She stopped, but didn't turn. "I'm going to pack. Then we'll start driving."

Vikous raised an eyebrow. "No questions about flying out there?"

"Well, you're not getting through a security checkpoint, are you?" Calliope looked back at him, sidelong. "They make you take your shoes off. That would be interesting." She turned away, but paused at the doorway. "Besides, he told me it had to be on the ground, that we had to stay close to the earth."

Vikous watched her back. "Gluen?"

"The message Gluen gave me." She waited, but Vikous didn't reply. "Josh."

Vikous kept his voice quiet. "Did he say anything else?"

"He told me who killed him." Silence filled up the space between them like cold water. "He said good-bye." Calliope turned and walked out of the room.

"The hardest part is getting started." Vikous stood outside the house in front of the Jeep. His hood was raised again, and his voice seemed to come from the dappled shadows beneath the autumn-colored tree that reached over the drive.

"No." Calliope turned toward him from where she had been looking out over the street. "The hardest part is hearing your friend's voice when you know that he's dead and that's all you have left." She locked the door, coming down the steps to Vikous. "Where's my stuff?"

"Packed it."

She gazed into the too-dark of his hood for a moment, glanced over his shoulder and back again. "I don't see anything in there."

"It's all the way in the back, behind the second row of seats."

"No way it could fit there."

He lifted the hood slightly, enough for her to see his caricature features. "You remember the clown cars in the circus? We're really good at packing things."

She blew air through her teeth and walked around to the back of the Jeep, peering in through the window. Her eyes widened, just a bit, then narrowed. For a few seconds there was no sound but distant traffic and a breeze running through the leaves over their heads.

"This trip is going to take a couple days." She was still looking in through the back window of the Jeep.

The hood bobbed. "Probably more, but yeah."

"You're going to have plenty of time to explain this crap." Without waiting for a response, she walked around the vehicle and climbed into the driver's side. Vikous seemed about to say something more, but he went to the passenger side and got in instead.

"I never liked this place," Calliope said.

"The house?" Vikous followed her gaze, tipping his head speculatively. "Doesn't seem too bad."

"We used to have this apartment," she murmured. "It was really . . ." She looked at Vikous, straightened in her seat, and started the engine. The Jeep pulled into the street and left the house behind.

Two blocks down, a young man Calliope would have recognized watched them from the confines of a reasonably new but nondescript vehicle. As they pulled away, he pulled out a cell phone and pressed a button. "Sir? It's Hyde. She just left the residence. The guide was with her sir, yes. The one you expected." He paused, listening. "Yes, sir. I'll call the others." Again, he waited. The smile below his mirrored sunglasses was broad and showed too many teeth. "Thank you, sir."

Vikous kept his hood up as they drove through the suburban streets. The angle of the opening indicated he was watching the streets scroll by through the side window. His body, over-large for the space it was crowded into, was tense. Calliope found herself glancing at him as she drove, waiting for him to say or do something.

"What's going on?" she finally said.

The hood moved slightly. "Unfriendly regard," he said in a strangely ritualistic cadence and tone. He shook himself, his shoulders shifting beneath the layers of clothing in ways that Calliope couldn't quite explain or follow. "Someone watched us leave," he explained in his normal, sandblasted voice.

"How do you—" She stopped herself. "Bad guys or good guys?"

"There aren't any good guys," Vikous said. His hood made an abortive move in her direction. "Besides us. Not involved in this business, anyway."

"Real informative," Calliope muttered.

"No offense, but you don't exactly react well when I play it straight with you." His voice was dry.

Calliope stiffened defensively. "I don't think anyone would blame me for not immediately running to my guide for answers when he looks like a reject from Barnum and Bailey's."

"You don't exactly make it easy. You're acting like this is a"—he waved his hand, exasperated—"a dress-up party you crashed." He paused. "I'd say you weren't taking it seriously, except for the time you kicked me in the chest, or the time you teargassed me, or the *other* time when you left me in a parking lot to go deal with Gluen by yourself."

Calliope's jaw was tight. "I can't *help* but think that all has one particular asshole in common—the one who never explains anything, just does something weird and waits to see if I freak out, like it's a test."

"*Everything* is a test," Vikous muttered. "If you haven't figured that out by now, I'm really not going to be able to help you. You'll leave me in another parking lot, or smack me with your little swagger stick." He turned in his seat as best he could, leaning back against the passenger door. "Or maybe you could get about halfway and turn around and run home," he growled. "Again."

Calliope yanked on the wheel of the Jeep and brought it to a screeching halt next to an open park in which the grass had gone autumn brown. Without a word, she ripped her keys out of the ignition.

"That didn't take long," Vikous said, his voice flat and harsh. He opened the door and swung his legs out of the vehicle. "This is a joke."

"That's a little ironic from someone who looks like a friggin' *clown*." Calliope's voice rose as she spoke; she shouted the last words through a door Vikous had already closed. She sat in the silence of the cab for a few seconds, then got out, stalking around to the passenger side of the vehicle. Vikous was already ten feet away by the time she got to the sidewalk.

"I'm *trying*," she shouted at his back.

Vikous stopped. His hood shifted as he looked up at the overcast sky, then he turned back, hands jammed deep in his pockets, walking stiff-legged back toward the Jeep. "You're *playing* at trying." He was nearly shouting, paying no attention to the sparse traffic on the sidewalk that first looked and then quickly looked away. His hood was still raised, but pushed back enough that she could make out his features. The snarl in his voice spread to his face, where the corners of his mouth had drawn up to reveal several uneven, yellowing teeth. Something along the line of his shoulders moved *wrong*.

Calliope felt a queasy surge in her stomach. "I don't know what you mean." She shook her head, as though to clear it. "I don't know how you know about . . . me. And I don't know what I've been thinking. I'm about to drive out of town on a weeklong road trip with a com*plete* stranger, a homeless man who's been stalking me for who knows how long." She glared at the sidewalk, working her jaw. "I'm going home."

"You'll never be *home*," Vikous said. "Not till this is over. You know there's something out there now and you know it killed White. You won't be able to shut down the last three days and fool yourself."

"You don't know anything about me," Calliope said, barely audible.

"I—" He clenched his jaw. "I know you're too good a liar to believe your own stories, and you notice too much to pretend you're not seeing what you're seeing." With one gloved hand, he reached up and yanked his hood back under the cloudy afternoon sunlight. "You want me to play it straight? *Look* at me."

Calliope looked, unable to keep her eyes from dragging over his features or dismissing anything as a trick of the light in a strobe-lit bar, or the shadows of a predawn street, or the dim haze of her shaded house. Eyes the color and sheen of hard plastic buttons bored into her, completely bereft of whites, despite the fact that they were open wide and staring right at her. The green spikes of hair on his head were too regular, too solid. His white face paint didn't flake or peel, didn't look like paint or stain at all, and the same was true of the crimson smear that surrounded his mouth—a mouth that was too wide, that opened too far when he spoke, dropped too far open when he drank . . .

and had too, too many teeth.

To her left, Calliope heard a gasp. She turned, confronted with the terrified face of a young boy clinging to his mother's side. The pair had been walking down the street but the boy was now hauling frantically backward on his mother's arm, his eyes locked on Vikous.

"Darien, stop it, quit acting so—" she managed a smile toward Vikous. "I'm sorry, he doesn't mean to; he's always been afraid of clowns."

Vikous smiled and Calliope couldn't help but see, now, that it went too far around his face, but the woman was struggling with her son and didn't notice. "It's all right, ma'am. They scare me, too." He turned to a bench facing the park and scooped up a discarded newspaper. Using it as a shield for his other hand, he made a gesture and a rose pivoted out of thin air and into his outstretched hand as he pulled the paper away.

The woman jumped, startled as she turned to find the flower in her face. "Oh! My . . . thank you." She hesitated a moment in reaching for the flower, then accepted it. "Thank you," she repeated, then turned to her son. "See? He's just a nice magician clown." The boy shook his head, his eyes still locked on Vikous, and shook free of his mother's grasp, running into the park.

At least I can see the whites of the kid's *eyes*, Calliope thought.

Clearly mortified, the woman called after her son. "I'm sorry," she mouthed to Vikous and hurried off into the park. Vikous watched her go.

"Maybe we should get back in the car now." He pulled his hood up.

"We're not done yet," Calliope said. Her eyes followed the woman as she approached her son, who had barricaded himself inside a jungle gym. "But yeah . . . let's go. I'll drive, you talk." She turned and walked around the back of their vehicle.

A nearly invisible smile played around Vikous's mouth. "Works for me," he murmured, his voice almost too low to carry. He rolled the newspaper into a tube, tapped it again with his hand, and climbed back into the Jeep.

"Before we get into this," Vikous said, rubbing at his eyes, "understand that there's only so much I'm going to talk about right now. There's too much to explain all at once, even just about the parts that have to do with you. Even if there weren't, there's parts that won't make any sense to you now and I'm not wasting my time on them." He took a deep breath. "Plus, there are rules about this sort of thing. Okay?"

"Sure, I guess." She glanced over at him. "Start out easy. What are you, exactly?"

He exhaled into something like a laugh. "I can't really say."

Calliope's eyes narrowed. "Oh, son of a—"

"Now wait." Vikous raised a gloved hand. "Explaining why I said that will tell you some things, so let's not go back to kicking me out of the car just yet." Calliope's face remained tense, but he continued: "The only real rule we've learned is to keep our heads down. All of us."

"All of you . . . what?"

He glanced in the side passenger mirror as they pulled onto the highway. "Well, rule out aliens and all that garbage. What I'm talking about are the sorts of things you heard about when you were a kid or when you read old stories. You know dragons and boogeymen, right?" Calliope nodded, her expression still set and cautious. Vikous nodded in turn. "Okay, which one of those can you describe?"

Calliope's brow creased. "Dragons, I guess. Boogeymen are just . . . scary; they don't look like anything."

"Which is why they're still scaring the crap out of little kids, but you don't have dragons burning towns down." He gestured out the window with the rolled-up newspaper. "You look out there and you see cars and trucks and highways; there's nothing magical in this world anymore—that's the nature of the people who control it." He looked at Calliope, then back to the window. "The things that don't match, the things that stand out"—he made a gesture with his hand—"they go away."

"They die out."

"Didn't say that." Vikous turned his attention to his own gloved hand. "This has been going on a long time. As a general rule most of the things we're talking about aren't very stupid; even trolls and goblins can learn to hide, but it's harder for them because most people would see a goblin and say 'oh dear, that's a goblin.' Being easily recognizable doesn't help when you're trying to keep your head down."

"So 'go away' means hide."

"Usually." He gestured, his eyes still following his hand. "For some of them, a long time ago, going away meant literally going someplace that's . . . Else. They had the trick of how to do it, the rest didn't, and now they're gone. They don't come back, ever, so none of the rest of us really know anything about it." He dropped his hand in his lap. "Mostly though, yeah, they hide." He looked up. "Some of them have names, and some of them never did: any things that could pass among people without getting noticed pretty much did exactly that."

Calliope raised an eyebrow. "So . . . every hobo clown touring around the country is a . . . whatever you are, hiding in plain sight? That's—"

"Whoa. No." Vikous frowned. "I don't think any of us—well, most of us—have ever been that numerous. In my case, what you're thinking of is a culture that built up, was built up a long time ago, on purpose, as camouflage. We passed ourselves off as entertainers and spawned imitators that we could then be mistaken for. I don't know what to tell you I am because we're always something else; fitting into the gaps has been our nature for so long we don't even exist as ourselves anymore. Even those who know about us call us by different names." His gaze returned to the highway. "It's a good trick, but compared to some folks I'm an amateur. There are things that can live in cracks and shadows, feeding on the prickles on your neck that you get when you walk back to your car at night."

"You have to know how crazy 'monsters hide among us in plain sight' sounds," Calliope replied.

"You're oversimplifying things." Vikous looked at the newspaper in his hand. "It's not just . . ." He unrolled the paper, flipped through to the center, then folded it back on itself twice. "Here. This."

Calliope glanced at the paper, then back to the road, frowned, and looked again. The spot Vikous indicated with one pointing finger was a perfect square of random letters on the puzzles page. "Yeah . . . I don't get it."

Vikous nodded as though he'd expected her answer, then

passed his hand over the page. Halfway through the movement he stopped and looked at her.

She glanced back at him. "What?"

"I'm going to do something." His voice was quiet. "One of the
weird things I do."

Calliope pursed her lips. "Should I pull over or something?"

"Just don't freak out and drive off into the ditch." Vikous
pointed at the page. "This is how the world works." He shook
the paper just enough to make the pages rattle. To Calliope it
seemed the letters in the puzzle shifted more than the paper
had, as though they'd been jostled loose. "Basically a big jumble
of stuff—so much stuff that you have to really concentrate just
to find the things that you're *expecting* to find." He gestured, and
the letters seemed to draw back from certain combinations
within their midst. Watching out of the corner of her eye, Calliope saw words like *work, family, vacation,* and *car payments* tumble
together, then fall back into the mix.

"Okay." She swallowed, working the muscles of her jaw.

Vikous didn't notice; his black eyes were focused entirely on
the page he held. "The thing is, when all you're looking for are
the words on the list—the stuff you're expecting—you miss
other things sitting right in front of you." His hand waved, and
the words on the page crawled again, cringing away from *troll,
witch,* and *monster.*

"Okay." Calliope tilted her head. "Put it that way, it makes a
kind of sense; still seems like people would *notice.*"

"It happens. Sometimes. But there are lots of things out there
that are even better at hiding than this; they write their names
upside down and backwards to make them even harder to
see." He looked down at the page again. "Then there's me."

"Yeah?" Calliope asked. "What do you do?"

Vikous held up the paper where she could see:

```
CLOWNCLOWNCLOWNCLOWNCLOWN
CLOWNCLOWNCLOWNCLOWNCLOWN
CLOWNCLOWNVIKOUSCLOWNCLOWN
CLOWNCLOWNCLOWNCLOWNCLOWN
CLOWNCLOWNCLOWNCLOWNCLOWN
```

She snorted a short laugh. "Nice."

He gestured out the window. "Mostly, people don't want to know this stuff—given any kind of explanation that *doesn't* involve flying cauldrons and trolls hiding under bridges, they'll swallow it, even if tastes funny." He grimaced, his face twisting in ways that were difficult to watch. "The real pain is the power of belief makes it—" He shook his head. "That's for later."

The interior of the Jeep was silent for a time. Outside, the city slowly pulled back from the sides of the highway and slid to the rear window of the vehicle, taking the afternoon with it.

"That's . . ." Calliope began, but shook her head. "That doesn't really tell me anything about what happened to Josh or why we're driving into the middle of nowhere or why you're involved in this."

Vikous tilted his head back, resting it on the seatback. "I'm involved in this because I said I would be, and for now you're just going to have to take that for whatever you want because I don't have anything else." He looked at her for a reaction, but she gave him none, and he turned back to face the front window. "The rest is more complicated."

Calliope gave Vikous a glance. "Try."

His expression grew resigned. "Okay . . . there are places that are easy for us to hide. Forests aren't what they used to be, but you can still get lost in one if you try hard enough." He paused. "Understand that I'm mostly talking about the lands I know about . . . you go into another land, there are different rules. These are the rules here, right?" Calliope nodded and Vikous continued. "So you've got forests and caves and sewers and dark alleys and mountain ravines and things like that, where it's . . . where hiding is easy. Easier, anyway." His lip curled up just a bit above a jagged eyetooth. "The home of the stupid and lazy."

"Says the thing that survives by pretending to be a homeless clown."

Vikous scowled. "I don't know a lot of trolls that could stand in the middle of the sidewalk next to a city park and have a conversation with a kid's mom while she apologizes for her kid thinking he's scary."

Calliope pursed her lips. "Okay, good point."

"She took a flower from me, on top of—"

"I got it, you're amazing. I give, please move on."

Vikous started to say something further, but gave up. "Anyway, those are the easy places. The things you find in places like that are mostly harmless."

"Mostly."

He made a face. "Crossing the street is dangerous if you don't know how to look for traffic, or if you don't pay attention." He glanced at her and continued. "What's more dangerous are the things that can hide in places where the hiding is hard. They're smarter and a lot more ruthless." He gestured broadly out the front window of the Jeep. "We're headed into the worst part of it."

"We're heading to Iowa." Calliope's voice was flat. "Nothing magical happens in Iowa."

Vikous seemed to ignore her, but paced his voice carefully.

"People's disregard made it possible to slip whole sections of the land out of view, like cutting off swatches for a patchwork quilt. The Hidden Lands." He paused. "Gluen mentioned 'em. What they left behind is what you remember: empty, boring chunks of landscape between two mountain ranges."

"The Midwest." Calliope's voice went from flat to scornful. "The last magical thing that happened there was about ten years ago, the summer of my sixteenth birthday, when I left, and it wasn't *good* magical. You're saying I managed to miss some secret kingdom?"

"You didn't miss anything." Vikous paused. "Well, okay, a few things, yes, but not the parts I'm talking about. The Hidden Lands aren't *there* to be seen in the first place." His voice sounded as though he were repeating something memorized. "Somewhere between the back of your mind and the corner of your eye, just beyond the edge of hearing—that's where the hidden things have gathered for years, finding their way there when the world got too hard for them, or too small, or too lonely." He looked at her. "That's the business that White got pulled into."

"What? Why?"

His black eyes gave no hint of his thoughts. "It would have been his choice. That's pretty much all I know." He hesitated, then, softly: "What did *he* tell you?"

Calliope didn't answer immediately, though she'd heard him clearly enough. "He said he was trying to save someone." Her voice was shaky. "And that they'd killed him. But he didn't say why."

Vikous shook his head. "I don't—" He glanced out the side window again and frowned. "How long did you plan to drive tonight?"

Calliope shrugged. "I can go for a while. We got started late and I wanted to get some distance before we stopped." She glanced at him. "Why?"

Vikous settled back and adjusted his seat to give himself more room. "Someone's following us."

Calliope swore and checked her rearview. "Which one?"

Vikous wriggled his shoulders, trying to get comfortable. "I don't know by the lights—I can feel it." He glanced across at Calliope. "'Unfriendly regard', remember?" He settled his head back. "We'll have to do something about them when we stop." He pulled his hood up and slightly over his eyes. "Don't worry about it now; they aren't going to try anything out here."

"What do we do when we stop?"

"We'll see." He shifted in the seat. "Wake me up when you get close to where you want to stop. I need to rest up."

After that, there was only silence.

9

THE RADIO WAS playing "Dead Man's Party" when Vikous lifted his head. It was hours past full dark, and the highway wound slowly into the foothills of the mountains.

"How we doin'?" he asked, his voice still muffled by sleep.

"Fine," Calliope replied. Vikous glanced up at her curt reply but said nothing and slowly readjusted his seat, rubbing at his eyes with a gloved hand.

"Are they still back there?" she asked.

He blinked at her, glanced over his shoulder, then settled back in his seat, inhaling through his nose with a loud and ungraceful snort while flop-shaking his head from side to side. Calliope looked at him askance. "Sorry," he muttered. "I don't wake up very fast." She remained silent, and he turned his attention to the side window through which only darkness and the occasional house light could be seen. His head tilted slightly to the left as he stared out the window, as though listening.

Finally, he relaxed back into the seat. "Yep, still there." He almost sounded satisfied. "Closer than they were before, actually."

"Great," Calliope said, her voice flat.

He looked at her, underlit by the dashboard lights. "What's the matter?"

Her expulsion of breath was equal parts astonishment and anger. "Oh nothing: 'We're being followed, Calliope, drive for a while so I can catch up on my no-one-could-call-it-beauty sleep.' The hell have I got to be *bothered* by?" She glared at the dark road ahead of her.

Vikous said nothing immediately, then: "What would you like me to tell you?"

Calliope's eyes widened. "What . . ." She made a visible effort to keep her hands firmly on the wheel. "All right, how about telling me who's back there and what they want."

Vikous watched her, his expression bemused. "I'm not sure."

"I'm . . ." Even in the pale green light of the dashboard, Calliope's face seemed to grow darker. "I'm really getting tired of that answer."

"Sorry, but that's how it is." He turned back to watching the oncoming road. "They could be waiting to grab us or kill us the next time we stop or they could just be watching us. It really doesn't matter."

"How could that not matter?"

"Where we're going, we don't want to be grabbed, killed, *or* watched. Any of those options and probably a half-dozen more are equally bad."

"And the obvious answer to this looming threat is a quick nap?" She made half of a raised-hand gesture from her grip on the wheel. "You've convinced me. Truly, your ways are mysterious."

He adjusted his position. "I was getting ready for what's coming up. I don't have any pepper spray, so—"

"It's in the back."

Vikous paused. "You packed it?"

"I didn't think I'd need it right away. Can we get to it? Will it help?"

"Probably." Vikous considered it for a second. "Probably it would help, I mean." He shook his head. "We can't get to it by the time we'd need it. It takes time."

Calliope's jaw was tight. "So that would be a drawback to your magical car-packing ability, then."

"Looks like. Don't worry, we'll be fine."

She favored Vikous with a dark look.

Vikous raised a hand in a warding gesture at her sour expression. "We can get this over quick; go ahead and pull over at the next motel sign you see." He fished in his pockets. "The older and more beat-up, the better."

It was six more miles before the Jeep pulled into the gravel parking lot of a roadside motel—a long, narrow brick building that looked like nothing so much as a stretched shoebox with a too-large lid for a roof, facing a loose-gravel parking lot that looked like it could swallow cars whole. Although it had been built over a half century ago, Calliope didn't honestly think the place had seen better days; she guessed it had been an ugly and unwelcoming last choice of travelers since the day it had opened. It was a nothing sort of place—the kind that grew up like fungus in out-of-the-way corners—and she'd seen thousands like it.

"Perfect," Vikous said. "Pull up in front of twenty-three."

Far beyond any sort of calm or rational comment, Calliope complied, shutting off the engine and killing the headlights as they rolled to a stop. Vikous immediately got out, swinging his ridiculous shoes to the ground as though he had not spent over four hours in a cramped vehicle. Calliope followed.

Vikous was already close to the door labeled 23. Something glinted in his hand under the illumination of the lot's single light. The metal-on-metal jingle helped Calliope identify it as a key.

"Where did you—" she began, but stopped as he reached for the doorknob and a light came on behind the thinly curtained windows of that very room. Vikous didn't seem to notice, and she hurried up alongside him. "Someone's inside," she whispered, but Vikous only glanced at her, his mouth set in a grim smile.

"I suppose there might be," he said, his voice low and taut. She could see sweat beading on his paste-white forehead as he wrestled the key back and forth in the lock. After a few moments, he let out a deeply held breath, gave a final turn, and withdrew the key. The old, diamond-shaped plastic tag hanging from it did not match the darkened sign near the road.

"No luck?"

"We'll see." He headed down along the concrete slab that fronted the motel, moving away from the light of the lobby. "C'mon," he called without looking back. The light in room 23 remained on.

Vikous stepped around the corner at the end of the building and stopped, glancing back toward the Jeep and the highway as Calliope walked past him, the truncated black shaft of an unopened police baton in her hand. Vikous spared it a bare glance, then turned back as a nondescript car pulled into the lot, heading for the Jeep.

"They're going to know we're around here. The Jeep's right there and we're not in that room," Calliope said.

"Good thing, too," Vikous replied, his voice slow and almost amused. "Because here they come."

The car pulled up. Four doors opened. Four large figures got out. Three of them slid things into the night air that gleamed and looked long and sharp in the bare lighting.

"Definitely not here to watch," Vikous whispered.

They descended on the door quickly and efficiently. One of them—the one not holding a sword—stepped to the center. Calliope could barely make out a few strident spoken tones from the group. Vikous smiled.

"Oh, very good," he whispered. "You're very good, aren't you?" His eyes were looking down and away from the figures, all his attention on listening. "Here we go . . ."

With the last spoken syllable, the door opened, spilling cheap golden light onto the walk and the front of Calliope's Jeep. The four moved inside so quickly that they barely seemed to cast shadows. The lot echoed with the slam of the motel room door.

The light in the window went out.

Calliope waited, noticing that Vikous's smile was back and spreading too far to look normal.

She squinted at the room, but couldn't make out anything. No lights. No sounds. The door remained shut. Vikous looked back at Calliope, the sweat on his face and his smile making him look like an exhausted but satiated demon clown, which she thought might be a fairly accurate summation of what he actually was.

"Good motel you picked," he said, his voice pitched at a normal volume. "Real shame we can't stay." He headed back to the Jeep, only glancing at the door to 23 once, a strange smirk on his face.

"You're going to explain what just happened," Calliope said from behind him as she walked.

"You kidding?" he said, almost to himself. "I'm going to be talking about this for *years*."

"Reality is like carpet," Vikous said as they pulled out of the parking lot. They'd checked over the other car for anything that might have indicated their followers' identity and Calliope, who had worked at just that sort of activity for several years, had found nothing that gave her any clues. The vehicle was a nondescript rental with no paperwork inside, not even proof of insurance, which meant that its absence was probably deliberate. If Vikous had noticed anything, he wasn't sharing.

"In some places," he continued, "special places, it stays nice and fresh and solid, practically like new for all intents and purposes—sometimes even normal people recognize a spot like that—maybe make a holy place out of it." His expression was unreadable. "In other places it wears down. Even then, the . . . carpet usually remakes itself; it builds its own inherent strength back up from the energy of the same living that's wearing it down—it's not new anymore, not like those really good places, but there's nothing wrong with it. Most places are like that." He gestured out the window and back, vaguely in the direction of the already-invisible motel. "Then you've got the opposite effect." He jingled the old motel key. "Places where there's no . . . soul, I guess . . . behind the living that goes on in a place. The carpet wears down to paper thin."

"That's very feng shui," Calliope interrupted. "Where did the bad guys go?"

Vikous shrugged. "I don't—" he began, but cut himself off at a warning look from Calliope. "Ahh, see, a magician's not supposed to give away his secrets, but basically what I did was shred what was left of the carpet."

Calliope frowned. "So they just . . . what? Fell through?"

Vikous shook his head. "I had to have it all *go* somewhere; just ripping open a hole would have been . . . bad."

Calliope cast him a glance. "Bad?"

"The stuff under the carpet isn't exactly friendly."

"Cute. So where'd they go?"

"It's a very inexact thing. They went somewhere like the place they'd just left—a motel like that, probably, but somewhere else—maybe not even realizing they were in the wrong place right away, except they probably did *not* all end up in the same place." He smirked. "Seriously, and don't hit me, I don't know."

Calliope nodded, feeling oddly calm. "So they could be ahead of us."

Vikous waved his hand in a broad gesture. "They could be lots of places, so yeah, they might be ahead of us, but if they aren't following us, we don't have to worry about them."

"At least for a while," Calliope said. "We couldn't have just broken their kneecaps and left them behind?"

Vikous glanced at her, his expression tired. "We'll have plenty of chances to fight. Usually we won't have a choice one way or the other, so I like to take advantage of it when we do. Besides"—he shifted in his seat—"at least one of them was real good. It's better that we didn't have to deal with them." He looked out the front window at the oncoming lights of a small exit-ramp town and pulled up his hood. "You hungry? I'm starving."

```
J B P D H I A D S O Q I N Y C Y L
H R C Y L D S E E M Y A Y R D S E
H Y M E S E G Z M C R G R S E M Y
F F D C M N I O C E U R E R A Y R
D E A X D O T F B T H A S E H Y M
T I O J M D I L N L H B I V E S E
I R S T Y N I P H R I I T O G Z M
L G C Z E A C E L M O N N L C R G
R J D X W B T U E V Y C S G R S F
Q Y R                         F D C
S X T                         M N I
S D R                         O C E
O K M W S R M J M Y D E S J U R E
X E E T L Q E D F T E S T E R D E
R M A N H T P T M W F P G J A X D
C L O H R U G E O G P H E T O T F
E A C E L M O N N L R J D X B T H
W B T U E V Y C S G Q Y R E A S E
H A R L E Q U I N I S X T E T I O
G L O I F R I E N D S D R A J M D
G O N L O G U I D E O K M W I L N
S R M J M Y D E S J X E E T L H B
L Q E D F T E S T E R M A N I V I
H T P T M W F P G J C L O W R S T
N E G I O H D T U L O H F D Y N I
B O J N M V R W Z O Y W Q J P H R
W R H Y V S I L P J N F C W O K S
```

STAGE THREE

10

THE WAITRESS TOOK their orders; the expression on her face said she didn't understand why Calliope was having a midnight meal with a homeless guy, but also that she didn't really care. From beneath his hood, Vikous glanced around the diner. "This place would have worked too," he commented, "if I'd had the right kind of key."

Calliope nodded, although she wasn't quite sure she understood. "That sort of thing—magic—that's . . . normal?"

"Nothing's normal with what we're doing," Vikous replied, his voice back to something like a lecture tone. "Some of it is more . . . common. Some"—he produced the motel key from somewhere—"isn't." He watched her for a second from the shadows of his hood, then pocketed the key. "It's all knowing how the world goes together, what pieces fit where, then figuring how to rearrange them a little bit." Without looking, he reached over and scooped up half of the individual jelly packs that sat in a bowl at the back of the booth and dumped them into a pocket. "Or a lot, like we did tonight, but that's harder." He glanced up. "I'm starving. Where's the food?"

Calliope looked around as well. "Actually," she said, her voice suddenly very quiet, "where are all the people?"

The waitress was gone, as were the two truckers at the front counter, the tall blond woman huddling in a ragged denim jacket in a booth near the entrance, and the tired couple with the sleeping baby that had been sitting two tables over. The kitchen was silent. Calliope turned back to the table, but Vikous was already standing.

"Run." He looked around the room, his expression equal parts hunter and hunted. For one electric moment, his haunted eyes reminded Calliope of a cheap black velvet clown painting that had hung in an even cheaper burger joint her family had visited when she was a kid.

"Who—"

"Run. Now." Without looking, his hands found Calliope's shoulders and he dropped his eyes to hers. "Someone else either has the right key for this place, or they don't *need* one." He nearly threw her, stumbling, toward the front door and the Jeep. "*Run.*"

Eyes wide, Calliope ran. Behind her, she heard the fire exit at the rear of the building slam open and the wind come howling in. Over it, just barely over it, Calliope thought she could hear Vikous shouting something in a language she didn't know. He sounded desperate, and the wind sounded very much like laughter.

Someone was standing just outside the doors to the diner, rock-steady in the tearing wind she could both see and feel, unaffected by the sudden violent flashes of lightning that had sprung up out of nowhere outside. Calliope froze, simply unable to process the shift things had taken in so short a time.

The landscape outside was barren, stark, and monochrome in the lightning illumination. Inside . . .

She turned.

Vikous stood where she had left him. His right hand, gloved, extended away from him like a claw. His ridiculous feet were spread wide and staggered to brace against the wind that tore in from the back of the L-shaped diner, pulling at his coat and clothes like a madwoman. Every movable stick of furniture in the place was sliding across the floor toward the rear entrance, moving *against* the blasting wind and piling itself before the opening in heaps, like a warped replay of *The Sorcerer's Apprentice*. Chairs stood in a haphazard pile atop one another, heaped over tables that had turned themselves on their sides.

And still something was coming through, hurling the debris away.

Calliope heard, in the rising pitch of the wind, the front door open behind her. She leapt back toward Vikous and pivoted. A tall man, wrapped in a long black coat that muffled him nearly to his eyeballs, took a few broad strides into the space and stopped. Slowly the door pulled itself shut behind him, and the volume of the wind dropped enough to hear the sound of crashing furniture.

Enough to hear Vikous's exhausted panting.

A voice, thin and reedy, like a sickly child's, came out of the crashing near the back door. "But when, Calliope, thy loud harp rang . . ."

crash

"in Epic grandeur rose the lofty strain . . ."

crash

"the clash of arms, the trumpet's awful—"

crash

"mixed with the roar of—"

Calliope lost the rest of the recitation in the ripping and tearing that rose up behind her. She turned, ignoring the large man, and saw an orgy of violence that cleared a passage through the heaps of synthetic and metal furniture.

Amid the wreckage stood a dusty brown old man no more than four feet tall: hairless, dry, and desiccated, with great, watery brown eyes that had, with age, bulged in their sockets rather than sinking. His shoes, pants, shirt, and ragged coat were all a simple unadorned black and he gripped the twisted metal leg of a chair in a knotted hand that might otherwise have looked too weak to make a fist. The wind had died completely away.

He looked only at Calliope, his mouth spread into a toothless smile as he spoke: "The ardent warrior bade his coursers wheel," he continued in his crackling voice, and he turned his wet gaze on Vikous with something like pity. "Trampling in dust the feeble and the brave." His gaze lowered and he made a simple gesture. Calliope felt the air *tense* like a stretched muscle.

Vikous flew to the side as though he were made of straw. The impact of his body against the painted cinder-block wall of the diner sounded like a baseball bat against a kneecap. He hung there for several moments; then, just as suddenly, he fell to the floor, utterly still.

"The feeble and the brave," said the shrunken man in his onionskin voice. "Truly, Vikous was both." He smiled, the skin around his mouth crinkling like old paper. "I suppose that would make me the ardent warrior." The old man turned his bulbous eyes back to Calliope, pivoting neatly on his heel and toe. "Hello, dear. I am called Faegos." He executed a tight but shallow bow. "I'm afraid I need a bit of your time."

The storm outside had subsided as quickly as it had come, once the fight was over. The tall, muffled man, still silent, had rummaged through the destruction and salvaged two reasonably intact chairs for Calliope and the one who called himself Faegos to use. These he positioned in the center of the cleared section where Vikous had been standing, setting them facing each other and adjusting both very precisely, even minutely, until he was satisfied, at which point he again withdrew out of immediate notice. Faegos pulled himself nimbly and easily into his chair, moving like a gymnast despite his age-ravaged appearance, and gestured for Calliope to take the opposite seat. His wizened face with its protuberant brown eyes was calm, confident—polite, in a slightly amused way.

Calliope was slowly starting to hate him more than she was worried about what was going to happen to her.

"Have a seat, my dear."

"I'd rather . . ."—*gougeoutyoureyeballsandbreakyourlegsandkillyou andcryandcryand*—she blinked—" . . . stand, thanks."

His head tilted, his face a mix of stern mocking and pity one might use on a disobedient but somewhat mentally handicapped child. "Calliope," he drawled, "please. Sit."

An iron band ratcheted tight on her mind at the words, dragging her to the chair. Pulling against the compulsion as much as possible, Calliope grabbed the chair and dragged it back to her, turning it backward and straddling it, her back straight. From its original position, she would have been forced to see Vikous's body just to the left of the old gnome sitting across from her; from the new angle, he was merely a disturbing shadow on her peripheral vision. She tried to push any thoughts about that out of her mind and kept her focus narrowed down to her growing anger.

Faegos's swathed assistant had started toward her as soon as she moved his precisely placed chair, but subsided at a negligent motion from the man's knobby hand. Faegos's eye ridge, as hairless as the rest of him, raised in mild amusement as she sat. "You are, I trust, comfortable?"

Don't look at the pool of blood spreading out like little fingers along the floor underneath his—

Calliope kept her expression cool. "I'm not really interested in chatting with you, so why don't we cut to the chase?" She glanced at the tall shrouded man who stood to the side. "You're going to torture me, find out what I know, and then kill me? Let me save you the trouble."

"Torture? Oh, goodness me, no." Faegos's wizened features twisted into a moue of distaste and gestured toward his companion. "Poor Kopro has no stomach for such things. Far too messy. For myself"—he laid a hand on his narrow chest—"I already know that you are sadly unaware of the realities that suddenly surround you." His face showed pity. "That much, I'm afraid, is painfully obvious."

"Then why are we wasting each other's time?"

He leaned back in the chair, at ease despite the fact that his legs, neatly crossed, only reached the floor with the toe of one shoe. "I would bargain with you."

Calliope didn't even bother to frown. "I don't have anything you want."

He smiled and raised an age-thickened finger, waggling it in the air before him. "Ahh, very good. That is essentially correct, but allow me to amend your statement; you do not have any-thing I want *at the moment*." He widened his already staring eyes. "I believe that might change."

Calliope narrowed her eyes, pondering. "You're the most powerful . . . thing that I've seen since I've gotten involved in this mess."

"Oh, how you talk," Faegos said and smiled, tipping his head bashfully as though receiving a compliment. He blinked his eyes. "Really, I am surprised. I was led to believe you were quite coarse."

Calliope thought of Gluen's angry pig-eyes and easily imag-ined the fat man selling information on her after they'd left his offices. "Some people just bring that out."

Faegos spread his hands, palms up. "Hopefully we will have a more equitable agreement."

"I'm just trying to sort everything out," Calliope said, barely listening. "See, if I'll eventually, maybe, have something you want, and if you want to bargain for it *now*, it's probably dan-gerous to you."

The diminutive old man's smile vanished. "Go on."

Calliope kept her eyes on his, tilting her head slightly. "What's to keep me from telling you to go fuck Kopro over there, then going and getting whatever it is you think I'm going to go get, and hunting you down like any other rat bastard?"

Faegos's face was grim. "I see I was not entirely misinformed as to your personality."

Calliope stared, her eyes wide and hard, holding on to her anger. "Some people just bring that out."

Faegos *tsk*ed. "I would certainly never let you leave this place, were that your choice. Nothing is so valuable to me that I cannot stand to see it destroyed, but I will most certainly not see it *lost*, or in the hands of such as you, which amounts to the same thing."

"So your bargain is whatever I might eventually get hold of that you find useful, in exchange for my life."

Faegos leaned a few inches forward, searching her face, then shook his head. "I regretfully must acknowledge that that would be a poor offer for one such as you." He eyed her shrewdly. "I suspect you might choose death simply to spite me."

Calliope didn't reply and kept her eyes locked on the old man's face, her jaw tight.

Faegos nodded as though receiving confirmation. "Obviously I would have to offer more tempting fare." He met her eyes, his gaze steady. "Perhaps the life of your young Joshua White would be sufficient."

The room seemed to tilt along its axis. Calliope's eyes felt painfully dry, but she could not bring herself to break eye contact with Faegos long enough to blink. "Say it again," she whispered.

"I have the means at my disposal to bring your lost young man back to you." Faegos's shoulders shifted as he gestured. "I am offering that to you as a trade for . . . certain hidden things . . . as yet undisclosed or discovered. It is quite a generous offer."

Calliope's eyes narrowed. "Alive? Actually breathing, not some shambling dead thing, or a ghost, or any other little trick?"

Faegos smiled. "I consider your caution commendable." He again spread his leathery hands, palms out. "I can bring Mr. Joshua White back to rosy-hued health, and not via some banal resurrection; I can make it as though what has happened never did. That service, executed on his behalf, is precisely and specifically what I am offering, to you." He leaned forward, his own glistening eyes bright. "As the late, lamented Vikous might have explained, there are ways to slip aside, away from, through, or behind this mortal coil." He smirked. "Or at the very least slip from one portion of the coil to another. Vikous himself dabbled at such things; it was, in fact, how we found you." Faegos shifted in his seat, his feet dangling. "But I . . . I can fold *time*, Calliope; I know where your young man died, and I know when. I will take him *around* that point in time, once we conclude our bargain."

A thin sliver of hope made Calliope's heart beat faster, despite her surroundings. She wrapped her arms around the back of her chair and leaned toward Faegos in turn. "What do I have to do?"

Faegos made an expansive gesture. "Nothing at all." He stopped, then raised a finger. "Ahh, that is not exactly true. You must continue on as you have. Pursue your quest to its fruition. I believe that will bring the thing I desire into your grasp."

Calliope managed a smirk. "Well, that's going to be difficult to do with a dead guide, genius."

Faegos ignored the slight, frowning. "Oh, do not be ridiculous; Vikous is a sorry guide in any case." He glanced over his shoulder. "Or was, rather." He shook his head and drew himself upright. "He has, I fear, been too long among your kind to be of much use; adopted so many of your ways—your false logic of violence, for instance."

"Sure. That's why *you're* the one that slammed *him* against the wall."

He scowled. "You manage to make your worth to me questionable through the simple act of speaking."

"It's a talent." She stood and crossed her arms. "Prove you can do the stuff you're talking about."

Faegos glanced at his companion. "You certainly don't expect me to follow through on my side of the arrangement when you cannot do likewise; goods neither seen nor inspected make a poor payment."

Calliope shook her head, her movements slow and deliberate. "No. Prove you can even do it at all. Doesn't have to be Joshua, just do it." She pointed, without looking, at Vikous's still form. "Fix that."

Like Calliope, Faegos did not so much as glance in the direction she was pointing. "You must be joking."

Calliope merely raised an eyebrow.

Faegos shook his head. "What you ask is essentially the benefit of my largesse twice for a single cost to yourself." He shook his finger again. "I think you are trying to trick me."

"You're getting your money's worth out of this."

He leaned back and folded his hands on his lap. "Explain to me how this is."

"This is how you convince me not to spite you," Calliope said. Her eyes and voice were clear. "You said you wouldn't let me out of here if I didn't agree to the deal." She leaned forward slightly, as if she were talking to a child. "I don't need Josh alive if I'm dead, do I?"

Faegos watched her for some time without moving; except for the wetness of his eyes, he might have been a dead thing left sitting in the blasted café for an age, long since dried to a husk. Finally he shifted, destroying the illusion with the ease of his movements as he dropped to the floor and wandered into the corner where Vikous lay.

"Such a petulant request, my dear," Faegos said, affecting the air of a disappointed teacher. He seemed distracted for a moment, as though listening to a fainter sound in the distance, then turned back to her. "We would have an agreement then? Provided, of course, I can prove myself to your satisfaction?"

Calliope shoved her doubts to the back of her mind. "Sure, yeah. I can't miss what I've never had, right?"

Faegos's toothless mouth curved into a smile that could never have been comforting or friendly. "As you say," he murmured, then: "Never mention this to your truculent companion."

"Why not?" Calliope asked.

"Why not what?" Vikous said from his side of their booth.

Calliope could only stare. Finally, her eyes still wide, she managed to force out a reply. "Umm. Nothing. Daydreaming."

Vikous watched her for a moment, his eyes narrowed, then turned to look over the sparsely populated diner. "I'm starving. Where's the food?"

Calliope tensed, but nothing happened.

Eventually, the waitress brought their orders. Calliope ate in silence.

—

Joshua White pulls on his jacket as he exits a downtown sky-scraper. The sun is bright, and he fumbles for his sunglasses with one hand, his cell phone with the other.

He will be dead in six days.

"Calli? This is Josh. You don't need to call me when you get this, I just wanted to let you know that I'm going out of town for a few days on a case, so if you need to get hold of me, call. My signal might be crap most of the time, though, so leave a message if you don't get me and we'll play phone tag." He glances over his shoulder and up at the building looming behind, wondering if the man he has just spoken to is watching the street. "I'll call and let Lauren

know what's going on so we don't have a repeat of the Seattle thing. See you soon. Be safe."

He looks back up at the glass and steel of the skyscraper. There is no question in his mind that he is being watched, or by whom.

There is also no doubt as to why, but Joshua tries very, very hard not to think about that.

"Red rover, red rover," he murmurs, "send Joshua on over . . ."

11

"I'M GOING TO make you a deal," Vikous said.

Calliope flinched at the words. The morning light shone through the frost-crusted glass of the front windshield, burning at her gritty eyes as she sat in the driver's seat and waited for the gas to finish pumping. They had spent what was left of the night in a (different) cheap motel in (different) double-bed rooms. Calliope's night hadn't been either long or restful, and she still felt edgy and tense. She glared at Vikous's puzzled look. "What?"

He continued staring at her, then shook his head and let his gaze drop. "Nothing . . . you just . . . nothing." He cleared his throat. "So . . . I have a deal to make with you."

"I don't like deals much right now."

"You'll probably like this one."

"What is it?"

Vikous pulled back his hood, revealing the pasty skin of his face in the morning light in order to make eye-to-shiny-black-eye contact. "Give us about five hours of driving and we can crash in a decent place for the rest of the day and night."

Calliope automatically opened her mouth to protest, then paused and conceded, "That . . . actually sounds pretty good."

Vikous nodded. "I know someone who can help us out a little."

"We won't be making ourselves late or something?"

Vikous laid a hand on his chest. "Trust the guide."

Calliope jerked her head in agreement. "Okay, we can—" She cut herself off and peered at Vikous. "Wait, what's the other part?"

Vikous blinked, his eyes wide, which in no way lent him an air of innocence. "Whaddaya mean?"

"'Deal' means I have to do something in return."

"You won't mind. It's easy."

Calliope's bloodshot eyes did not suggest trust.

"It's something we need to do anyway; I just want you to get some rest, all right?" Vikous started to pull his hood back up, but paused halfway. "All right? Trust the guide?"

The pump handle release *thumped* from outside the cab and the electronic display began to beep faintly. Calliope looked over her shoulder at the pump, then back to Vikous.

"Fine." She pushed open the door and swung out of the seat. "As long as I can sleep for a while."

⌁

"You and Mr. White both work in the same detective agency, Ms. Jenkins?"

Calliope is sitting in a chair in Lauren's office again, the glare through the office window turning both men into silhouettes. Only Special Agent Walker's eyes stand out—shining like lozenges of silver.

"Yes."

"I see. Do you know the nature of this case?"

"Josh handled this one from the beginning. I only knew he was

*flying out of town, not where, and I knew when he thought he'd
get back. I can check the office for records but I think he had all of
them with him when he left."*

"You're familiar with the area Mr. White was found in."

"Yes."

"Was Mr. White?"

" . . . not really."

"Had he been in the region before?"

*"When he was a kid, with his younger brother, yeah. Then once,
later."*

Don't ask don't ask don't ask don't—

"What was the nature of that later visit?"

. . .

"Miss Jenkins?"

"He . . . I took him there."

"For a case?"

"No. It was personal."

"You took him to meet your family."

"Yes."

"Did they like him?"

"No."

"Did they like you?"

Walker is smiling now, and his teeth glitter out of the darkness
of the office.

"What?"

"Does your family like you? They don't, do they, Miss Jenkins?"

"No. Yes."

"Which is it?"

"They don't like . . . some things. Didn't. Don't. I don't know."

"Are they going to like your new boyfriend? The clown?"

"He's not my boyfriend, he's—"

"Will they like him?"

"They don't know him."

"But you do. You've known the clown a long time, haven't you?"

"No."

"Haven't you?"

She is standing at the very top of the blocky jungle gym. It's her favorite place to stand because she can see so much of the playground and everyone can see her. She's standing at the very top, on the little block of bars that sits on top of a larger block.

Joshua is at the other end of the playground, playing Red Rover with the other ki—

> That's not right; Josh can't be here. We didn't know each other.

—she's singing. It's her favorite thing to do and she likes it very much. It makes her feel good and strong and warm. She can see Joshua is climbing up the jungle gym to her. He's shouting something at her, but Calliope just sings louder so that she doesn't have to hear it. Josh keeps climbing, keeps getting closer, and finally Calliope can hear him shouting to stop, to stop singing, to let someone else on top of the jungle gym.

Calliope gets mad. She wants to keep singing. It's the only thing she

> has

wants to do. She reaches out with her foot and shoves and Josh falls back away from her.

Too far. Right out over the edge of the big block and down to the ground. He lands funny and when Calliope looks down, she can see a big sharp white thing poking out of his arm, and the skin curls back on both sides of the white thing like sheets of old paper.

> That must be a bone, *Calliope thinks, but she keeps singing—keeps singing and doesn't come down until a teacher*

pulls her right off the jungle gym and carries her back into the school.

Across the playground, outside the fence, Calliope sees a man watching her be carried away, and it makes her feel bad. He looks familiar, so very familiar. Calliope is sure she would know who he was if his hood wasn't up. She can still see his shiny eyes, though— shining out of the hood, the same way Walker's shine in the dim of Lauren's office.

So familiar.

"You see, Miss Jenkins? You've known the clown a long time."

"No."

"Haven't you?"

"No. That wasn't me. That didn't happen to me."

"It happened."

"But it wasn't me. Someone told me about that happening. The pushing, the falling . . . all of that."

"Really?"

"It was . . ." She frowns. She can almost remember. "It wasn't me."

Calliope jerked awake.

"Calliope?" A knock on the door. "Calliope?"

She looked around the room, wide-eyed and trying to make sense of the strange, nonmotel surroundings.

"Calliope?"

"Yeah." Her mouth tasted like something evil had died inside it. "Yeah, I'm up."

"I thought we could go do this thing in a little bit."

Calliope blinked, still groggy. "What thing?" she called back.

"The deal, remember the deal?" Vikous sounded as though he was at least trying to be patient.

"Right," she said to herself, then called, louder, "Right. Give me a few." She sat up on the edge of a twin bed Vikous's friend had made up for her.

So familiar . . . The thought clung to the back of her mind, but Calliope couldn't remember why.

"You, ehh, you sleep all right? You get, ehh, a good, ahh, nap?"

Calliope smiled across the small table at their host. He was only a few inches taller than Faegos, but when it came to the man Vikous had introduced as Gerschon, all similarities to the vicious old man from the diner ended there. Their host moved around the room like a duck that had swallowed a bowling ball. His dark olive complexion was leathery, and his body sprouted tufts of wiry gray hair from any number of unlikely places. When he spoke in his worn and crackling voice, he paused frequently, struggling to think of the correct word and waving one or both of his hands around in random patterns, as if the perfect phrase were a mosquito he could swat out of the air and quickly pop into his mouth.

"I slept very well, thank you." Calliope smiled and lied with equal ease. "I'm glad that Vikous knew someone nearby who was so caring and helpful."

"Oh, heh heh, you are . . . ehh, kind, I think." The older man chuckled, obviously pleased, and reached back for a steaming pot on the stove, lifting it by its bare wire handle and carrying it over to the table. "I, ahh, make the coffee? You?" He raised the pot by way of an offer.

Calliope smiled and meant it this time. "Yes, please."

He chuckled. "You kids and your coffee, eh? Always *go go go.*" He poured. The powerful scent washed over Calliope as she raised the cup.

"It smells strong." She took a careful drink and grimaced, though she tried not to. "It *is* strong." She smiled at his concerned look. "It's all right. I like it strong."

Gerschon smiled. "Ahh, tha's good. Vikous wanted you . . . ehh, bright-eyed for the . . . ehh, visit my club, no?"

Calliope took another sip from the cup. "I guess so."

Gerschon nodded, his thoughts obviously elsewhere. "He, ahh, Vikous"—his thick accent turned the name into *Vee-koosh*—"he is a good—" Gerschon said some word Calliope couldn't quite understand. "You are lucky, ehh, I think."

Calliope shook her head. "I'm sorry, I don't know that word. Gregory? Gree-*gor*-ie? Is that his name? Another nickname for him?"

Gerschon waved his hand as though to brush aside a fly. "Oh, not 'Gregory' . . . Is . . . is old word, I use." He paused for a second. "Is also *wrong* word, made by people who did not understand . . . eh . . . things. But is almost not *too* wrong. Means . . ." He frowned, staring into the middle distance, as though trying to read the word he wanted from the wall behind Calliope.

"A guide?" she suggested.

He turned back to her and smiled broadly. "Ahh, guide. Is . . ." He tapped the table soundly with one hairy knuckle. "Is . . . close enough, I think." He glanced at the clock. "And . . . I think we have to get going." Gerschon turned back to her, peering at her face. "Lemme as' you something." He leaned in. "You are . . . ehh, okay with this? The club?"

Calliope raised an eyebrow. "Well, it's not a strip club or something, is it?"

Gerschon's eyes opened wide. After a moment's silence, he sat back in his chair, laughing and waving his hands back and forth. Calliope would have sworn he was blushing. "A, ehh, a strip club? With the . . . ahh, I . . . no." He chuckled again. "No. No strip club, not for Gerschon. Not . . . ahh . . . anymore."

Calliope smiled. "Then I guess I'm fine with it."

Gerschon searched her face, then slapped his hands against the tabletop and pushed himself upright. "Oh-kay," he said, and smiled. Calliope returned the smile and stood up, finishing the coffee in one bitter gulp. Gerschon had continued talking. "We . . . ahh, we get the coat . . . here you are. Would you like help wi— No, you got it. Ladies today get the coats . . . and Gerschon gets . . . ehh . . . *my* coat." He chuckled to himself and moved to the door that led out the back of the kitchen and into the side yard of his small house. "And . . . we have the door, which . . . ehh, you will have to let Gerschon get, because I am old-fashioned . . . And out we go . . . going to the club." He flipped off the kitchen lights and turned on the yard light for Calliope to see by. "And we will get to . . . ehh, hear you sing and . . . ehh, then we see what—"

"Excuse me." Calliope turned fully around on the steps that led down from the door. "Hear me what?"

Gerschon's club was essentially a small bar with a fair number of open tables, some booths along the back wall, no dance floor, and a small stage about the size of a bathroom stall. Calliope looked over the sparse collection of college-age kids, thirtysomethings, and lonely singles fingering their drinks and watching the crowd. The stage was set up with a TV on one side, two mikes, and a number of mismatched speakers. A soundboard and playback unit sat just to the side of the stage.

"This is a karaoke bar," Calliope said.

"Only on . . . ehh, Saturdays," Gerschon said as he eased past her and into the bar. "Excuse me, I must see to the business." He smiled and roll-walked through the crowd, nodding to the bartender.

Calliope turned to Vikous, standing next to her with his hood raised. "This is a karaoke bar."

"Only on Saturdays," Vikous murmured.

Calliope glared. "You're not funny. This"—she gestured to the bar—"isn't funny."

Vikous pushed his hood back and raised an eyebrow at Calliope. "I'm not trying to be funny." He indicated the stage with his chin. "This is something that I—we—need to check."

"This is crap."

"Hey, what happened to trust the guide?"

Calliope snorted. "The last time—" She cut herself off abruptly.

Vikous gave her a puzzled look. "What?"

"Nothing." She turned her attention back to the stage, moving out of the way of the entrance.

Vikous looked around. "It's just like any other karaoke bar." On the stage, a young man stepped up to the microphone and began a rendition of something that the screen next to him insisted was Jimmy Buffett.

"I've never *been* to a karaoke bar," Calliope growled.

"No kidding?" He looked mildly surprised. "I figured . . ."

"You figured what?"

He nudged her in the direction of an open booth, moving through the tables with a dexterity that seemed impossible. "Well, you sang in a band, right?"

Calliope rolled her eyes. "I played drums first but yeah, what's your point?" She dropped into a seat and glared across the table. "Do you know a lot of triple-A baseball players who do local coed softball on the weekends?"

Vikous's eyebrows shot up. "Nice attitude."

"You are *hearing* the sounds that guy is making right now, right?" The bar's lone Saturday-night waitress stopped at their table.

"That's Jerry," she said, pulling out a pad. "You should have heard him do "Henry the Eighth" a few hours ago. He walked through the crowd."

Calliope winced. "Oh god."

"I recommend a painkiller," the older woman murmured. "And the boss says it's on the house, so go crazy."

"Strychnine?" Calliope asked.

The waitress shook her head. "Only have a beer and wine license, honey. Sorry."

"Beer then," Calliope replied. "Whatever's on tap."

"Liquid bravery, on the way." She gave Calliope a perfunctory smile and wove her way into the crowd without so much as a glance at Vikous.

Calliope closed her eyes, speaking only after several seconds had passed. "What, exactly, is the point of this? What am I supposed to do?" She glanced back at the stage where Jimmy Buffett had been replaced by a Foreigner ballad sung by a balding man in his midforties. "If it's some sort of rite of passage in which I have to suffer through a gauntlet of pain, and you thought this would be easier than cutting off a finger, let me tell you: I can spare a finger."

Vikous's face was blank. "I want you to sing."

"Why?" Calliope turned back to him.

"Because I think it might *matter*," he said, his voice low and hard. "People are interested in you and it's not all about your dead friend; it's you. Do you know why?"

Calliope shook her head.

Vikous handed her a piece of paper. "Then you can sing. If I'm completely wrong, the worst thing that happens is Gerschon gives you free food and drinks, and you have to hear a pair of newlyweds sing 'Endless Love.'"

Calliope frowned at Vikous, then glanced at the paper. "What's this?"

Vikous turned back to the stage, where a girl in her twenties was leading the crowd through "My Guy." "You have to write down the songs you want to do. I picked out ones I thought would—"

"No." Calliope held up the paper so Vikous could see it and pointed. "'Me and Bobby McGee'? 'Mickey'? Are you cracked?"

"What's wrong with—" Vikous cut himself off. "The song list is on the bar. Big book, can't miss it."

"Was there any Green Day?" Calliope asked.

"I didn't—" Vikous began, his voice starting to rise, then he caught sight of Calliope's expression. "Okay, now you're just screwing around."

"Were you joking about the newlyweds?"

Vikous snorted. "Count yourself lucky you slept as long as you did—saved you from the warm-up performances."

The waitress dropped off a mug on her way to a large table. Calliope ignored it and looked around the club. "Okay."

"Okay to what?"

"I guess I'll go check out the song list."

Vikous's expression was neutral as he toyed with the plastic rapier sticking out of the cherry in his drink. "You could do that."

Calliope stood. Vikous watched her go, his mood not at all helped by the woman starting "I Say a Little Prayer" on the stage.

It would normally have been about an hour before they got to Calliope's first turn at the microphone, but Gerschon spoke to the young man running the soundboard and within twenty minutes she heard her name called. She moved through the crowd on heavy feet. There were no stage lights to speak of— half the people she'd seen so far hadn't even gone up to the stage, simply standing at their tables as they sang. The closeness of the room made her unusually aware of the dozens of pairs of eyes watching her. It had been two years since she had performed, and every familiar element—the murmur of the crowd, the hiss of the open mic, even the simple act of stepping up onto the humble stage—dumped adrenaline into Calliope's system.

She pulled the mic to her and looked over the nearest patrons. "Hi." She tried to smile. The sound wasn't set up so she could hear her voice as it came through the system; to Calliope it sounded as though the mic was off. In the back of the room, she could see Vikous, his hood still pulled up. At that moment she hated him, hated the bar, and hated herself for agreeing to do anything this ridiculous. The music began without warning or signal and Calliope started in surprise, glanced at the smaller video screen angled in her direction, and decided to get it over with.

With nothing to lose, Calliope sang.

> At the end of the night, no one could remember the songs the girl from out of town had sung.
>   The first one, they were able to say, was angry. Or maybe she was, but one way or the other that was what they remembered.

When she was done, everyone sat there for a second, long enough for her to make it halfway through the tables before they started clapping. They hadn't waited all that long, but she had nearly run from the mic when she finished up. The applause had stopped her cold; they remembered that, too.

When they called her second song, someone had started clapping while she was still walking up to the stage.

That had made her smile. They recounted that and smiled to themselves when they talked about it, warmed by the remembered fondness.

That second song had been slow, slow and sad. Some of the women had cried; nearly, anyway. Everyone had clapped when she was done.

The third time, people started clapping when the sound guy called her name.

Her name? No one was quite sure. The little weird guy who ran the club said he didn't know. People had stood up the third time; some had tried to dance—that, they remembered.

No one could say what happened after that. The girl stayed on the stage and sang for . . . well, till just about the end of the night, but she was gone afterward, before anyone could stop her, and she hadn't come back.

People still talked about her every Saturday night when they got the song list and the microphones out.

They said she sang her soul, and their eyes were far away, remembering.

Calliope, Vikous, and Gerschon sat around Gerschon's small kitchen table with steaming cups of coffee. Gerschon was smiling.

"I think"—he waved a hand through the air—"ehh, she is found something very strong, Vikous, yes?"

Vikous's coat-button eyes were on Calliope, but he spoke to Gerschon. "That's what it looks like." He took a drink of coffee, grimaced, and set the cup carefully on the table. "What do you think?" he asked, directing the question to Calliope.

"Waste of talent and time." Calliope murmured to herself, the words hardly intelligible.

"Calliope?" Vikous said.

"Yeah?" Calliope looked up from her coffee cup and blinked, shaking her head. "Sorry. Umm, I guess it went all right."

"All right?" Gerschon chuckled. "She makes joke, I think." Vikous said nothing.

Calliope looked from one to the other, her expression bemused. "I don't really remember . . ." Her voice was quiet. "It's always kind of a blur."

Vikous nodded, his garish face as close to serious as was possible. "How do you feel?"

"Great," Calliope replied without thinking, then blinked. "I mean . . ." She looked up at Vikous, clearly confused. "Great. I'm not tired or anything. I need a shower, I guess, but otherwise . . ." Her gaze became unfocused, as though she was trying to recall something just at the edge of memory. "Great."

Vikous looked at Gerschon, who smiled broadly and slapped him on the shoulder. "I think you have hit the nail on the first . . . ehh, swing, my friend."

Vikous nodded to Gerschon in acknowledgment, but like Calliope his expression was distracted.

⌁

Calliope rolled her window down, raising her voice over the noise of the wind. "I still don't know what we're doing."

Vikous glanced at her, sucking on his cigar hard enough

to make his cheek bow inward as he held a flame to the tip. Moving it to the side of his mouth, he blew smoke out of his own partially opened window. "We've got to keep moving. We can think while you drive."

"Burning tires," Calliope said, her face twisted. "That smells exactly like burning tires. God, I hate that smell; always have."

Vikous frowned at her, moving the cigar nearer the window. "Well, why'dja tell me I could start it up if you're gonna go all martyr on me?"

"Because it still smells better than *you*," Calliope said. "We were at Gerschon's for over a day—you couldn't have taken a shower and washed your clothes?"

"It's a little more complicated than that." Vikous took another draw from his cigar.

Calliope raised her eyebrows. "What?" She looked over his rumpled, stained clothing. "Please don't tell me that you melt if you come in contact with water or something, because that would be really stupid."

Vikous snorted. "Hardly." He rubbed at the corner of his mouth with a gloved finger. "It just wouldn't help, is all."

"Then what would? Because I'm willing to try most anything."

With a wordless sound, Vikous extinguished his cigar and tucked it somewhere within his clothing. "There, it's out, roll the windows back up, please."

"You didn't have to—"

"If I'm going to die, I'd like it to not be hypothermia that takes me down."

Calliope glanced at Vikous, then rolled up her window without comment. "There's not much chance of that, is there?" she said after a few miles had passed.

"Of what?"

"Dying quietly," Calliope said. Her voice was solemn, reflecting her morbid mood. "Not really one of the options."

Vikous met her eyes in the rearview mirror, his expression blank. "Well, it'd be all right by me if dying didn't come into it at all, but yeah, if it happens it won't be quiet." He glanced at her. "*You* definitely won't go quiet, anyway," he deadpanned. "I doubt you do anything quiet." He chuckled. "Like that time when your parents let you sign up for that school play."

"What?" She glanced at Vikous, her brow furrowed. "I don't—"

"You were, what? About fourth grade or so? The counselor said you needed to participate in some school functions to help you socialize. You hadn't been going to the town school for that long or something, right? Help build your confidence."

"Something like that," Calliope said, still frowning.

"Yeah, but confidence wasn't the issue, was it? Absolutely no problem with stage fright for the Jenkins girl." Vikous grinned and his mouth stretched back much too far, which Calliope never liked to see. "You got up in front of everyone and just took *over*. Your folks were so embarrassed." Vikous shook his head. "Snow White's Evil Stepmother tries to kill everyone and take over the world on opening night—just a *skosh* over the top."

Calliope shook her head. "That isn't what happened. I was trying to explain how she was just . . ." Her frown deepened. "I never told you about any of that. How do you—"

"I found out after I died," Vikous said, his eyes tracking the snowflakes that were starting to come down.

Calliope's heart thudded in her chest. "You . . . I didn't think you knew that had happened."

"What do you mean?" Joshua turned to look at her, scratching at a long, shiny scar on his forearm—the one from the jungle gym accident. "Good grief, Calli, I called you *twice* afterward. Pay attention."

He grinned and his mouth stretched much too far back.

Calliope screamed.

The sound of it shocked her awake.

"You, ehh, you sleep all right? You get, ehh, a good, ahh, nap?"

Calliope stared across the table at Gerschon. His ears, still hairy, ended in tufted points that waved in unison with the movements of his bushy eyebrows. She was surprised she hadn't noticed that before, or the points of his canines dragging at his lower lip. His leathery skin shone in the kitchen light, the fur-smooth hair along his jowls and arms a mix of salt and copper.

"I had a weird—" Calliope cut herself off and forced a smile. "I slept very well, thank you."

"Oh, heh heh, you are . . . ehh, lying, I think." He chuckled, his eyes slitted and sly, and reached back for a steaming pot on the stove, lifting it by its bare wire handle and swinging it over to the table. "I, ahh, made coffee. You?" He raised the pot, leering at her over the brim.

Calliope kept her smile locked in place. "Sure."

He chuckled as he poured, shaking his head. Steam rose from her cup, but no smell. "Is good, you drink. He wanted you . . . bright-eyed for the . . . ehh, visit."

"I guess so." Calliope felt her forehead crease, but took a sip, tasting nothing but hot, slightly metallic water. "He's a good guide."

"Guide?" Gerschon made a mock-confused face—the kind adults use when a child gives the wrong answer to an obvious question. "You use the wrong word, ahh, I think." He tilted his head and waggled his free hand back and forth. "Is close in sounding, but . . . guide? No . . . is *goad*, what Walker is."

"Walker?" Calliope cut in. "What—"

"Sounding same, meaning different." He paused for a second. "And . . . ehh . . . wrong, anyway. Is what he *was*. What Walker is now, ehh, I think there is no—"

"Gerschon likes to talk." The narrow-faced special agent stepped past Calliope and walked around to stand behind the old man. Gerschon hung his head, his expression ashamed, the small horns on his forehead—something else Calliope hadn't noticed before—pointing nearly at the floor. "Sometimes he talks too much." Walker patted him on the shoulder, then wiped his hand on his coat as he looked up at Calliope. "I only mind when it's to the wrong people."

Calliope's eyes narrowed. "Like you?"

Walker's pin-bright eyes met hers, but he spoke to Gerschon. "Miss Jenkins and I need to have a talk." His face was blank. "Give us a minute."

Gerschon started to stand, but caught Calliope's gaze. He hesitated. "You are . . . ehh, okay with this? This talk?"

Calliope looked up at Walker, her face deliberately calm— the kind of bored look she knew irritated most people—then back to Gerschon. "It's fine," she said. "I'm dreaming, right?" She leaned back in the chair and folded her arms. "It's not like he can do anything."

Gerschon opened his mouth to say something, but his eyes slid sideways—to Walker—and he nodded. "Oh-kay," he said, the word a rough whisper. He shuffled out of the room, his small hooves dragging on the linoleum as though his legs were in shackles. Calliope watched him go, watched his tiny cloven feet, then turned back to Walker, eyebrows raised in silent challenge.

"Right." Walker sniffed, the nostrils of his hatchet-blade nose flaring. "Let's talk."

"Whatever," Calliope replied, her voice thick with boredom. "But I don't see the point. I know this is fake." She gestured around the kitchen. "We left Gerschon's place almost a day ago."

"Oh, I know. Sorry about that." Walker's face—except for his eyes—took on a look of apology. "It's the best I could manage, since I was never able to find that bloated stain you got White's message from." He leaned on the table, stretching across the open space toward Calliope. "Help me make it more accurate."

"H—" Calliope cleared her throat. "How?"

Walker smiled, the too-sharp angles of his face pulling up into harsh V's. "If you're not at Gerschon's, where are you?"

The lights in the room went out, and the darkness filled with whispering voices.

Calliope jerked upright, heart thumping, fumbling through the darkness for a light switch. A blocky red alarm clock LED near her grasping hands showed 1:43. Next to the clock, she found a lamp, then the switch at its base.

A motel room. Dark windows. No one else in the room.

Calliope got out of the bed and padded to the window. Pulling aside the curtains, she could see that the snow that had kept them off the roads for the last twelve hours had stopped falling. In the reflection from the darkened window, she could make out the room behind her clearly.

Still no one else here. Her gaze came back to her own face. *Except me.*

In the reflection from the window, her dark eyes looked like black plastic.

12

"**WE'RE MAKING LOUSY** time," Calliope said.

Vikous looked up from his breakfast and mumbled something around a mouthful of toast and scrambled eggs. He kept his hood raised in the diner, but Calliope found that she had no trouble seeing his face within its shadows anymore.

"We left my house four days ago and we haven't gotten halfway there."

Vikous lifted a gloved hand and extended his index finger in the air while he swallowed. "First day we got started late, then the trouble at the motel." He extended a second finger. "Short day to get to Gerschon's, which was sort of out of the way, but worth it." He extended a third finger. "Then the snowstorm came on in the middle—"

"I know," Calliope said. "I know why it happened."

Vikous speared hash browns with one hand and grabbed packets of jelly from a dispenser on the table with the other, the former going into his mouth, the latter into a pocket. "Then what's the problem?"

"I want this to be done; I want to get where we're going and find out what's going on." Vikous gave her a look. "What?"

Vikous continued to watch her face, then set down his fork and wiped his mouth with the back of his gloved hand. "You've got some sort of notion that getting where we're going will fix everything. This isn't a fairy tale—it really *couldn't* be, at least not the kind they tell little kids. There's more to it than that."

Calliope set down her coffee cup, hard enough to slosh some of the liquid over the edge. "Then what's the point?"

"You tell me," Vikous said. "You're the one that got Gluen's supersecret message from behind the grave."

"I've told you what the message was," Calliope said. "So maybe you could quit—" She stopped. "Tell me what you just said."

Vikous paused. "You're the one White sent a message to?"

Calliope shook her head. "No. You used a phrase for it."

"Behind the—"

"*Yes*, that." Calliope said. "Where did you learn it like that? It's not behind, it's beyond."

Vikous shrugged, looking puzzled. "It's how it's said with . . . well, *us*, I guess . . . all of us. What difference does it make?"

"Walker. Walker said it that way."

Vikous searched her face. "The one from back at your office?"

Calliope nodded. "You know him."

Vikous's mouth twisted. "Walker's a potential problem, but I think we dodged him. I'm pretty sure those guys from the motel were sent by him, and we lost them, so he's out of the picture."

"Not *my* picture," Calliope muttered.

Vikous raised an eyebrow, his expression wary. "I'm not following."

"I've been dreaming about him." She frowned. "I think. I don't really remember much about the dreams, except he's there and asking me questions."

"Walker is?"

Calliope nodded again, her body tense for reasons she couldn't name.

Vikous searched her face, then set down the fork and started to slide out of their booth. "We'd better get moving."

⌒⌐

"The number of people tangled up in this," Vikous said, "is getting hard to keep track of."

Calliope pulled into the passing lane for the third time in twice as many minutes. "At least you know these freaks. I'm completely lost." She glanced at Vikous without turning her head fully. "Sorry."

He shook his head, barely listening. He worked his unlit cigar between his fingers, but paid it no other attention. "The way I figure it, that makes at least three groups, not counting Gerschon, tied up in this."

"He's one of the—"

"He's a satyr." Vikous said, answering the question before she asked. "Was. Gave it up."

Calliope tilted her head, something half remembered inside her knowing it was the truth. "Gave it up?"

"Some of it." Vikous shrugged in his peculiar, hard-to-watch way. "Enough to fit in."

"Another way to hide."

"Not . . . no." Vikous shifted in his seat. "What Gerschon is doing isn't hiding as much as . . . removing just enough of himself that hiding isn't required."

"I like him." Calliope felt defensive on the little hairy man's behalf.

"I like him too," Vikous replied, "but that's what he did. He let some of himself go to fit in. Gluen did the same kind of thing." His jaw muscles worked. "Walker took it a lot further."

"And you . . ." Calliope's voice was even, but sounded distant to her own ears. To hear Gerschon equated to the sour-faced Walker made something in her chest go cold and hard. "You *hide*. That's better?"

"It's not—" Vikous cut himself off, but Calliope could feel his glare even though she kept her eyes on the curving road. "We all pay prices. The prices Gerschon and I pay are different. Neither is *better*. Okay?"

"Okay." Calliope let the hum of the tires on the highway fill the cab before changing the subject. "Three groups?"

"Three groups."

"You don't think there's overlap somewhere?"

Vikous considered it, then shook his head. "No one's reach goes that far. White's killer would have had to plant someone ahead of time. Walker might have sent the goons at the motel, but he definitely wasn't there, and *that's* weird, because he's the sort of guy who wants to be hands-on."

"You know him." It wasn't a question, but Calliope felt unexpectedly tense, waiting for his reply.

Vikous's expression soured further. "I do, and that's not great news."

Calliope considered mentioning Faegos, trying to explain his involvement without mentioning the diner or the deal she had made with him. She shoved the idea away. "I just want to figure out what happened to Joshua. He said—" She swallowed. Her mouth was dry. "Or why. He told me what happened, I guess, but not why."

Vikous did not ask for more. "If we keep going and nothing gets any worse than it is, we should be fine. Nothing's come apart yet."

Calliope thought of the encounter with Faegos and shook her head a bare fraction of an inch—almost a warding gesture. "Sounds good," she said.

Vikous glanced at her, then settled his head back, a slight crease in his brow. He said nothing, but in Calliope's relatively brief experience, his silence was usually significant.

"What?" she asked.

He looked at her, frowning. "'Scuse me?"

"What's the look for?"

"What look?" He gestured at the front window. "I was looking at the road."

She worked her jaw. "You had a look."

"I did *not*—" He stopped himself and turned back to the road. Calliope let the silence build up, a trick she had taught herself in the last few years. It didn't come naturally to her, but she'd met very few people who could leave a conversation unfinished when faced with a long stretch of—

"I was expecting another round of questions," Vikous said. He looked at her, wearing a vaguely irritated expression. "I say something like 'as long as things don't get worse, things probably won't get worse,' and I kind of expect you're going to bust me on it. You didn't. It caught my attention."

Calliope smirked, shaking her head. "I'd just been thinking that the fact that *you* hadn't said anything probably meant something."

Vikous grunted. "Apparently we're both more interesting when we aren't talking."

Calliope's mouth quirked. "Wouldn't be the first time someone's told me that."

"Likewise." Vikous leaned his head to the side, stretching his neck. "I don't mind the questions, though, just so you know."

"Really?" Calliope cocked an eyebrow.

Vikous made a sour face. "I can't always explain everything, but that doesn't mean they aren't good questions."

"I'm supposed to be good at that," Calliope said. "Detective agency."

"Sure." He frowned. "Actually, *I've* got a question about that."

Calliope kept her hands loose on the wheel and her tone light. "Why a crappy skip trace agency?"

Vikous rocked his head back and forth. "Sure, if you want to put it that way." He made a gesture with the hand resting on the door's armrest. "I've heard you sing, so you can't tell me that chasing down bail jumpers and taking pictures of cheating husbands is the thing you do best."

"It's not," Calliope said. "But sometimes you can be really good at something and still not be able to do it very well, you know?"

Vikous looked at her, his expression made even more blank by his shining black eyes.

Calliope sighed. "Being a good singer doesn't actually mean I'm very good at being in a band."

"Ahh," Vikous leaned back in his seat. "Yeah. Okay." He smirked.

Calliope scowled at him, sidelong. "What?"

He shook his head, as though it wasn't important enough to repeat. "Just wondering if you were McCartney or Lennon."

She considered that, watching the dotted lines of the highway slip past. "Buddy Holly," she finally said. Her voice was soft, nearly lost in the noise of the road.

"Ahh." Vikous paused, as though choosing his next words carefully. "So no Nick and Nora Charles fantasies behind the White Agency, then?"

"What?" Calliope shot him a look. "Josh and I weren't together when he started the agency."

Vikous frowned. "I didn't—"

"It was his idea," Calliope continued, speaking over him. "I had to get my cert as we went. Took more than a year. It wasn't *fun*."

"Whoa, hey." Vikous raised his gloved hands. "Sorry, I didn't—"

"Just . . . you know what?" Calliope cut in. "Let's not. Okay?"

"Okay." Vikous settled back in his seat. A few seconds later, he murmured, "You just ask good questions, is all I meant to say."

The road rolled by beneath them, filling the small cab with its drone. Vikous almost didn't hear Calliope's quiet "Thanks."

"It's always how I thought Weathertop would look," Calliope said. They had emerged from the mountains and were driving north along I-25. Vikous didn't need to ask what she was talking about. A monolithic slab of native stone jutted out of the tall hill that rose just to the east of its namesake city of Castle Rock. It had loomed ahead of them for the last twenty minutes of their approach, drawing attention with a casual authority.

"You've been through here before?" Vikous said.

"I drove back home to visit my sister a couple times," Calliope said. "Then I came to my senses."

"You flew after that?"

"I stopped going at all." She turned her attention back to

the massive hill. "The last time I came through here was with Josh, sightseeing." She paused. "Stalling, really. We were going to stop and hike up to the top, but they've got all kinds of . . ." She shook her head. "It wasn't something we could set up in an afternoon."

"Why not set it up on the way out and do it on the way back?" Vikous scanned the hill that dominated the skyline, almost as if he was looking for something in particular. When Calliope didn't reply, he turned toward her.

"We didn't feel like it on the way back." Her eyes drifted down to the dashboard dials and displays. "I'm going to stop for gas and get something to eat."

Vikous nodded and pulled up his hood.

While Vikous filled up the Jeep, Calliope went in to the station to pick up something that passed for food. Neither cared for eating while they drove and both preferred (if that was the word for it) meals in diners, where the quality of the cook could be determined by the number of professional truck drivers sitting inside. But a sense of urgency had grown between them, hour by hour, and Vikous didn't stop her when she went inside.

She emerged from the station with a flimsy bag in one hand and a cardboard tray holding two massive plastic soda cups in the other. Vikous didn't acknowledge her return; when she went around to his side of the Jeep, his attention was focused beyond the silent pump to the highway exit visible down the street. "What's going on?" she asked.

For several moments, Vikous didn't reply. Calliope pulled her coat more tightly around her against the cold. "Something's here," he finally said.

The statement chilled Calliope more than the mountain air. "Do you . . . who? Was it waiting for us?"

Vikous's hood moved back and forth. "I don't think so. I think they've been following us."

Calliope frowned. "For how long? I thought you could tell when—"

"Maybe since we got back on the interstate, which I'm suddenly thinking might have been a mistake. I can't tell, though. Someone's been shielding them." His eyes narrowed. "They aren't now."

Calliope didn't ask why; that was one of the million-dollar questions to which they never seemed to have the answer. She could come up with a number of reasons herself, all equally likely and none of them comforting. "Can we keep going? Lose them going through Denver or taking back roads?"

Another head shake. "Not being found is one thing; losing them is something else entirely. Besides"—he glanced up at the mountains that crowded in at the town from the west—"I don't think they're going to wait around after it gets dark."

"So tell me you have a plan."

Vikous turned toward her. She could see him wink within the depths of his hood. "Let's eat, and you can tell me what kind of problems you had when you tried to do that hike with White."

Dusk comes early to a town that lies directly against the eastern face of a mountain range. By four thirty in the afternoon, the streetlights were already brightening. Atop the rocky slab that gave the town its name, the lights of several radio towers winked in the gathering dark like sentries.

Calliope and Vikous climbed the steep incline of the hill

from which the massive stone formation rose up, pulling themselves along in places with handfuls of chaparral that dotted the rugged slope.

"Tell me again," Calliope said as she pushed herself along, "why we're doing this?" The cold night air burrowed into her lungs. The region was only a few spring thunderstorms away from officially being a desert—throw in the fact that they were right alongside a mountain range, at night, in the first part of November, and Calliope was certain that she was, at that moment, as cold as she had been in the last ten years. She hadn't missed the sensation.

"We need to . . . lose . . . whoever's following us," Vikous said between breaths. Calliope was perversely glad that, uncomfortable as she was, she wasn't the one suffering the most from the climb. "That means . . . need to . . . jump."

"Jump?" Calliope's gaze traveled up the nearly vertical cracked stone face that rose above them. "I don't think I want to lose them that bad."

Vikous could barely get enough air to chuckle. "Not that kind of jump. We need to find a way . . ." He shook his head. "Ask me once we get to the top and I've had a chance to puke."

Calliope nodded and kept going.

The ground was loose and almost sandy near the base of the rock itself. Vikous sat on a flat stone, his hood up and his head lowered between his knees, his breath hard but steady. His hands were tucked into his midsection, and in the dark of the new moon his silhouette looked like nothing so much as a nesting bird.

With skis tied to its feet, Calliope thought. Aloud, she said, "You ready to go, iron man?"

Vikous made a deep grating noise in his throat that made Calliope cringe, then spat noisily. "Oh yeah." He spoke directly to the ground. "I'm fantastic. Top of the world. Kill me when all this is done." He leaned back and tilted his parti-colored face toward the clouded sky, inhaling shallowly through his nose. "I'm really too old for this crap."

"Move now, bitch later," Calliope said. "I'm freezing."

Vikous threw her a glare that almost seemed to warm the air around her, but he got up. "You sure you're ready for the next bit?"

"I don't know. Where are we going?" Calliope's tone was clipped, reflecting the tension she felt whenever their trip took a stranger turn. So far, those twists had not been in their favor.

Vikous's expression was unreadable. "Someplace else," he replied, picking up a small, sharp stone and walking up to a deeply shadowed crevice in the stone. He glanced back and Calliope moved to join him as he bent and drew a line in the sandy dirt that stretched from one side of the crevice to the other then, standing, simply stepped over the line and into the shadows beyond. He vanished utterly into the darkness.

Calliope watched the crevice for movement but saw nothing. "What the hell," she muttered, then stepped over the line.

"Borders are important," Vikous said in the close darkness. "If you can't find one, make one."

In the face of the stone wall in front of them stood a small iron door, limned all around its edge by a flickering light whose source had to lie somewhere behind it.

Calliope looked back to where she'd just been standing and gasped aloud. Down the slope of the hill they had just climbed, the lights of the city had vanished.

Not really, said a small voice in the back of Calliope's head. *There's just a lot less of them.*

"What . . . ?" Calliope's voice trailed off, robbed of all forward momentum. It felt to her as if every time she got used to the way things worked, someone dropped the ground out from under her.

"Welcome to the Hidden Lands." Vikous banged on the door.

The portal swung open almost immediately, spilling torch-light into the crevice. A squat, bowlegged figure peered up at Vikous's face without surprise, although his bloodshot eyes widened almost comically when he turned to Calliope. "Oy now, what's this?" the thing nearly shouted, turning back to Vikous. "We don' like yur kind aroun' anysight, an' these"—he jerked his bare, misshapen head toward Calliope—"r' fur other things." A dim spark of intelligence flared in the depths of his muddy eyes. "Or didjya bring us a pressent, paint face?"

Calliope knew exactly what a goblin looked like now. She also knew why they had been forced to hide; she wanted to beat this one bloody already. It was instinctual—a long-forgotten imprint flaring back into life. "Okay, Vikous," she said, "every time you take me to meet someone new I want to kick their ass into their throat. It's getting old." The goblin snarled.

Vikous glanced over his shoulder at Calliope and stepped directly in front of the twisted guard. "I am Vikous," Calliope heard him say in what she had dubbed his on-the-job voice. "I seek audience."

The goblin frowned, obviously puzzled by the shift in mood. "Err . . . what's she got to do widdit?"

"I am her guide," Vikous replied in the same tone. The guard's eyes twitched in surprise to Calliope, then back to Vikous. He pulled himself more erect, which almost seemed painful.

"Err . . . awright." He frowned in thought again. Finally: "Err
. . . what's yer purpose of . . ." He squinted. "Whattayer here for?"

"Trade," Vikous said without hesitation.

The goblin snorted. "Aww, yer shoulda said 'at from the firs'
bit." He glanced at Calliope and cleared his throat. "I mean,
err . . . come on in and be welcome in the Keep a' the King."

<hr>

It's not Weathertop, Calliope thought. *It's Goblintown.*

They followed the bobbing gait of the goblin as it descended
into the hill. Its skin was a mottled gray–green that hung in
wrinkled folds from its twisted, rawboned frame.

"Nice friends you've got here," Calliope murmured. "What
are we trading for?"

"Travel," Vikous said. "Their king can arrange to get us farther
into the Hidden Lands. If we can arrange to do it quietly, we'll
lose the guys following us."

"And we're going to offer what for this?"

Vikous glanced at their guide. "These guys like to have bits
of human culture. It doesn't even really matter if what you
have is valuable, they're like pack rats."

In the shadowy light of the torch, Calliope's eyes widened as
one tiny piece of the puzzle her life had become dropped into
place. "*Oh.*"

Vikous glanced at her. "What?"

"That's why you've been grabbing all those jelly packs at the
restaurants. You must have been planning for this for a while."

"Umm . . ." Vikous frowned, shaking his head. "No, I just
really like jelly."

Calliope blinked. "Oh, sure. That makes . . . sense." She scanned
the walls as she tried to recover her train of thought. *You can deal*

with magic and monsters, she thought, *but petty shoplifting leaves you speechless? Come on.* She cleared her throat. "What . . . what were you going to use for—" She paused, looking at Vikous, whose face had twisted into an expression she could not interpret in the near-dark. "What's wrong?"

Vikous shook his head, obviously struggling with some internal conflict. Suddenly, with a shock of expelled air, he burst into a low chuckle. Calliope stared at him. "You were joking?" she said.

He nodded, still laughing. The goblin glanced over his shoulder. "Oy, shut yer soup-hole."

Calliope ignored him. "The jelly *is* for the trade?"

Again, Vikous nodded.

Calliope turned away from him. "Asshole," she said, the sting of the words stolen away by Vikous's redoubled laughter.

"I . . . I just . . ." Vikous gasped out. "I just . . . really like jelly." His words dissolved into another laughing fit. Calliope elbowed him in the ribs to no effect; he was still chuckling quietly to himself when they arrived in the main cavern of the goblin king.

So, Calliope thought as she blinked back tears, *this is what being buried in a giant cat box is like.*

"Reminds me of your pepper spray," Vikous murmured, his laughter all but faded away. Calliope could only nod; she didn't want to risk taking the deeper breath that speech would require. There were few torches burning in the room; the light, such that it was, seemed to come from clumps of glowing matter that had been smeared in strange patterns on the walls and floor.

The goblin they had followed was taking a great deal of

pleasure in his suddenly increased importance. Leading them across the center of the nestlike cavern, he announced their arrival by banging on whatever bit of metal or hard plastic could be made to clash or thump and calling out *"vis'tors, vis'tors, vis'tors"* at the top of his cracked voice. By the time they had crossed a quarter of the cavern, others had begun to stir, which only seemed to make the stench worse.

Their escort led Vikous and Calliope up to a recessed alcove in the far wall of the cavern into which a threadbare recliner had been jammed. An almost childlike goblin perched in the large chair, its sticklike legs jutting straight out from the front edge of the seat cushion. A tin crown smeared with filth tipped precariously on its head. It . . . he, rather, Calliope amended, was quite clearly naked except for the crown, and licked his lips lasciviously as they approached.

"Shek," the crowned goblin said in a high and surprisingly clear voice.

"Vis't— ehh, yes, m'lord?" Shek managed a clumsy bow.

"Shut it," the king said.

Shek opened his mouth to speak but, at a glance from his liege, clearly thought better of it. The king turned back to Vikous and Calliope. "You have come to trade, flatfeet?" the king asked Vikous.

Vikous executed a stage bow, flamboyant and graceful while simultaneously foolish. "Indeed, king of the earth kin. We seek to travel farther into the Hidden Lands to which your home is a noble gateway." He raised his face to meet the shrunken monarch's gaze. "We also desire secrecy, which all know only the earth lords truly master." He bowed to the throne again.

The emaciated thing atop the chair dipped its head, its eyes half lidded. Calliope couldn't decide if he was trying to look wisely thoughtful or regally bored. "What do you bring in trade?" he asked.

Vikous swung his right hand low, bringing it up the left side of his body and across his face. As he did, packets of Smuckers and Knott's Berry Farm jelly tumbled from the hidden space behind his fingers and dropped into his waiting left hand. The crowd pressed in around them made appreciative noises. "Foodstuffs from the lands beyond," he said, his voice brazen and set to carry. "Reflections of the rainbow, fuel for your finest forges, fit only for a king and his most loyal followers."

The king nodded, a sad parody of a potentate in his flabby and wrinkled nudity. He fixed his eyes upon Vikous. "Truly, the jester's talents are not exaggerated." His oil-slick eyes flicked to Calliope, then back to Vikous as he licked his lips. "No," he said. His high voice somehow carried the length of the cavern.

Vikous froze, caught halfway through an acknowledging bow. "No, Highness?" He straightened and raised an eyebrow, motioning with one hand to stop a movement that Calliope hadn't realized she was about to make. "If I may presume to ask, why do you decline?"

"I think I can answer that, Vikous," said a voice behind them. "First, though, I'd like you to secure Ms. Jenkins for me."

Calliope spun to face the speaker, already recognizing the voice. A few dozen feet away, Special Agent Walker's sharp, saturnine expression seemed to glow softly in the place's pale luminescence. Anger overwhelmed her surprise. "Unless you bribed these guys to help you, Walker, I think the only thing that's going to happen right now is a righteous ass-kicking."

Walker smiled, and Calliope remembered again how much

that smile had bothered her. He opened his mouth to speak, shook his head, and pulled a gun from inside his coat.

Why am I on the ground? Who tripped me?

Calliope was having trouble breathing. She tried to get up but couldn't quite get her balance to shift forward. She looked up and saw that Vikous was standing over her, tried to tell him to help her, but couldn't get the words out. She tried rolling over, but her right arm wouldn't work.

He used a spell on me, Vikous, like that one you did on Lauren. Help me.

"You didn't have to shoot her," she heard Vikous say to someone past her line of sight. Calliope couldn't remember to whom he was talking, which was strange, because it seemed like it should be important.

He shot me? I thought . . .

And then she didn't think anything at all.

13

"**I KNOW WHAT** you've been doing, Vikous," said someone Calliope couldn't see. Above her, Vikous scowled in the direction of her feet. "You've been trying to do your job while staying away from me, because you know what will happen if you don't." Walker slid into view above Calliope, his gun still leaking a thin line of smoke that somehow reminded Calliope of Vikous's cigar. "You know what you owe me."

Vikous's face twisted. "I don't *owe* you anything."

Walker made a dismissive gesture with his empty hand. "Fine. You know your oath, sworn to me for services . . ."—he smiled, his face stretching—"rendered." Vikous looked away, but Walker continued, "You know its conditions, and you *knew* what I would ask of you should we cross paths." Walker's expression was bitter. "I'm tired of this game. I want it to end."

"Then you want everything to end." Vikous's voice was a growl. "Stagnate and rot."

"Yes." Walker's voice snapped at the air. "If that's the only way to break this cycle, I want it dead on the vine. I'm not

going to let this one"—his hand chopped down at Calliope—
"or anyone else reach the effigy."

"Because you've given up." Vikous spat the words out. "You
lost your faith before you ever rejected your nature."

"This role has always been my nature, my calling, and my
desire." Walked looked down at Calliope through what seemed
to her to be a long, dark tunnel. "This time . . . let's say I'm
investigating more permanent solutions to the problem. Plus
the disagreeable bitch has had it coming from minute one." He
tucked the gun away within his coat and looked up at Vikous.
"Now, pick her up and let's go."

Vikous turned his gaze on Walker, and for a moment it
seemed as though he would leap over Calliope to get to the
man. Instead, he seemed to deflate, bending down and easing
his arms under her.

"Vik'ss," Calliope heard another voice say. After a few seconds,
she realized it was hers.

Whoa, I sound bad.

"Quiet, Calli," Vikous murmured. "Save your strength."

"Vik'ss. Don' havt do this."

Vikous closed his eyes, his face gone slack and sorrowful. "I
do, Calli. I tried to stay clear of him, but . . ." He shook his head
and opened his eyes. "I have to do this."

Calliope didn't understand. The room was starting to spiral
away, but she focused her attention down to her left hand and
clutched at Vikous's sleeve. Her eyes locked onto Vikous's own.
"No. Y'don't."

Vikous frowned, his eyes first scanning her face, then
growing unfocused, as if searching within for some dark
thing they could not find. "I don't . . ." His eyes returned to
Calliope. "That's not possible."

"Get that bitch up and let's go, cousin." Walker was suddenly looming over them, the V's of his face pulled down and bitter. "I'm not going to—"

To Calliope's shock–addled perception, it seemed as if Vikous *flickered*—one moment, kneeling over her, the next, standing— motion compressed between two heartbeats, effortless as a hummingbird's wing beat. But the sound that echoed through the cavern as Vikous's hand shot out and clamped around Walker's throat—like a baseball bat swung into a side of beef— conveyed violent momentum. Walker's feet swung away from the floor as he dangled from Vikous's outstretched arm.

"What'r you *doing?*" Walker choked out, his hands scrabbling at Vikous's arm.

"Whatever I like, apparently." Vikous's lips drew back and back into something that could never be called a smile. His arm swung in an arc, and Walker flew across the cavern. Calliope didn't hear him land, but the goblins all made an impressed noise.

Vikous's face loomed over hers again and she was floating in the air, held aloft by his arms. Her shoulder was starting to hurt, but none of his movements seemed to jar her.

Solid, she thought, *he's solid.*

She tried to smile her thanks up at him, but when she saw his expression, the movement died on her lips.

Whatever Vikous was feeling at that moment, Calliope was absolutely sure it wasn't gratitude.

There were rules.

Vikous slipped through the goblin tunnels like fear in the veins of a coward: unstoppable, and bound to break out onto the surface before long.

There were very set rules for all the Hidden Things.

The king's minions scoured their lair for him, but they were creatures of darkness, dependent on scent and sound to track their prey, and he was what he was; the tunnels filled with the scents of roasting peanuts and stale cotton candy; cheap, tinkling organ music echoed from the walls.

Respect the Songs of Power. No blasphemy. All Oaths to be honored.

Vikous scowled, glancing down at the woman cradled in his arms.

She knew. It was right in her eyes. The thought filled him with a kind of sick rage.

"Oy! Who goes there?"

One. They only put one on the exit.

Vikous smiled, the corners of his mouth stretching back and back and back as his jaw opened.

Too wide.

Too many teeth.

The goblin's screams alerted its brethren, but by then it was far too late.

Morning sun pushed in through the curtains of a motel room. Calliope blinked grit from her eyes and tried to focus. She shifted slightly and agony speared through her right side. The pained hiss of air through her teeth drew movement out of the shadows in the corner of the room. Straining, gritting her teeth, Calliope could raise her head and make out Vikous's hunched form leaning forward in a chair. His hood was raised.

"How are you feeling?" he said.

Calliope settled back into the pillow, trying not to jostle anything too hard. "I . . ." She tried to take a deeper breath, thought better of it. Her entire right side felt stiff and constricted. "I'm awake and I hurt like hell."

"Good." He stood up and walked over to the side of the bed so that she could see him without moving. With the window behind him, he was little more than a silhouette. "I've figured out a plan."

Calliope grimace–smiled. "Sounds good," she said. "Let's hear it."

A pause, then: "Once we get some food into you, you're going to tell me what happened back in that diner the first night."

Time seemed to slow down for Calliope. "Why—" She licked her lips to buy time. "I mean, what's important about the diner? You were there with me the whole time."

"Was I?" Vikous said. He hadn't moved.

Calliope ignored the question. "What's that got to do with Walker? Do you think he's been following us since then?" She frowned, trying desperately to turn the conversation while keeping her face calm. "He couldn't have been, could he?"

Vikous shook his head, moving the hood only slightly. "He didn't catch up to us then."

"Then what—"

"I've been thinking about it." Vikous moved away from the bed and wandered, first to the door, then across the room. "Playing everything back. There are things that linger, like a headache; where you can have it on you for so long that you don't even know it's there anymore. It still hurts, but that's just background noise." Reaching the far side of the room, he turned and started back in the other direction, not looking at Calliope. "It becomes part of how you feel all the time until you don't even think about it, you just suffer, and when it's gone, sometimes you don't even realize it immediately." He reached the door of the motel room and turned back again. "You maybe know something's different, but it was so much a part of you that until someone asks you 'How's the headache?' you don't realize you don't have one anymore." He turned to look down at Calliope. "I had something like that, something I've been carrying around for a long time." He shook his head and looked away. "It's gone now. I didn't know it until you told me I didn't have to listen to Walker and I realized you were right."

In the shadowed gloom of the room, Calliope couldn't read Vikous. "That's . . . that's good, right?"

Vikous's voice was flat. "In the world I live in, oaths means something, Calliope. As far as I know, nothing could have broken the hold that oath had on me." He was holding himself completely still, as though he was afraid of what he might do if he moved. "I've thought it through—the binding went away the night we were at that motel and the diner afterward." Vikous's head shifted slightly; Calliope could feel, if not see, his eyes on her. "Something happened there, and I think you know what it was."

From her pillow, Calliope stared up at Vikous. "I don't . . . believe that," she said.

She could hear herself breathing, but not Vikous, and it startled her when he spoke. "Excuse me?" he said.

"The oath. Things don't have to bind you if you don't let them. Words are just"—she started to gesture the way Gerschon might have, but a flare of pain from her right side made her think better of it—"words."

Vikous did gesture, the motion of his arm short and sharp. "Those are the sort of rules your kind live by."

"My *kind*?" Calliope forced herself a few inches closer to sitting position, hissing through the pain. "I thought we were on the same side. I've got a kind now?"

"Humans," Vikous said, his voice grating and thin. "You walk in wherever you want, changing things to suit whatever it is that you think is true." His hand twitched. "You twist everything until it fits whatever flat little image you have in your head." He leaned in toward Calliope. "It's either arrogance or stupidity," he said in the silence of the room, just over the sound of her breathing, "and either way you manage to kill off everything that doesn't fit. Tear it out and throw it away, whether it mattered or not. *What did you do to me?*" Vikous's voice nearly choked off in his own throat and he leaned in close over the bed.

"I didn't *do* anything. I don't know *how* to do anything." The pain in Calliope's shoulder and side pushed up and out with each deep breath. Vikous's face was inches from hers; his breath, almost like lemons and probably the only part of him that never smelled bad, puffed in her face with each panting breath.

"You don't need to know how," he said in a whisper. "You never have; *none* of you ever have, but somehow something happened, and you were there, so tell me what you did."

"You *died*!" Calliope yelled, pressing upward as tears ran down her face against any will or desire of hers, brought on by the bright white pain that was reaching up from her shoulder and scrabbling at her mind. "You died, you fucking sociopath, and I made them bring you back and I wasn't supposed to tell you about it so I probably just blew one of the all-important rules that you nut-bags follow, and screwed everything up." Her face was bare centimeters from Vikous's; she could see herself reflected clearly in his flat black eyes, saw the bandages on her shoulder, saw the pain in her face, and the fear.

Vikous must have seen it as well. He blinked, pulling back a few inches, then reached out and lowered her down to the pillows.

It still hurt, hurt worse than anything she could think of that had ever happened to her, and she hated crying in front of anyone, especially—right at that moment—Vikous, but when she was finally lying back down, she couldn't help but smile in relief through the tears. He turned away.

"I shouldn't have gotten you worked up," he said, still facing the doorway.

"It's all right," she said.

Silence dropped down into the room, leaving only the echoes of the things she'd told him. Calliope didn't move until Vikous turned and sat down on the corner of the bed. He didn't look at her.

"What . . ." He cleared his throat. "Who did you . . . who was there?"

"Faegos," Calliope said, all reluctance gone out of her with her outburst. "Some taller guy who never spoke—"

"Kopro." Vikous inhaled through his nose and glanced up at the ceiling. "Actually, they're the same person, sort of. Shit-eater."

Calliope stared at him, surprised by the profanity. "Wow. You don't like him."

Vikous looked back at her. "No, that's . . . well, *no*, I don't, but that's not what I meant—that's what his name means, Koprophagos."

"Shit-eater? And the two of them are really one person?"

"Close enough." Vikous shook his head. "He's . . . very old. It's complicated." His eyes narrowed. "What did he want?"

Calliope carefully did not shrug. "He wanted me to promise him something I didn't have that he thought I might find later. He said he could bring Josh back to life in trade."

Vikous's eyes were steady on hers. "Did you say yes?"

Calliope looked away. "I told him it would be okay." Her eyes went back to Vikous. "I didn't know what he was talking about, and I still don't think I'll ever—"

"Did you," Vikous said, each word measured out. "Tell him. Yes?"

Calliope frowned. "Yes." Vikous sagged within his coat. She thought for a moment, then shook her head. "No. I don't— Maybe?" Vikous continued to watch her face, and Calliope shifted her weight. "It was days ago. I don't remember, but I don't—"

"It's—" Vikous cut off before the words could build to a shout. "It's sort of important."

Calliope glared. "I can't remember."

"Okay," he relented. "We'll burn that bridge when we come to it. What did—" He frowned. "How did you make him . . ." He gestured to himself.

"I made him prove he could do it," Calliope said.

Vikous stared at her, his too-wide mouth gaping just a bit. "I would have paid many jelly packets to have seen that," he finally said.

Calliope smiled, already beginning to tire. "So . . . that did it? Fixed your oath?"

Vikous's gaze seemed to turn inward, contemplating as he blew out a breath. "Well, yeah." He scratched at his green-spiked head with a gloved hand. "I suppose being dead pretty much voids the agreement. Never thought of trying that . . ." He made a face, annoyance mixed with amusement. "Of course, if

I'd done it on purpose, it would have broken the oath, which I couldn't do, so . . ."

Calliope quirked an eyebrow. "Your life is complicated." Vikous snorted, pushing himself back to a standing position. "Is it . . ." Calliope started. Stopped. Vikous looked down at her. "Are you all right with it?"

He thought for a moment and nodded. "Not exactly the way I would have wanted to go out, but yeah. It's weird, even for me, but it's all right." He shrugged. "Nothing I can do about it now, anyway."

Calliope watched his face. "You were very brave," she said, then looked away when his eyes met hers. "When it happened."

Vikous blinked. "Umm . . . thanks, I guess." A small smile. "Now I wish I could remember it."

"No," Calliope said. "You don't."

Vikous turned back to her, then nodded. "Heh. Fair enough." He glanced around the room. "Well, the goblins are out of the picture now; they already made a deal with Walker and even if they hadn't, we can't get back in there till a moon has gone by, so I figure you'll have to rest up and we'll do it the old-fash—"

"CALLIOPE JENKINS, THIS IS THE POLICE." The sound echoed through the room from the front parking lot of the motel. Vikous let out a growl that was the closest Calliope had ever heard him get to cursing and moved to peer through a break in the curtain. "WE HAVE THE BUILDING SUR-ROUNDED. YOU ARE TO DISARM AND EXIT THE BUILDING IMMEDIATELY, SURRENDERING TO THE CUSTODY OF FED-ERAL AGENTS ON-SITE."

"Federal—" Calliope began, then grimaced. "Cripes, didn't you kill that son of a bitch?"

"I didn't have time, you were bleeding all over the place," Vikous said. He turned back from the door and the covered window, assessing Calliope. "Can you stand up?"

"Can you get us out of here?"

"Maybe," Vikous answered. His eyes became distant for a moment and he smiled, though it wasn't pleasant. "Yeah, I can."

Calliope pushed at the covers with her left arm. "Then I can stand up."

It wasn't as easy, Calliope realized, as it sounded. She'd taken the bullet just about halfway between her breastbone and the point of her right shoulder. The exit wound was clean and nothing major had been destroyed, but it was still a bullet that she had taken at close range less than twenty-four hours ago; it would be months—if ever—before she completely recovered. Her right arm was immobilized and someone— Vikous, obviously—had pulled a T-shirt on over the whole mess—something she was profoundly glad she hadn't been awake for. She was wearing a pair of jeans, unfastened. When she checked the floor for socks and shoes, the room tilted and suddenly Vikous was standing next to her, looking tense.

Calliope managed to smile. "Need a little help, I think." Vikous nodded, had her sit down on the edge of the bed, and got to work. It took several minutes, during which Calliope had to tell the cops that they were coming out but had to get some clothes on first. It hurt to shout. Vikous arranged her leather coat around her as best as possible and stuffed a sweater down the front before zipping it up.

He looked around the room, nodded to himself, and extended his hand to Calliope, who took it and stood. The room tried to tip again, but she was prepared this time and got herself under control after a few seconds. She nodded and they moved for the door.

"When we get out there, raise your hand and don't say anything. Don't be threatening. I'll do what needs doing."

Calliope eyed him. "You're not going to try anything stupid, are you? I don't want to get shot again."

Vikous grinned in a thoroughly unsettling fashion. "We'll see." He pulled open the door, moved Calliope into the open, and turned to pull the door closed.

"PUT YOUR HANDS IN THE AIR!"

Calliope raised the arm she could and squinted into the afternoon sunlight. Unlike the movies, the police hadn't done anything stupid like parking their vehicles in a perfect half circle around the door. The closest uniform was down at the corner of the building. He had a rifle trained on her and was peering down the barrel from within a very solid-looking riot helmet. As far as she could see, no one else was within thirty yards. The other cops were using cover to their best advantage, blocking exits from the area but in no way putting themselves in danger. The guy calling out orders was all the way across the parking lot and hunkered down behind a vehicle. Calliope thought Detective Johnson would have been impressed with the setup.

Speaking of setup . . . Walker stood right next to the detective using the vehicle-mounted amplifier.

Behind Calliope, Vikous was doing something with the door.

"TURN AWAY FROM THE DOOR, DROP YOUR POSSESSIONS, AND PUT YOUR HANDS IN THE AIR."

"I think they're talking to you," Calliope muttered out of the side of her mouth. "Sorry, Officer," she called out, noting with something between amusement and scorn that several of the cops twitched at the sound of her voice. "Some jack-off shot me yesterday—I've only got the one arm to raise." She moved enough to make her empty right coat sleeve sway to illustrate, wincing as she did so.

"MOVE TO THE GROUND. OFFICERS ARE MOVING IN." There was a flurry of motion and raised voices behind the vehicle, barely audible from across the parking lot, then the bullhorn clicked again. "STEP AWAY FROM THE DOOR OR WE WILL FIRE." Calliope heard the jingle of a key behind her and Vikous gasping for breath.

"What are you *doing*?" She turned halfway around. "They're going to shoot us." She could hear boots scuffing on the pavement as pairs of police clad in full riot gear began to move in.

"I dunno," Vikous said, grinning at the door latch as he rotated the old motel key. Sweat poured down his face. "It's kinda liberating to know you've already died once."

Calliope tried to grin back. "That's great for you, but *I* haven't."

His black eyes, bright in the afternoon light, turned to Calliope and the grin stretched farther. "Hang on, I want to try something." He snaked an arm low around Calliope's waist and swung her into his arms like a parent with a sleepy child, then kicked open the motel door and stepped back into the room they had just left.

Calliope just had time to realize that there wasn't anything where the room should have been before Vikous stepped over the threshold. The sounds of shouting policemen—all sound, in fact—cut off as the door snicked shut behind them and vanished.

Vikous stood on nothing, cradling Calliope in his arms. His breath came in gasps and sweat poured down his face.

"What—" Calliope began.

"Sshhhhuddup." Vikous's jaw worked. "Causentray."

He was wiped out just opening *the motel door last time.* Calliope glanced around the smeared bruise color of the nothing that surrounded them. *How can he do this?* She tried very hard not to think of the obvious answer.

Vikous trembled, vibrating with the effort to do nothing but hold still. After a timeless moment, his right foot moved, dragging across the nonspace as though pulling a weight. Calliope's chest was burning before she realized she was holding her breath; her gasp was a ragged sound in the silence that matched Vikous's own. His eyes were lifeless, like a doll's, in a way she had never seen.

Planting his foot, he began to turn, his body still trembling.

"C'mon," Calliope whispered, clutching at the front of his coat with her left hand. Her one useful arm was trapped between her body and Vikous's heaving chest. "You can do it," she said, unsure what she was urging him toward.

Vikous halted. Again, there was a pause measured in years, and then he moved his foot.

Racing ahead of conscious thought, Calliope's urging melted into a wordless singsong; from there, the sounds slid into a simple tune, nursery rhyme words she had known since she was a child, nonsense that she didn't even hear—the point was the urging, the sound, the direction—Calliope sang her strength into Vikous, willing him forward.

Vikous continued moving. To Calliope, nonsense words still trailing off her lips like water, it seemed they had turned about halfway around when Vikous raised the hand under the crook of her knees, extending the key out and in front of them.

Calliope's eyes locked onto the key; her words, meaningless and tumbling, pushed at the hand and key until they seemed to meet Something within the Nothing. She blinked, and saw a door.

She turned to Vikous and saw a strange motel room over his shoulder.

"Go't," he said. For a moment, Calliope thought he would drop her out of exhaustion and tensed in anticipation but, still moving with a trembling, glacial strength, he sank to his knees and set her on the old, worn carpet in front of the door as she whisper-sang to him.

His eyes, glistening, met hers. He nodded and a small smile moved his lips as Calliope pushed herself into a sitting position.

Then he dropped backward like a dead thing, utterly still.

Son of a bitch. No no no not again. Calliope pushed herself onto her knees and shuffled over the carpet. "Don't you die on me, dammit." She lurched alongside him. "I'm not doing mouth to mouth and I don't know where your heart is or if you've got one or two or three or . . ." She held her hand over his open mouth, angry that she was trembling and unable to stop it. "C'mon now . . . I don't know where we are . . . I don't know where we're going . . . please don't die . . ." She rocked on her knees as she held her hand over him, tears shining on her face. "Please please please please please oh you son of a bitch please do something, please . . ."

His chest moved. Breath puffed, weak and warm, against her hand.

Air burst from Calliope in a sob that turned into a disbelieving, choked laugh.

Another breath. Another. Calliope held her hand in place.

"That's right," she whispered, "you . . . you just k-keep

doing that." She drew a shuddering breath, her lips trembling. "I'll wait."

In the darkness of an empty motel room, Calliope Jenkins
sat on her knees next to the clown-faced man lying on the
floor, singing lullabies she hadn't known she remembered,
holding her hand over his face to feel him breathe.

```
J B P D H I A D S O Q I N Y C Y L
H R C Y L D S E E M Y A Y R D S E
H Y M E S E G Z M C R G R S E M Y
F F D C M N I O C E U R E R A Y R
D E A X D O T F B T H A S E H Y M
T I O J M D I L N L H B I V E S E
I R S T Y N I P H R I I T O G Z M
L G C Z E A C E L M O N N L C R G
R J D X W B T U E V Y C S G R S F
Q Y R                       F D C
```

STAGE FOUR

```
S X T                       M N I
S D R                       O C E
O K M W S R M J M Y D E S J U R E
X E E T L Q E D F T E S T E R D E
R M A N H T P T M W F P G J A X F
C L O H R U G E O G P H E T O T F
E A C E L M O N N L R J D X B T H
W B T U E V Y C S G Q Y R E A S E
H A R L E Q U I N I S X T E T I O
G L O I F R I E N D S D R A J M D
G O N L O G U I D E O K M W I L N
S R M J M Y D E S J X E E T L H B
L Q E D F T E S T E R M A N I V I
H T P T M W F P G J C L O W R S T
N E G I O H D T U L O H F D Y N I
B O J N M V R W Z O Y W Q J P H R
W R H Y V S I L P J N F C W O K S
```

14

"Josh?"

"Yeah?"

"What're we gonna do?" The younger boy turns and looks up at the older boy sitting beside him on the fence.

Josh scowls. "I dunno."

"But—"

"I don't know, Mikey. Jeez!" Joshua boosts himself off the fence and turns to walk along it. The younger boy hurries to catch up.

"Are they gonna split us up?"

Joshua makes a face. "What? No." He tries putting a hand on the boy's shoulder, but he's awkward and unfamiliar with providing comfort, and turns the gesture into a shove instead. "They'll send us to live with Aunt Patricia or something. That's all."

Mikey scowls at the shove, but falls into step without retaliating. "She's old."

Joshua looks sideways at the younger boy. "We'll be okay."

"Sure."

"We will," Joshua repeats, trying to make it sound sure. "They

aren't going to split us up, okay? It'll be okay, and if it isn't, I'll
make it okay. I promise."

Mikey sighs. "Okay."

Josh looks at his little brother as they walk, then punches the boy
on the shoulder. "I promise."

"Ow!" Mikey glares up at Joshua. "Why'd you hit me for?"

The older boy grins. "So you'd remember." He raises his fist again.
"Don't!"

"You gonna remember?"

"Yes! Jeez!"

"Remember what?"

"You'll make it okay." The younger boy's voice is low. "You promise."

"I promise." Josh loops his arm around his brother's head,
giving him a quick noogie, but he leaves his arm around Mikey's
shoulders. His eyes shift, belying his words, but his voice is steady.
Reassuring. "I promise."

Vikous woke up on the floor seventeen hours later. Unable to
move at first—his arms and legs felt so *heavy*—he concentrated
on getting his surroundings to come into focus, blinking re-
peatedly.

"Hi." Calliope's voice came from somewhere toward his feet
and to the right.

He managed to lift his head for a moment, squinting. She
was all right. Good. He let his head fall back, not caring if it
hit the floor and surprised when it didn't. "Looks like I've got
a pillow," he commented.

Calliope pushed herself out of the chair near the curtained
window. "Least I could do, since there was no way I was getting
your ass onto the bed."

Vikous chuckled. "No doubt, but how did—" He frowned, then his face cleared. "Oh yeah."

"Oh yeah." Calliope moved to stand next to him and looked down. "That was really stupid, by the way."

Vikous grimaced, abashed. "Yeah. Kinda think it was." Calliope walked back to the chair. She sat down facing a small break in the curtains. "What's the good news?" He propped himself up on his elbows, trying to make it look like a less exhausting effort than it was.

Calliope kept her eyes on the break in the curtain. "We're in a motel and I've paid for the room."

Vikous's eyes narrowed at her expression, which was the kind of calm she tried to project when she was especially upset and didn't want anyone to know. "What's the bad news?" he said.

Calliope's eyes never strayed from the window. "I think I know where we are."

After a brief silence, Vikous said, "If you say 'somewhere back in California,' I swear I'm gonna start crying right here on the floor."

Calliope's smile was faint. "We're not back in California. Nothing that interesting." She turned away from the window. "It's Portsmouth."

Vikous's eyebrows furrowed in disbelief. "I don't think we're on the East Coast, either."

Calliope shook her head. "Portsmouth, Iowa, a few miles north of Persia and a few miles south of Panama." She tugged at the curtains, leaving them parted only an inch. "Lots of places with names from somewhere else, filled with lots of people who wish they were."

"Sounds like it's awfully familiar."

"I spent some time here on the way out to California the first time." Calliope's eyes wandered around the room. "This is where I decided to keep going, to really leave." She slouched, leaning back in her chair, looking at nothing with the tip of her pinky caught between her teeth.

Vikous took his time choosing his words, sensing the tension clinging to her. "Doesn't sound like that bad a place, then."

Calliope's jaw clenched. "I also decided that I'd never be caught dead sitting in a motel room like this one again, trying to figure out what was going on in my life." She shook her head. "And here I am. Ten years later and I'm right back where I started."

Vikous sat up, moving with a certain care. "It's not the same thing."

"It doesn't feel that different." Her face twisted. "Except for the teleporting across two states and sharing a room with a demon clown."

Vikous smirked. "So what's the same?"

"The feel." Calliope huddled closer into her coat. "The people I see outside."

Vikous frowned. "You recognized someone?"

"I recognized their expressions." Calliope looked over at Vikous, her eyes narrowing. She sat up in her chair and leaned forward toward him, her arms still tight around her. "You know how they say that owners start to look like their pets if they live around them long enough?"

"Sure."

Calliope's eyes locked on Vikous as though she were imparting a great secret. "These people raise cattle; they raise sheep. Those are their pets, and they have them for their whole lives."

She dropped backward into the chair, but her eyes stayed on Vikous. "Those are the faces I remember: cattle and sheep. I've been watching them walk up and down the street all day."

"There weren't any human sheep walking around on the streets where you've *been* living?"

Calliope scowled. Vikous didn't press the point. Reaching over to the foot of the bed, he turned sideways and pushed himself to his feet.

Calliope was standing over him. Rough, threadbare carpet pressed into his cheek where he lay on his side, staring at the floor under the bed. "What the hell just happened?" she said. Her voice was hard and held more than a hint of something he'd never heard from her before. Turning his face slightly, he could see that her own face was almost as white as his; she held her right arm close to her side, tense with pain.

"Ahhm," Vikous managed. His tongue felt thick in his mouth. "I'd say I blacked out a little bit. Still tired, I guess."

"Tired," Calliope replied. Her voice had lost its unidentified quality and exchanged it for something much more readily identifiable. "You nearly killed yourself with that trick yesterday. You stopped breathing when we got here."

Vikous lay there for a moment, letting the sound of her voice sink in. "Wouldn't be the first time, I guess."

Calliope's face grew taut. "I just got you brought back two"— she frowned, shook her head as though to clear it, wincing at the pain the movement obviously caused her—"four days ago . . . or something. You don't get to throw yourself away for the hell of it."

"Wasn't—" Vikous cut himself off, lowering his voice. He

had no desire to start a fight, and he suspected Calliope didn't either. "It wasn't a whim." He pushed himself off the carpet for a second try. "Needed doing."

"Whatever." She sounded tired, exhausted actually, her words almost slurring; it seemed unlikely she'd slept since they'd gotten here. "What was so damn . . . why was it so hard?" she said.

"It's not, usually." He pushed himself to his knees and lay his head against the foot of the bed for a moment. "If you just want to hop in the door and come out wherever, it's like going down a slide."

"And?"

Vikous pulled himself up to the edge of the bed and collapsed backward, taking long, hard breaths. "You . . . you remember when you would try to walk up the playground slides at recess instead of going down them?"

Calliope's eyes widened and she turned toward him. "How do you know I did that?"

Vikous frowned, lifting his head a bare inch to look at her. "I didn't. Didn't mean *you* specifically, just that some kids do that and it definitely *seems* like you." He looked up at her again, puzzled by her expression. "What?"

"Nothing." She turned away. "What about the slides?"

"Going down is easy." He tried to slow his breathing. "Going up them—or standing still in the middle of the slope—that's a lot harder than just riding them down. That's what I was trying to do, to get us somewhere close to where we were going." He closed his eyes and wiped at his face with a gloved hand. "Now imagine doing that and carrying someone."

Calliope's shoulders hunched unconsciously, making her wince. "You didn't have to carry me."

"I did if I wanted you to come out at the same place."

Calliope's eyes widened for a second. "Oh." Vikous said nothing. The effort to get most of his body onto the bed had left him shaking and sweating. Calliope looked down at him, made an amused sound in her throat, and sat down beside him without bouncing the bed. "We're a pretty sorry pair right now."

"And no car," he murmured, an arm across his closed eyes.

"And no car, yes, thank you." She stared at the blank screen of the television standing on the bureau across from the bed. "Any ideas what we're going to do?"

"Order pizza," Vikous replied, his words distorted by a yawn. "Sleep. Then I've got a plan."

"A plan."

Vikous didn't look up, but he could imagine her expression. "You gotta remember to—"

"Trust the guide, yeah." She shifted on the edge of the bed. "I've heard that before, but I'd like to know what's going on for once."

Vikous waved his hand through the air above him, turning his head just enough to see her. "We're in the Hidden Lands. Close to them, anyway. Anything's possible."

At his words, Calliope forced herself to turn despite the pain in her shoulder. Her eyes were flat and hard as she looked back and down at Vikous. "I used to live in these so-called magical lands and, in case you're wondering, this is my skeptical face."

"Duly noted. Who's ordering the pizza?" Vikous studied Calliope's unresponsive features. "Hello?"

"I'll get it." She turned and pushed off the bed with a hiss of annoyance and pain. "Watching you move right now is pathetic."

"You have a lovely bedside manner. It's a real gift; you should know that."

She paused next to the side of the bed nearest the nightstand that held the phone. "I'm just going to remind you, just once, that I was shot. Yesterday. Next time I'm going to use my one good arm to drop a fucking lamp on your head."

"Fair enough." Vikous rolled himself laboriously onto his back. Silence filled up the room, broken only by the faint sounds of intermittent traffic outside. He licked his dry lips. "Are you going to—"

"Don't." Calliope picked up the phone with her left hand and tucked it against the crook of her neck as well as she could. "Don't say it." She wasn't looking at him, but Vikous nodded anyway.

They were already asleep when the pizza delivery driver knocked. Calliope paid with cash. They ate, and were both asleep again twenty minutes later.

Interlude

"Baby?"

"Calli? Honey?"
    "Mmm . . ."
    "You sleepin'?"
    "Mmmmm . . ."
    "'Kay, I'll leave you alone."

"Heeeeey . . . aahh. Wh-what're you doin'?"
    "Nothin'."
    "Tha— mmm . . . that doesn't feel like nothing."
    "Glad to hear it."
    "I . . . I was sleepinngg."
    "Couldn't be."
    "I was."
    "I'm a perfect gentleman, I would never disturb you when
you're sleeping."
    "Hmm . . ."
    "Am I disturbing you?"
    "Just . . ."

"Hmm?"

"Just shut up and keep doing that."

"This?"

"No."

"Oh. Okay. This?"

"You're smiling."

"You can't possibly know that. The lights are off."

"I can hear it when you're smiling. I always can."

"Huh. Neat trick. This?"

"Calli?"

"Y-yeah . . . yeah, do that."

"You sure?"

"Bastard."

"Now you're smiling. And what a mouth on you."

"I learned it all from y— tha-that's new."

"I've been reading in my spare time."

"It's . . . 's a good book. C'mere."

"Calli?"

"Mmm . . . yeah."

"We need to get going."

"Calli?"

"Yeah. I know. I'd just rather stay here."

"It'll be good to see everyone. I'm looking forward to meeting your folks."

"I'm not."

"You don't want me to meet them?"

"No, you go and meet them. I'll just stay here."

"Heh. Funny girl. We really should get going though. We're gonna be late."

"Mmm. I'm tired. Someone woke me in the middle of the night."

"Hotel pixies. Deadly little guys."

"Mmm . . . c'mere."

"Sure, what's up?"

"I think the pixies are back."

"Hey now, we need to—"

"You said something?"

"Didn't say a thing."

"That's what I thought. You like the pixies?"

"They . . . must have been reading that book of mine."

"I don't need a damn book."

15

WHEN CALLIOPE WOKE up, the hotel room looked wrong. Shabby. Smelled wrong. Also, her shoulder ached and she couldn't remember when—

"You talk in your sleep."

Memory came rushing back. "Hmm."

Vikous sat in the chair Calliope had sat in the day before, his ludicrous feet up in another chair, legs crossed at the ankles. "Yeah, something about 'plowing the graveyard would make for good corn.'" He glanced down at the motel key he was toying with. "Some other stuff."

Calliope could feel heat creep into her face. She rolled onto her left shoulder, which faced her away from Vikous and was marginally less uncomfortable. "How . . . how long have you been up?"

"A few hours. You hog the bed, too."

"Sorry."

"It's all right. I wasn't sleeping that well, either." She heard him shift in the chair, set his feet on the carpet. "You think you're up to a little hike?" He waited. "Calli?"

"I was thinking," Calliope said, but didn't continue, suddenly nervous.

Again, Vikous waited before speaking. "Yeah?"

"Nothing."

"Doesn't sound like nothing."

She closed her eyes as if bracing for impact. "Maybe we should just forget about it."

Vikous didn't say anything immediately, but Calliope was certain it wasn't because he was waiting on her. "Forget about it." His voice was flat.

"Not *forget* forget, but I don't know if we should . . ." She rolled to her back and slowly sat up, swinging her legs to the floor. "I mean, what are we going to find? Are we going to find the guy that killed Josh? 'Cause right now we aren't exactly going to beat a confession out of him."

Vikous watched her, his expression as blank as the white, red, and greens of his face could be. "You're scared about what's coming."

Calliope shook her head. "Not scared, I'm just . . ." She paused. "Well, yeah, actually I am scared about it. We've been dealing with Faegos, Walker—they don't even have anything to do with this and we're getting our asses handed to us—what's the big bad going to be?"

Vikous gestured with a gloved hand. "This isn't a video game, Calli. The big boss with a thousand hit points doesn't have to be the one waiting for you at the end. Who says the *end* is even at the end? Life keeps going."

"Maybe."

"Sure. Maybe. We could die. We could save the world. Lots could happen."

"We could turn around and go home."

Vikous hesitated. "Yeah. Doesn't sound much like you, but yeah, we could do that."

Calliope glanced up at Vikous, caught his expression, and looked away. "It's just . . . Josh is already gone. I don't want to find out what else I can lose. I'm tired of losing."

Vikous's eyes never moved. "You said you made a deal that could bring him back."

Calliope met his gaze. "And you made it sound like a bad deal."

"It's your deal to make." He shifted in the chair, his shoulders moving in the slightly wrong way they had. "I'm not going to tell you how this has to go. I'm the guide, and that's my job—I show you the way, and you make your own choices. You don't *have* a job, you have a *life*; if you want to make a deal, you can; if you want to turn around, you can." He leaned forward, resting his elbows on the knees of his worn and stained pants. "I'm ready to go on. You tell me if you are."

Calliope didn't immediately react. Her eyes were wide and unfocused as she stared without blinking at the old and faded carpet. "You're wrong, you know."

"Mmm." Vikous grunted. "About what?"

"Turning around and going home," she said. Her voice was distant and flat, the emotion sapped out of it by exhaustion. "It sounds ex*act*ly like me." She thought of the argument they'd had as they'd left Los Angeles. "But you know that."

"I know some history, Calli," Vikous replied. His voice was low and had lost some of its perpetual rough edge. "And I know you, today. They aren't always the same thing." He blew air through his teeth. "But all *that* means is you're stuck deciding yes or no."

Calliope nodded, still facing the opposite side of the room, her thoughts—perhaps inevitably—on another trip.

You don't want me to meet your folks?

"Let's keep going."

Vikous looked up. "Yeah?"

Calliope still didn't look up. "Yeah. Give me a few minutes, but yeah."

"All right." She heard the now familiar rustle that signaled the donning of his concealing hood. "I'll wait outside. Scream in agony if you need help with the shoulder. You'll want the sweater." He stood.

"Sure. Hey, can you do me a favor?"

Vikous didn't reply, merely waited.

"Could you—" Calliope pulled at the edge of the unused bed cover. "It's not personal, but could you not call me Calli?" She looked up at Vikous, then down. "It was sort of Josh's thing."

"Sure," Vikous said. "Sure. Consider it done." The motel door opened. Closed.

Calliope was alone.

"Josh?" Mikey sits on the floor, shoving matchbox cars around the carpet.

Josh sighs. "Yeah?" He doesn't like being interrupted when he's reading, and his brother does it all the time.

"Do dragons really have beaks, like it says in the Pooh story?"

Josh shrugs. "Just some of 'em."

"Yeah?"

"Yeah." Josh leans back and looks at the ceiling. "But the ones around here have lots of teeth instead."

"Cool."

"And scales."

"Coool . . ." Mikey picks up a car and swooshes it through the air like a plane. "I want to meet a dragon."

"It'd eat you."

"Would not."

"It'd eat the whole house, then the town."

"I'd make it like me, then we'd do stuff together." Mikey lowers his arm to the floor. He is staring out the window. "We'd have adventures all the time, like forever."

Josh snorts. "There's no such thing as forever, doofus."

"There is too!"

Josh rolls his eyes at his younger brother's back. "Whatever. Anyway, you'd grow up and have to do grown-up stuff."

Mikey shakes his head. "We're not going to."

Josh makes a face, scratching under the edge of the cast on his right arm. "You're a dork; of course we are."

"NO we're NOT!" Mikey jumps up, face red, hands knotted in fists at his side. His whole body is shaking.

Josh looks away from Mikey, back to his book. "Cool your jets, little man." The words are out before he even knows they're coming.

Words their dad used to say.

Tears are running down Mikey's face. Josh raises a hand toward his brother—the one not in the cast—but the boy whirls and runs from the room, yelling. At Josh, at the world, at nothing; repeating his denial over and over until the words lose their meaning; empty echoes in the empty house, holding nothing but the anger.

⁓

"This would be a lot easier," Vikous remarked, "if we were along an interstate." They were walking on the shoulder of

Highway 19; had been doing so, without any real explanation from Vikous, for the last hour. Calliope had stopped at one point, refusing to freeze to death before Vikous revealed what they were doing, but he had pulled a pressed flower out of one of his pockets and done something with it that had made the midwestern November cold die away all around them.

Out of gratitude, she had let her questions go even when he stopped to pick up and sniff cast-off tire treads that lay along the side of the road, but this comment was too much for her to take quietly. "It would be a lot easier," she replied, "if I knew what the hell we were doing."

"Hunting dragons." Vikous scanned the highway and shoulder ahead of them in the waning afternoon light.

Calliope didn't reply for the space of twenty more yards. Finally she said, "First of all, you told me that all the dragons were dead; second of all, I know I've been gone awhile, but if there were dragons in Iowa, I think I would have—"

"I never said they were dead," Vikous said. "I said you didn't see them destroying towns anymore. Doesn't mean they're dead."

"You remember my skeptical face?"

Vikous sighed. "Just—"

"Trust the guide. Yeah, I'm trying." Calliope continued on in silence, glancing at a mile marker. "What is it you're supposed to *do*, exactly?"

Vikous scanned the road and shoulder as they walked, paying only cursory attention to the question. "Do for what?"

"As a guide. What do you—what are you supposed to do?"

Vikous glanced at Calliope, his eyes narrowed and careful, then turned back to the ground before them. "I thought the message Gluen gave you explained that."

Calliope shook her head. "Just told me to go with you."

Vikous nodded, blowing out a puff of steamy air and glancing at her sidelong. "There's people like you that get . . . involved in things. To keep everything from coming apart at the seams, we . . . there's someone to guide them and try to—"

"Keep them from wrecking everything?" Calliope's tone was sour.

Vikous tilted his head and made a face that said she'd almost got it, but not quite. "Some think that. I'd say help them figure out enough that they understand what they're doing."

Calliope raised an eyebrow and glanced at her shoulder, her mouth quirking upward at the corners. Vikous scowled. "Also, there're people who try to keep anyone from messing with anything at all. Like Walker." Calliope could hear the emotion Vikous had penned up inside that name.

"Whom you already know," she said.

"We've been on opposite sides before."

"Before," she said. Vikous nodded.

She hesitated. "How did you end up swearing an oath to him?"

Vikous continued walking for some time as the waning sun left orange and purple streaks across the sky. Just when Calliope thought that the topic had been closed and was starting to form an apology, he spoke. "I was with this . . . someone I figured would really do all right. It looked like it was going to be a big deal." He shifted within his coat. "We got turned around and ended up in the Badlands, which I don't recommend as a vacation spot if you're in the Hidden Lands. Walker rigged it; got us stranded."

Calliope waited, walking alongside him through the cold November afternoon that she couldn't feel.

"I cut a deal," Vikous said, his voice barely audible above the gravel scuff of their feet. He glanced at Calliope. "Not for me."

"For her."

"Him, actually. A kid about twelve . . . thirteen years old."
Vikous hunched his shoulders in the coat. "I thought . . . I
made a deal with Walker that I'd stand down the next time we
butted heads, if he'd let the kid make it through. I thought I
could stay clear of him if I had to."

"Walker came through on your deal?" Calliope asked.

Vikous snorted. "Yeah. You'd have thought he knew—" He
shook his head. "I was wrong about the kid. Didn't end well.
For anybody."

Calliope's voice was quiet. "I'm sorry."

Vikous said nothing. The expression on his face looked as
though he'd bitten down on something rotten. Looking up, he
squinted into the middle distance. "That looks good."

Calliope followed the direction of his gaze. In the middle of
the right-hand lane, a solid black line about ten inches wide
and forty feet long stretched down the pavement. "That's a tire
streak. We've passed fifty of those already."

"Wait," Vikous said.

They walked up to the end of the streak and Vikous nodded.
"Good. Real good." He glanced at Calliope, who was alternating
bemused looks between him and the mark on the road. "Look
at the mark. Do you see any treads?"

Calliope frowned and looked back at the streak. Still frowning, she walked along the shoulder to the other end. Her frown
deepened. "That's weird." She pointed at the end of the mark.
"If this were a guy peeling his tires drag race style, there'd be
tread marks visible on this end where the tire finally started to
grip." She turned and walked back down to Vikous. "If it were
someone hitting the brakes, there's be tread marks down here,
before the wheel locked."

Vikous raised an eyebrow. "You know a lot about tire marks."

"When you grow up in rural America, you learn way too much about the very few things you can do for fun."

Vikous nodded and motioned at the streak. "So?"

Calliope stared at the scored pavement. "That's not a normal skid mark."

"No." Vikous turned and peered at the shoulder of the highway. "Now, if we're real lucky—"

"You're hilarious."

He ignored Calliope's interjection. "We might find . . . *oh yeah.*" He walked down the shoulder past the end of the streak, reached down, and picked up a dark object. Calliope trailed along after, in no hurry once she saw Vikous was simply sniffing another piece of tire tread. His lips stretched back in what passed for a smile. "Oh yeah. Real good." He held it out toward Calliope's face.

She recoiled just enough to keep her face clear. "Yeah. Thanks. Maybe I can lick a used ashtray instead."

Vikous frowned, looking annoyed. "Just, for the love of . . ." He gestured with the hand-sized chunk.

Calliope scowled at him, leaned forward, and sniffed. *Summer. No, spring. Late spring, when the rainstorms have stopped and the clouds are high and white, and the end of school's just a few weeks away.* Confusion flashed across her face and she took another sniff. "It's . . ." She looked up at Vikous. "Lilacs?"

"I would have said violets, but around here you're probably right." He waggled the thing that looked exactly like a chunk of burnt, black tire tread in the air between them and dropped it into Calliope's left hand. It was so light she almost dropped it, overcompensating. "Congratulations," he said. "You've found your first dragon scale."

Calliope looked at the thing in her hand and back to Vikous. "And we do what with this?"

Vikous's smile broadened, looking even less reassuring. "We summon a dragon." He looked up at the fading colors of dusk. "Let's walk; the last sign said there was a rest area about a mile up and we need to get there before it gets late."

Carrying the alleged scale in her pocket, Calliope started after Vikous, walking in silence for a quarter of a mile before speaking.

"So . . . dragons."

"Dragons." Vikous kept his eyes on the shoulder ahead. Cars passed them in both directions at a regular rate, but none slowed or stopped.

"You said . . ." Calliope frowned, trying to remember. "You said that the things out here were good at hiding." Vikous nodded. "But there's . . . dragons buzzing the highways?"

"You'd be surprised what tricks your eyes can play on you at night," Vikous said. "Besides, they're only out there when they're hungry."

Calliope raised an eyebrow. "Hungry? Something that big lives on roadkill?"

Vikous snorted. "Just because they don't attack towns any-more doesn't mean they don't need a lot of food." He waved a hand up and down the highway. "They can usually get by on wild animals, but with this food supply right here and all their—"

"Food?"

Vikous gave her a look. "Do you have any idea how many hitchhikers go missing in a year?" He shook his head. "Don't assume it's all abductions and kidnapping. Sometimes they just take a whole car."

They walked in silence for a time. "You know the weirdest thing about this whole trip?" Calliope asked.

"I've got no idea."

"You just told me that the highway disappearances I read about aren't always criminals and abductions—that some-times it's dragons hunting for food—and that actually cheers me up." Calliope was still smiling to herself when they came to the rest area. Snow was starting to fall.

16

VIKOUS BEGAN PREPARATIONS while Calliope explored the rest area. The vending machines were all empty or marked "Out of Order" on sheets of paper that had been taped over the coin and bill slots. The restroom stalls had seen more than the usual share of graffiti.

In the antechamber of the unheated building, several maps were mounted on the wall behind Plexiglas. Calliope traced her finger along highways and secondary roads to an area in the northeastern section of the state that she had once called home. Like a great deal of the map of Iowa and the highway map of the continent mounted on the wall to the left, the Plexiglas was heavily obscured by more graffiti done with permanent markers in various colors. Names of several towns had been entirely blacked out or renamed (Grinnell became Grinner; Storm Lake has been left untouched, but was circled three times in different colors). Other nonexistent places (Wrathburn, Needlehole, Western Marches) had been added. It wasn't until Calliope noticed the words *Goblyn Kinge* scrawled over what should have been Castle Rock on the larger map that she realized there was a pattern to the haphazard cartography. She was looking at a map of the Hidden Lands.

Vikous called to her while she was still searching through the additions made to the area of the state with which she was most familiar. He had started a fire in one of the painted fifty-gallon oil drums that served the area as a garbage receptacle, but she was looking over the parking lot. "This place is a little off."

Vikous did not look up from his preparations. "How so? Can you hand me the dragon scale?"

Calliope gestured to the parking lot with the scale as she took it out of her pocket, then handed it to Vikous. "There's no cars out here."

Vikous smiled, his lips pressed together. "And?"

"There weren't any when we got here, and that was ten minutes ago. Even on a secondary highway at a shady-looking rest stop—which this one definitely is—with all the traffic we saw on the road, someone should have stopped here by now." She watched Vikous for a reaction. Receiving none, she said, "And someone's drawn in a map of the Hidden Lands over top of the normal maps in the main building."

"Really?" Vikous glanced back at the building. "Maybe I should take a look at that when I get a chance."

Calliope's frown deepened. "We're in the Hidden Lands already, aren't we?" She glanced around them in the dim lighting that the stop provided. "You should have told me."

Vikous straightened and shook his head, still smiling. "We're at a rest stop," he said, as though he had explained everything with five words. Calliope looked at him and did not return the smile. Vikous folded his arms across his chest, eliciting the same unnatural motion beneath his coat as always. "I told you before that borders are important."

Calliope nodded but said nothing, blinking random snowflakes from her eyelashes.

Vikous rolled his eyes. "Borders are just things in between other things. This"—he gestured at the rest area—"is a place that lies in between."

"It's a border?"

"A natural border," Vikous said. "I don't even have to do anything to it. Someone already hid it—probably after it was closed down for some other reason—and now we're ready for the next thing."

"Which is what?"

Vikous's smile widened to uncomfortable dimensions. He held up the dragon scale and threw it into the fire.

The smell of lilacs filled the air.

Minutes passed. Calliope shivered. "Cold again."

Vikous nodded, scanning the skies. "Couldn't keep everything going at the same time. Trust me, you'll be plenty warm in a few minutes." He frowned, turning slowly as he watched the clouds. "Assuming this works."

Calliope watched the highway beyond the parking lot. "This place is hidden from normal people, right?"

Vikous nodded but didn't turn. "That's the way it works. Otherwise people would wander in, take a weird turn on the way out, and find themselves out of gas in a very bad place—it's generally best to avoid that."

Calliope nodded, only half listening. "Then why is a semi pulling in?"

Vikous whirled, the frown on his face melting into something Calliope could only call wonder. "Oh, jackpot," he said
as the truck's headlights, coming right toward them, flashed
over his face.

Calliope squinted into the light, shielding her eyes. "What's
the big deal? It's just a—" She lost track of the next thing she'd
meant to say as the truck turned

wheeled, actually, like a bird

and came to a stop perpendicular to them. With the light
out of her eyes, Calliope could see that whatever it was, it was
definitely not a truck. Black, lit only by sparks of light here
and there along its body, it could be mistaken for any number
of things, at least at night, but when the shining claws settled
to the ground—when great, midnight wings like a bomber
plane's furled in from where they had stretched out and away
from the body a hundred yards in either direction—when the
heat from the thing washed over her and what she had first
thought were headlights turned, and dimmed, and blinked—
Calliope knew what she was really looking at.

"WE HAVE COME TO YOUR SUMMONING, HARLEQUIN,"
thrummed a voice that seemed to vibrate out of the ground
and straight into Calliope's body. *"SUCH IS THE AGREEMENT,
TIME OUT OF MIND."* The great thing shifted. Even now, in the
flickering illumination afforded by the lights of the parking
lot, Calliope could only guess at its exact size and shape. *"BUT
YOU HAVE INTERRUPTED OUR HUNT, AND WE WILL HAVE A
PLEASING EXCUSE FOR THAT OR KILL YOU FOR AMUSEMENT'S
SAKE AND CONSUME THE HUMAN GIRL."*

"I think you might have forgotten to mention a couple of
details," Calliope murmured to Vikous, who ignored her and
stepped forward.

"Ancient Majesty," he said, "I am guide and escort to this woman." He paused. "We must reach the effigy."

"WE FAIL TO HEAR ANYTHING IN YOUR WORDS, HARLEQUIN, THAT COULD POSSIBLY INVOLVE OR ENTERTAIN US." The low thrum of its annoyance in the vibration of the thing's voice made Calliope's jaw ache. She saw Vikous swallow and straighten his posture imperceptibly, and she couldn't help but think that her companion might have overestimated his abilities.

"We would ask the boon of transport, Majesty."

The low ache that had accompanied the creature's annoyance was less than nothing compared to the pain that burst behind Calliope's eyes when the growl–explosion erupted out of the air around her. She tried to track what was being said, but the white agony in her skull pushed everything else away. After several moments, the surge of pain faded to the point where she could understand the words she was hearing.

*" . . . IS NOT ENOUGH THAT YOU SHOULD PRESUME TO PARLEY, PRESUME TO COMPEL, BUT THAT YOU SO MUCH AS MENTION THAT MOST UNWORTHY OF TASKS IS GROUNDS ENOUGH FOR YOUR UTTER DESTRUCTION. ARE WE **BEASTS**? WORSE, ARE WE A MINDLESS, IMPROBABLE, AND IGNOBLE MACHINE, SINCE BEASTS THEMSELVES ARE NOW TOO LOWLY A CONVEYANCE FOR HUMANS? **WE THINK NOT.**"*

The last words redoubled the previous agony and drove Calliope to her knees, sobbing. When she could see again, after a fashion, she realized that Vikous was kneeling next to her. In his case, however, it seemed as though he had assumed the position willingly; though he looked down and away from the dragon, there was no pain on his face.

Eventually, as the discomfort faded and the susurrus of dry winter grass replaced the ringing in Calliope's ears, Vikous stood. "Your pardon, Majesty, but I believe there is a misunderstanding."

*"YOU INTIMATE THAT THERE IS A THING—**ANY** THING—WE FAIL TO UNDERSTAND?"* The ache-drone of the thing's disdain was almost a relief.

Vikous dipped his head. "I have spoken unclearly and without proper distinction. The fault in understanding lies in my own poorly chosen words; we would only ask the favor of your company on our journey. In return we offer what small entertainments we have."

*"YOUR MEANING IS CLEAR TO US, HARLEQUIN. BUT DO NOT THINK THAT YOUR PALTRY TALENTS MAY BUY THE PRICE OF OUR COMPANIONSHIP. WE ROAMED FREE WHILE YOU AND YOURS HAD YET TO **DISCOVER** YOUR CRAFT."* The sound of a massive body shifting filled the air in a way utterly unlike the voice. *"WE CARE NOT FOR YOUR BANAL TRICKS AND FOOLISHNESS."*

"I . . ." Vikous's face became slack, unprepared for this latest pronouncement. Calliope saw desperation in his eyes; an aborted glance in her direction. "I meant to—"

"He meant"—Calliope forced herself to her feet against the constriction of her bound right arm—"he meant me, Highness."

Majesty, Vikous mouthed.

"Majesty," Calliope amended. "I'm the . . . I sing."

"DO YOU THEN SING MORE DEFTLY THAN YOU SPEAK, HUMAN GIRL?"

Damn, I hope so, Calliope thought.

"You're going to have to cut me loose," Calliope said under her breath. Vikous stared at her, uncomprehending. Calliope motioned toward her shoulder. "Help me get the coat off and cut the bandages holding my arm down."

Vikous frowned. "What? What for?"

Calliope was already pushing out of her coat. "This thing's a straitjacket. I can't sing if I can't breathe."

"It's not going to do your shoulder any good."

"I'm pretty sure having a dragon chew on it isn't going to do much for the healing process either, so let's cut the goddamn bandages."

Vikous nodded and helped Calliope lift the sweater over her head. Beneath, she wore the very tired-looking white T-shirt that Vikous had gotten her right arm into two days ago and which she hadn't had the guts to remove since. Her arm was held tight to her side with bandages that Vikous had wrapped entirely around her midsection.

"*YOU ARE INJURED, HUMAN GIRL.*" The thing's voice sounded vaguely intrigued.

Calliope managed a deferential nod while Vikous worked at the impossible task of pulling tape off her arm without moving her shoulder. Ten minutes ago, the movement might have caused her to cry out, but compared to the dragon's recent anger, the sharp, sullen ache in her shoulder was more than bearable. "Yes, Majesty. I was shot."

"*BY WHOM?*"

"By the goad, Majesty," Vikous answered.

"*WE ASKED THE GIRL.*"

Calliope blinked. "Walker. My"—she glanced at Vikous—"my goad. The one who's trying to stop me, I guess."

"*THAT IS NOT THE GOAD'S TASK.*"

Calliope looked a question at Vikous, who continued working on the bandages as though he wasn't listening. "I'm sure you're right, Majesty, but he did shoot me."

"*WHERE WAS YOUR QUEST-GUIDE?*"

Calliope frowned. "He was with me."

Motion whispered in the night air as the great, flowing shadow of the dragon shifted in the darkness. It was the sound waves made on a shoreline. Or wind in a cornfield *"WE BEGIN TO UN-DERSTAND THE GREATER STORY. YOUR GUIDE IS INCOMPETENT."*

"Hey—" Calliope began, but cut herself off when she felt Vikous's hand on her good shoulder.

"YOU HAVE SOMETHING TO ADD, HUMAN GIRL?"

"Just . . ." Calliope frowned, looking up, doing her best to meet the gaze of a creature she couldn't really see. "I have no cause to complain about my guide, Majesty."

"INCONGRUOUS."

"Maybe," Calliope began to shrug, thought better of it. "It's the truth."

The sparks of light along the dragon's body shifted a few inches, the movement oddly contemplative. *"THERE IS A STORY HERE,"* said the dragon. *"PERHAPS WE WILL HAVE IT FROM YOU, IF YOU LIVE."*

Calliope bowed her head. "I would be honored, Majesty," she hesitated, "by both events."

"AS YOU SAY," said the dragon, but Calliope thought she caught the barest hint of amusement. *"NOW. YOU ARE READY. SING."*

Calliope glanced down, realizing that the dragon was correct. Vikous had removed the bandages as she spoke. She stood, wearing only a pair of worn jeans and a wrinkled and stained T-shirt outside a midwestern rest stop in the middle of November, but she felt perfectly comfortable, blasted by the heat of the dragon's existence. Above her, snow fell, but not a flake reached the pavement as anything more than a mist. Watching the droplets condense on her crumpled coat as it lay at her feet, Calliope began to sing.

It filled her up with a kind of sad warmth, like sitting safe but alone by a roaring fireplace. Her voice lifted up through the snowy darkness and into the empty border-world around her, and the words, which she sometimes couldn't even remember afterward, clung to her and swirled along the ground like half-seen images. The song was one she had known for years and sung for many different reasons, but in this place, at this time, it was about what she had done, where she had come from, where she still had to go—the alien world in which she suddenly found herself.

It was about Joshua.

It was about everything.

By the end, it was angry—still filled with loss, but colored with uncomprehending confusion and rage—the song sung eternally by those who had lost what they loved and didn't understand *why*. She sang-screamed at the sky above her, letting the lyrics ask that simplest of questions and, when she was done—when the song had gone out of her like a withdrawn candle—she slumped, hanging her head and letting the damp strands of her hair hide her face. She hadn't felt her shoulder while she sang, but now the ache glowed like a banked fire that was starting to flare up. Her clothing clung to her in the mist, cool and clammy.

Vikous cleared his throat. It was only then that Calliope realized that the song was probably not what anyone could consider decent payment. She looked up at the light and black where the dragon loomed. "I'm . . . that was . . . I can sing something else for you if—"

"*WHAT IS YOUR NAME, CHILD?*"

Calliope blinked and, after a nudge from Vikous, gave her name. Silence answered her, then: "CALLIOPE," the voice thrummed through the pavement. *"MUSE, MOTHER OF OR-PHEUS, ASTEROID, MUSICAL INSTRUMENT."*

Calliope cleared her throat. "It's also a kind of hummingbird."

The lamplike eyes turned toward her, brightening for a moment. Calliope squinted but did not turn away. *"IT IS AN UN-COMMONLY COMPLEX NAME,"* the dragon said, *"FOR A HUMAN."*

Calliope couldn't think of a reply, so she nodded.

A vast undulation shifted the glints of light along the dragon's body as it moved toward her, sinuous and cumbersome at once. *"WHERE WOULD YOU TRAVEL, CALLIOPE?"*

"My . . ." Calliope glanced at Vikous, who had been uncharac-teristically silent throughout the exchange. She didn't recognize the expression on his face and, frowning, turned back to the dragon. "My guide tells me we have to go to the effigy." Vikous nodded, but stopped in midmotion when Calliope continued. "But before that, I need to stop somewhere else."

The dragon's bright eyes stared down at her, unblinking. After several seconds, they moved slightly. *"AS YOU SAY, CAL-LIOPE."* The massive body shifted. *"WE WILL TRAVEL WITH YOU FOR A TIME AND, AS YOU ARE SORRY, EARTHBOUND CREA-TURES, WE WILL SHOW OUR BENEVOLENCE BY CONVEYING YOU IN A MANNER BEFITTING OUR NATURE."* It paused, then turned to Vikous. *"WE PERCEIVE THAT YOU ARE DECEPTIVELY COMPE-TENT, HARLEQUIN, WHICH SHOULD NOT SURPRISE US, GIVEN YOUR NATURE, YET STILL DOES SO. IN ALL THOSE THINGS, YOU ARE A TRIBUTE TO YOUR KIND."* Vikous bowed his head as the creature drew back to look at both of them. *"WE WERE CALLED MAHKAH IN THE TONGUE OF A PEOPLE WHO ONCE DWELT IN THESE LANDS. USE THIS NAME AS WE TRAVEL."*

Vikous froze for a second, then bowed very, very low. Calliope did her very best to do likewise.

"COME," Mahkah said. *"WE WILL SHOW YOU HOW DRAGONS MOVE OVER THIS WORLD, AND YOU WILL TELL US YOUR STORY."*

Vikous helped Calliope pull her sweater and coat back on, though they hardly seemed necessary, this close to the dragon.

"A thousand–jelly–packets performance," he barely whispered in her ear as he worked the right sleeve over her arm. "There," he said in a normal voice as he stepped back. Calliope could only smile and give his arm a squeeze. He winked. "Where are we going?" he asked, but Calliope thought he already knew.

17

CALLIOPE WATCHED THE sere grass of the highway's ditch blur by as she sat perched on the neck of a dragon. It didn't seem normal, not by any stretch of the imagination, but it wasn't impossible. Not anymore. The most telling thing was that, despite herself, she was starting to get drowsy.

They had been flying—gliding, almost—for several hours, jarred only occasionally when Mahkah reached down to the road with one trailing claw to adjust the path of their flight, laying another mark along the pavement. Calliope and Vikous had recounted their story to Mahkah as they traveled, watching oncoming cars sweep by without so much as a second glance from the drivers or passengers.

"It's partly magic," Vikous had explained after the fifth or sixth pickup truck had gone by. "Enhancing shadows, implying a little more to the shape than what's actually there, obscuring the wing shadow as cloud cover or an overpass." He gestured at the highway. "Most of it's just that people see what they want to see." His hand swept back over his shoulder, indicating the massive bulk of the dragon. "And some of it's the natural coloration and the sparks of light. Luminescence, whatever."

Calliope nodded, but didn't bother to look the way he'd gestured. She'd found that even now, sitting atop the creature, she still couldn't really *see* it; her eyes slid away, or her mind wandered the way it did on long drives. "That's natural? They've always looked like that?"

Vikous shook his head, but it was Mahkah who answered. *"ALL BEINGS ADAPT TO SUIT THEIR ENVIRONMENT. WHAT WONDER THAT THE GREATEST AMONG THEM DO LIKEWISE?"*

To this observation, Vikous added nothing. Calliope decided to follow suit, and let her eyes slowly close.

"You don't want me to meet your folks?"

Calliope sighs, eyes closed. She pushes her fingers halfway through her hair, then grips it tight, focusing on the pain. "No; I don't want to meet my folks."

Josh blows air through his teeth. "You know, it's funny to joke, but this is a little more serious than just not calling them on the weekends."

"I know it's serious." She glares at him. "I don't think you get how much." Again, she tugs on her hair, turning to stare at the ground. "I don't—"

"We drove," he interrupts, "for two solid days. We are"—he turns, pointing down the road that runs past them and their parked car—"ten minutes from your house."

"My parents' house."

"What d—"

"It's not my house," Calliope continues, raising her voice to shut down his protest. "That was made very clear when I left."

Josh drops his chin down to his chest the way he always does when he's swallowing words he doesn't want to say. "Fine. Okay. Your parents' house. But it's still your family. They're not going to leave you standing on the front step."

Calliope's eyes go wide, her expression incredulous. "Ha!" She tips her face up to shout the sharp, barking laugh at the sky. "You . . . that . . ." She gives Josh a look of pure, astonished disbelief.

He turns away from Calliope, pacing between her and the car, hands on his hips, looking at the sky. When he gets back to where she's standing, arms wrapped around her midsection, he tries again. "Why?"

She shrugs. "They wanted me gone."

"That was seven years ago," he says, his voice quiet and intense. "We walk up and knock on the door—"

"They never forget," she manages, barely above a whisper. "They'll ruin everything." She winces at Josh's explosive exhalation. "Please—"

"You've got a family." His bites off each word. "I don't think you'll ever understand how much that's worth."

"I understand them." Calliope turns away. "Honestly? You're the lucky one."

As soon as the she says the words, she knows she's gone too far.

She is right. The next sound from Josh is the driver's-side door of the car opening and closing.

Calliope turns. Josh sits behind the wheel, eyes forward, not looking at her or anything else. Through the glass of the side window he looks pale and bloodless, like a ghost.

She walks to the car, gravel crunching under her shoes, and stands next to the door. She doesn't say anything; knows that

anything she could say now won't matter. Eventually, he rolls the
window down, but doesn't turn to look at her.

"Baby," she begins.

"Let's go home." She can barely hear him.

She starts to protest; stops. Shakes her head. Tries again and fails.

He rolls up the window and, with nothing to say, Calli can only walk
around and get in. Tears stand in her eyes, and she doesn't know why.

There are too many reasons.

It was nearing dawn when Mahkah's voice thrummed Calliope awake. *"WE HAVE ARRIVED AT YOUR FIRST DESTINATION,*
CALLIOPE."

Calliope blinked her eyes into focus, staring at the half-
harvested cornfield they sat in. With help from Vikous and
some assistance from Mahkah, she slid to the ground without
too much pain and looked around. There were buildings in
the distance that were familiar, if not comforting.

"This will take me most of the day, Mahkah." She turned
back to the dragon. "I hope you—" She stopped, staring at an
empty field.

"HAVE NO WORRIES ON OUR BEHALF." The voice shook out of
the earth, everywhere and nowhere. Behind Calliope, dried
cornstalks rustled in what might have been the wind. *"WE*
WILL FIND YOU HERE AT DUSK."

"Look out for the hidden things," she murmured to herself
and turned to Vikous, who stood with his hands in his pockets,
poking one great oversized shoe at a severed stalk of corn. "I
think it might be—"

"—better if you do this alone, yeah." Vikous smirked. "Sounds
good. I'll wait out here."

"You sure you won't be cold?" Calliope asked, but Vikous's smirk only broadened.

"Don't worry about me; this last bit's been like a vacation." He looked up from the dirt. "It's your journey; I'm just the guide. If you know where you're going, then I can pretty well take it easy." His eyes flicked to the buildings in the distance.

Calliope said nothing and Vikous nodded. "Get walking. We'll be here."

Calliope turned down the long driveway that led to the cluster of buildings she'd seen from a distance. Surrounded on three sides by thick ranks of trees planted back in the late '30s, the farm was clearly visible only after she walked into the yard.

Nothing had changed. She didn't recognize the car in front of the garage, and the barn and machine shed both needed paint, but that was it. Calliope had walked down the drive a thousand times—more—dropped off by the school bus in the late afternoon. It had always looked the same.

No one noticed her approach. No one came out to meet her. That was pretty much the same as well.

She almost turned around at the mailbox by the road, again by the driveway gate no one ever shut, again when she walked into the main yard, and finally when she got to the base of the steps.

"They're not going to leave you standing on the front step."

"Oh, but they might," Calliope murmured, her breath swirling around her in pale wisps. "They might."

She stood at the steps for a long time, then climbed them and lifted her left hand toward the door. It shook visibly.

"We walk up and knock on the door . . ."

Calliope let out a short, nervous laugh. "God, I wish you were here."

She knocked and jammed her hand back in her pocket.

A few seconds later—the time it takes to wipe off your hands and walk from the kitchen—the main door opened. Calliope watched the face of the woman on the other side of the screen change from polite curiosity to confusion to worry and finally, as expected, drop back into its familiar stoicism.

"This is a surprise," the woman said.

"Hi," Calliope said, hoping the wind muffled the shake in her voice. "Mind if I come in?"

It was probably only a second before her mother answered, but it seemed to Calliope that the question hung in the air between them for hours; dangerous, giving off a kind of poisonous heat.

"Good grief, like you need to ask." Phyllis Jenkins pushed open the screen door, still holding the rag she'd been using to wipe off her hands. Calliope stepped past her into the house— their unfamiliar proximity awkward for only a second—and Phyllis glanced at the snow-packed drive. "How'd you get here?"

Calliope turned, unzipping her coat halfway as her eyes scanned the pictures on the walls. "I had a friend drop me off. They'll be back this afternoon, if that's all right." She motioned to the walls, where each portrait had been updated over the years, except for Calliope's sophomore head shot. "Everyone's aged except for me, I guess."

Her mother glanced up at the walls. "Sort of Dorian Gray in reverse."

"God, do I look that bad?" Calliope forced a smile.

Her mother made a dismissive grimace. "Oh, I didn't mean it like that."

Calliope chose not to reply and nodded toward one picture. "Dad's lost some weight."

"That's because of the cancer, actually," said a voice from the archway leading into the hall beyond. "Hello, Cal."

Calliope turned, startled, to the speaker. Her sister, wearing a faded apron that Calliope recognized, leaned against the door frame, unsmiling. "Cancer?" She shook her head. "Sorry. Hello." She turned back to her mother. "Cancer?"

Phyllis shook her head. "Just some melanoma—your dad never covered himself up on the tractor like he should have." She motioned toward the kitchen. "Let's go sit down."

Calliope glanced at the couch and several armchairs in the room they were already standing in, but said nothing and followed her sister out of the room.

—⁓—

"Your hair looks like you've been standing in front of a leaf blower." Her mother set a cup of tea in front of Calliope at the kitchen table.

"The . . ." Calliope took a drink, not using her right arm, but trying not to favor it. "The ride I got was windy."

Phyllis raised her eyebrows. "In this weather? Didn't you freeze to death?"

Calliope tipped her head. "I guess not, Mom, since I'm sitting here."

"Probably a motorcycle, that sounds crazy enough," said her sister, sitting across from Calliope and looking at her over her own cup. There was no playfulness in her expression.

Calliope matched the look. "Sure, Sandy, it was a motorcycle."

She tilted her head. "Aren't you working anymore? I thought you'd be in town in the middle of the day."

"It's Saturday, Cal. Did you lose track of time?" Sandy's jaw was tight.

"A motorcycle." Her mother's expression was a mix of disbelief and embarrassment.

"It had a heater, Mom. It was fine."

Her mother frowned. "One of those big . . . what do they say . . . Goldwings?"

Wings like a bomber, Calliope thought, *furling in toward its body.*

"Yeah." She hid a small smile behind her cup. "Something like that."

Sandy set her cup down. "Did you steal it?"

Calliope stared at her sister, her lips parted in astonishment. "Excuse me?"

"Sandy . . ." Their mother shook her head, her lips pressed together.

"Oh, *please*, Mom; you were thinking the same thing." Sandy made a sharp gesture toward Calliope. "She shows up looking like she's been living in a ditch, smells like roadkill, and you said the sheriff was through here two days ago asking about her."

"I wa—the sheriff?" Calliope's pulse rose as her stomach dropped.

Sandy turned back to Calliope. "That's pretty good. You almost sounded surprised."

"I *am*—" Calliope shook her head. "What's going on?"

Sandy's eyes narrowed. "That's what I'd like to—"

"You've been on the warpath with me since I *got* here. I haven't done anything—"

"You've got that right." Sandy glared at her sister.

Calliope sat back in her chair, her expression slack. Her older sister had seemed her first and best friend all through her childhood, but the woman sitting across the table from her was, in light of those memories, worse than a stranger. "You don't . . ." She shook her head. "You don't even know me. You'd rather listen to some ignorant hick cop than—"

"Jim Fletcher isn't some—"

"—even hear anything that I'm trying to—"

"Stop, stop, stop, *stop!*" Phyllis smacked the table with one hand, and both younger women subsided, each glaring at the other. Their mother reached out and put a hand over one of Sandy's. "Sandra, we don't know anything that's going on, and this is your sister." She reached out her other hand. "Calliope—"

Calliope, blood still pounding in her ears, jerked her hand free and instantly regretted it, not least because of the look of superiority in her sister's eyes when she did.

Steel—the sort of strength that saw a person through year after year of living on the edge of profit—slid into Phyllis Jenkins's eyes. "You will be *civil* in my house, young lady." Her hand snaked out and gripped Calliope by the shoulder.

The pain pinned Calliope to her seat. The wound in her shoulder seemed to stretch, like strips of Velcro being pulled apart, and her muscles locked in shock. To her credit, Calliope didn't scream or cry out, and at first her mother didn't realize why there were tears in her daughter's eyes, only that she had gone rigid beneath her hand. When a bloody flower began to stain the shoulder of Calliope's sweater, she let go with a gasp, staring first at the widening blotch, then at her own stained thumb. "What? . . ." she said in a whisper.

"Just a bullet hole, Mom," Calliope said through clenched teeth. "It's nothing; ask Sandy."

"Perfect." Sandy stood up and yanked her coat from a hook by the back door. "*You*, you just stay away from me."

For the third time in fifteen minutes, Calliope was left slack jawed in the face of her sibling's rejection. "Because . . . getting shot is *my* fault."

Sandy dropped both of her hands to the table and leaned over it. "I have *kids*, little sister," she said, her own eyes bright with unshed tears. "Until people stop shooting at you, stay away from them. *And* me." She pushed away from the table and turned. "Bye, Mom. I'm—I'll call you." The two women exchanged a look and Sandy left, closing the outside door behind her as she went. A few moments later, Calliope heard the car out front start up and pull out. After that, the kitchen was silent. Calliope sat, mute and still, left hand gripping her right biceps as if she could cut off the flow of pain to the rest of her body.

Finally, her mother said, "Are you running from the poli—"

"No," Calliope said. Her mother didn't respond. "I've got a phone number of a detective in the city. You can call him and ask."

Her mother shook her head, still not looking at her. "How did you get hurt?"

Calliope simplified things as much as possible. "A bad guy shot me."

"On purpose."

"Bad guys do that." Calliope snapped, goaded by the pain in her shoulder and the shock of her sister's words. She glanced at her mother, then away, uncomfortably guilty at her own reaction. "Some people don't like me much, Mom," she continued, her tone subdued. "It's a mystery."

A faint, sad smile ghosted across her mother's face. "Why are you here?" She caught the look on Calliope's face and shook her head, closing her eyes as though to retract her words. "I mean . . ." She looked at Calliope, then got up and moved to a cupboard drawer. "It's been a long time. And an awfully long drive for some coffee."

"I'm working," Calliope said, "kind of." She sighed, trying to figure out where to begin. "I started this job a while back."

"Two years from September."

Calliope blinked. "Good memory." She frowned. "Wait, how do you *know* that?"

"Your sister read us the last letter you sent her."

"My last—" Calliope's brow furrowed as she pieced things together. "That letter came back Return to Sender. The last *two* did, actually."

"Well, she read it to me," her mother replied. She pulled a bundle from a drawer and walked to the sink, wetting down a fresh dishtowel. "I don't know how you'd get them back if she opened them."

Oh, I do. Sandy had been a secret ally after Calliope had first left, always staying in touch and keeping her up to date (mostly), but a few years ago something had changed, for reasons Calliope had never been able to figure out. Resealing a letter and sending it back apparently unread no longer seemed out of character for her older sister. "Anyway, my partner's"— she hesitated, remembering that the deal with Faegos might still hold—"missing. The police and the feds got hold of me last week and told me about it. It happened out here—"

"Here?" Phyllis returned to the table. "Let's pull that sweater off and see how bad I got you."

Calliope sat forward and started to pull her left arm in through its sleeve. "Not here exactly; Iowa in general. I thought

I might be able to help figure out where he was." She pulled the sweater over her head with her left arm and, with her mother's assistance, moved it off her right arm and shoulder. The T-shirt underneath was soaked in a circle the width of an outstretched hand.

Phyllis blew out a long breath. "I hit the bull's-eye, looks like."

"It's all right," Calliope said. She opened her mouth to say something, but stopped, heat rushing to her face.

Her mother caught the hesitation and the hot flush on her cheeks. "What?"

Calliope gave her head a short shake. "I think you owed me one anyway," she murmured, her eyes averted.

Silence was Phyllis's only reply. She turned her attention back to Calliope's shoulder and clicked her tongue. "It sounded like that job might be dangerous; I guess it is." Her nose wrinkled. "And your sister wasn't wrong about your clothes. Get that stuff off and I'll get 'em in some water after we look at you."

Calliope started to comply, but paused—somehow reluctant to give her mother some kind of advantage. "I don't want to be a hassle."

"I just shoved my thumb into a bullet hole in my daughter's shoulder," Phyllis replied. "I think you can impose a little."

The blood looked worse than it was. Whoever had stitched up Calliope's shoulder (Vikous, spooky clown of many talents, most likely) had done a good job; two or three stitches had been pulled hard but none had torn loose. Calliope took a long, much-needed shower, and her mother found her something to wear while her clothes washed. An hour later, Calliope was back in the kitchen in a pair of sweatpants and a flannel shirt, eating her first real meal in two days.

"Where's Dad?"

"In town, working on tax stuff. He'll be home late." Her mother folded clothes as they talked. Early afternoon light shone through the west-facing windows.

Calliope frowned. "It's not even January."

"This is still from last year." She paused. "Or the year before last, maybe."

Calliope made a face. "I don't know how you do it . . . this."

"Oh, neither do I, most of the time." Her mother's voice was light, but Calliope could hear the strain. "We'll have to retire when we're fifty-five so we have time to get jobs that pay."

Phyllis glanced at Calliope and pulled another article of clothing out of the basket. "The sheriff said that a federal agent was asking if you'd been in the area. He wasn't sure if the police were hunting for you or just trying to get in touch."

"The police are not hunting me, Mom." Calliope hoped she was at least telling the literal truth.

"But they don't know where you are."

"No."

"They don't know you're doing this."

"Officially?" Calliope took another spoonful of thick soup. "No, but they didn't say not to." Her mother sighed. Calliope glanced at her sidelong. "What did you tell the sheriff?"

"I told him the truth." She turned to Calliope. "I told him I didn't know where you were, what you were up to, who you were with, or how to get hold of you. Which he already knew and has known for years."

Calliope searched her mother's face. "I'm sorry."

"Please don't apologize. I'm the one who got you in the shoulder."

"No," Calliope said, reaching out to lay her hand on her

mother's arm, making her stop folding clothes for a second. "I'm sorry. About everything." The apology hung in the air between the two women. Phyllis's face fell into an expression Calliope couldn't read. After a few seconds, she shook herself like someone casting off a daydream and moved aside the folded laundry.

"So," she said. "You came looking for your boy."

"My partner."

"Your partner." Phyllis rotated her coffee cup on the table in a way that reminded Calliope of Vikous. "Someone you know well enough to drive across the country for."

"Yeah," Calliope cut in, "it's complicated, Mom. We've known each other a long time. He dropped out of the band we were in and decided to do something with his degree. I wanted to—" She shook her head. "He offered me a job, and I decided to get into the new business with him." She sat back in the chair, rubbing at her hairline. "It's complicated."

"You were in a band?" Phyllis said.

Calliope winced, internally. "We could never get a record deal," she explained, unasked. "I sang, and it was really good in the clubs—when we were live—but our demo tapes could never—"

You were never happy with them, came Joshua's voice; from a dream, or her own memory, or both. *You got nervous whenever things looked like they were becoming real—just like with us.*

She grimaced. "They never came out right."

Her mother set her cup down on the table. "That sounds like it would have been good for you," she said. "Better than playing detective, certainly."

Calliope blinked. "What?"

Phyllis looked at her, her eyes showing some surprise. "Well, you always loved singing, and you were so good."

"You . . ." *told me it was a pointless waste of time* " . . . never told me that," she finished, looking away. "You made music sound like a . . . very bad idea."

"I never said any such thing." Her mother looked affronted.

Calliope leaned forward, as though to make sure the words made it clearly across the table. "I was fifteen. It was June. It was a Saturday. I told you I wanted to sing. I told you I wanted to be a star."

Her mother frowned. "Honey, I don't remember you saying that."

"I—"

"Not specifically," she continued. "I remember the sentiment well enough. And that summer. Do *you* remember that summer?"

Calliope nodded. "It was hot."

Phyllis stared at her. "It was hot, yes." She took a drink of her coffee. "It was the worst drought in twenty years. Nothing was growing. Your father didn't know how we were going to make our loan payments. Your grandfather had died three months before. I think . . ." She looked into the middle distance. "I imagine I was worried you might end up in some crazy situation with no stability, like what we were going through. If I said something that bad, well, I'm sorry. I am. I don't see why you'd never tell us about—" She shook her head. "You've always been so secretive."

Calliope opened her mouth to speak twice before she could get the words to come. "*I'm* sorry, but I seem to remember something about Dad having *cancer.*"

"Oh." Her mother waved her hand as though to sweep the words away. "That was just your sister blowing things out of proportion. It was a couple of lumps on the back of his neck;

they cut 'em right out. We would have called you if it had been important. He wears sunscreen now, and . . ." She trailed off, watching Calliope's expression. "I suppose I shouldn't be calling the kettle black."

Calliope shook her head, the corners of her mouth twitching.

Phyllis returned her wry smile. "Maybe we could catch each other up."

━━

"I'm sorry," Calliope said. "I really wanted to see Dad." Afternoon light slanted through the windows, and Calliope's throat had the pleasant ache that came from a lot of talking, but she'd turned the conversation away from uncomfortable topics or stepped around the land mines of old arguments more than a few times, and it was wearing her down. Also, she was becoming increasingly conscious of the time.

"Oh please." Her mother smiled without showing teeth—it looked more like a pained grimace. "*I* ought to be the one apologizing." Her expression took on that same distant, daydreaming look she'd had earlier in the day. "When you—" There was a knock on the front door. Her mother's eyes snapped back to the present. She looked at Calliope, the corners of her eyes tense.

Calliope's brow creased, and a surreal sense of danger sparked in her chest. "Mom?"

Phyllis shook her head and stood up. "Better get that."

Calliope sat alone at the table for a few moments, bemused, then pushed herself out of her chair with her good arm and moved after the older woman. "I'd be happy to just stay and wait for him to get home," she said, her voice raised just enough to carry, "but I should get going."

"Maybe you could hold off on that," replied a man's voice.

Phyllis stood next to the open door, her arms crossed. She had stepped back and to the side to reveal her visitor, but Calliope had already caught sight of the broad, flat-brimmed hat over her mother's head.

The man in the doorway rested his hands on his hips, making it look as though he was simply stretching after sitting in a car for too long, not imposing his size on the two women or putting his hand closer to the firearm hanging from his belt. "Hello, Calli. Haven't seen you in a coon's age."

"Hello, Jim." Calliope tilted her head, letting a hint of sarcasm creep into her voice to mask her nervous concern. "Or is it 'Hello, Sheriff' today?"

"Oh . . ." Jim Fletcher shifted and looked away from both women and out over the dry and rustling cornfields surrounding the farmstead. His breath puffed in the cold air. "I suppose sheriff is the right idea, at least for a little while."

"Mmm." Calliope folded her arms, unconsciously mimicking her mother's stance. "You want to come in, or should I get my coat?"

"Oh," her mother admonished her. "Calli, you don't have to be—"

"How about we go for a drive," Fletcher interrupted, with an apologetic nod to Phyllis. "No reason for me to track mud into your mom's house."

"Jim . . ." Phyllis breathed.

"Right." Calliope hadn't moved, and her face was impassive, but the adrenaline wash at the local lawman's words made her breathing short and tight and left her hands tingling. "Am I under arrest, Sheriff?"

"Ahh . . ." The older man spoke the word as though it hurt. His face sagged. "Do you think you need to be?"

Calliope pursed her lips and tried to remember that the sheriff was a friend of her family's—someone who'd let her off the hook on two tickets when she'd just been learning to drive, and fined her three other times when she had no good excuse and should have known better. "I really don't," she said, turning toward the kitchen, "but I'll go for a drive if you like."

He nodded after her. "That sounds about right. I just want to get things straightened out," he added, to Phyllis.

"She hasn't—"

"It's fine, Mom." Calliope pulled her coat off the back of the kitchen chair and returned to the room with it hanging over her bad arm—which conveniently gave her an excuse not to use it. She walked over to the door. "I'm assuming your car's warm enough I don't need to put this on."

"Sure, sure . . ." The older man made room for Calliope to pass, holding the door as he did.

"Jim—"

"It's fine, Mom," Calliope repeated. She stepped through the door and started down the steps, her eyes taking in the open yard and the tracks of the car her sister had left in. She stopped, remembering the look Sandy and her mother had exchanged just before the younger woman had left. "You should probably call Sandy and tell her you stalled me long enough."

Her mother said nothing at all as Calliope walked the rest of the way to the sheriff's vehicle.

As the sheriff's SUV pulled out of the driveway and headed down the gravel road that led to the highway back into town, Calliope watched the cornfield on Jim Fletcher's side of the vehicle.

Don't come after me, she thought. *Just . . . let me work this out before you show up and eat the local police department.* She didn't expect that anyone out in that field might have heard her, but that wasn't the point—her thoughts were more a prayer than a message.

"Something on your mind, Calli?" The sheriff had his eyes on the road, but he could obviously see the direction of her gaze out of the corner of his eye and thought she was looking at him.

"Not much," Calliope said, sitting back and turning her attention forward. "I think we probably could have straightened things out back at the house, but it means a couple calls back to L.A., and I'd rather the long-distance fees got charged to you."

Fletcher chuckled. "Well, thank you for not sugarcoating it for me."

"I do what I can." Calliope allowed herself a small smirk. Although he was taking her in to his office, the sheriff hadn't put her in the backseat cage. In fact, he'd opened the front passenger door for her even though she'd stood next to the rear door. From where she sat, she could reach him, his gun, a vertical rack-mounted shotgun, and the steering wheel. Either he didn't think that Calliope was really any kind of danger, or he was pulling off the mother of all con jobs to get her guard down as far as possible.

That last was a sobering thought; the only reason the sheriff would have to play that sort of game would be if he were bringing her to Walker, and the supposed special agent had shown up unexpectedly so many times that Calliope couldn't bring herself to rule out the possibility.

She glanced at Jim Fletcher, and her misgivings faded. The older man had stoic and unreadable down to some kind of martial art—she imagined he was a terrifying poker player—

but she didn't think he was a very good liar. It was a subtle distinction, but one that mattered a lot to her, and it didn't feel wrong.

"Think your mom's going to beat us into town, at this rate," Fletcher said, interrupting her thoughts. Calliope looked in the rearview mirror on her side of the vehicle and saw her parents' pickup closing the gap behind them. "Guess she thinks I'm not going to give you a ride home afterward."

"Are you?" Calliope turned to look at the sheriff. "'Cause if you already know you're going to, I'm not sure why we're driving into town."

"Oh . . ." That familiar, pained expression crossed the older man's face again. "I guess I don't know. It's a little complicated."

"Sounds like you've got a lot of badges being shoved in your face." She tried to keep her voice neutral. "That's usually what complicates things for me."

"Just the one," the sheriff replied, his voice tinged with just a hint of disapproval. Calliope filed that away for later. "One's enough, sometimes."

"Sure." Calliope said, pronouncing it *shoore*. She could hear the verbal tics and phrases of her youth creep back into her voice with almost every sentence she spoke, as though her mouth was dropping into old habits with some kind of relief. "We'll get 'er all fixed up in town."

"Mmm." Fletcher's eyes went to his own rearview, and Calliope caught the faintest of twitches at the corner of his mouth and eye. "Think your mom'd be too happy if I pulled her over for speeding?"

Calliope raised her eyebrows. "You're the one with the gun, Jim"—she blew air between her teeth—"but I'm not sure that'd be such a hot idea."

"You're pr'y right," he said, holding his poker face. "Don't need that kind of trouble today."

"Good," Calliope replied. She let a few more miles scroll by in silence, then: "That badge flasher you mentioned . . ."

Fletcher didn't obviously react, but the air around him seemed to go still. "Yeah?"

"Is he still around?"

Sheriff Fletcher motioned Calliope into a seat in his office. "We'd better make this first part quick." He lowered himself into his chair. "I have a sneaking suspicion that I'm not going to get a Christmas card if I don't let your mother in here pretty soon." He raised his eyebrows and opened both his hands, palms up, in Calliope's direction. "Unless you don't want her in here while we talk. It's not like I need to have your guardian present."

"Let her sit out there all day if you want," Calliope replied. Her voice was even, but the last few silent minutes of the ride into town had given her time to review the way her mother had played her, and cast a gray pallor over what had seemed an impossibly good reunion.

The sheriff's eyes flickered at her tone, taking in the high spots of color that shone on her cheeks. He rested his arms on his desktop blotter. "Calli, look at me." His tone was private and familiar—so far from his "sheriff" voice it surprised her into meeting his gaze. "When your mother came to the door," he said, "her eyes were wet. Now"—he raised a hand to forestall Calliope's angry reply—"maybe you've got good reason to be upset with her, but you need to know that if she could have wished me off her front step right then, she would have."

Calliope opened her mouth, closed it, and turned away from the sheriff's look. Jim Fletcher had always been hard to fool but, worse, he'd been a hard man to make trouble around—a talk with the sheriff back in high school had left Calliope feeling like she needed to apologize to everyone for being a bother.

Fletcher nodded as though she'd given him some kind of agreement and leaned back in his chair. "So . . . a couple questions before we bring everyone in?"

Calliope glanced back through the office window. Her mother stood near the dispatch desk, her arms crossed tightly over her midsection, talking with her father, who stood with his back to them.

He's thin, Calliope thought. *Thinner than the pictures.*

"Sure." She turned back to the sheriff. "Just a couple; I'd like to see my dad."

Fletcher nodded, his lips pressed together. "Fair enough. Back at your folks' house, you said you could straighten this out with a long-distance call. Can I have that number?"

Calliope pulled out her cell phone, scrolled to Darryl Johnson's name, and handed it to the sheriff. "That's the detective who was investigating my partner's disappearance back in the city."

Fletcher squinted and copied the number onto his blotter. "And . . . he'll be expecting a call?" He handed the phone back to Calliope.

She shook her head, dropping the phone back into her left pocket. "Expecting it? Not really."

The sheriff made an attempt to look confused; as a result, he looked like a police officer who was pretending to look confused. "Then how do you know he's going to vouch for you?"

Calliope shrugged. "Don't you know people who'd vouch for you even if you didn't warn them ahead of time?"

The older man dipped his chin. "Sure . . ." he said, pronouncing it the same way Calliope had on their drive to town.

"So do I," Calliope said. A small, less confident voice in the back of her head hoped she was right. She ignored it.

Fletcher gave a short chuckle that someone might have mistaken for a throat clearing. "Fair enough."

Calliope kept her eyes on him. "He worked with Special Agent Walker for a couple of days too."

The sheriff's face gave nothing away, but Calliope did notice his hands pause for the barest second as he moved a paper on his desk. "That's interesting, that you bring that name up."

"Not that interesting." Calliope settled into the chair, working hard not to favor her shoulder. "He's the kind of guy who likes to push badges into people's faces. Not very likable."

Jim Fletcher met her eyes. "You're not wrong about that, but that doesn't mean he's not someone a county sheriff has to at least listen to." Before Calliope could answer, he picked up the handset of his phone. "I'm going to call your detective friend and run the county phone bill up a bit," he murmured, his eyes on the number scrawled on the blotter. "Go give your dad a hug and tell Dwight we all want some coffee."

Calliope considered any number of things she wanted to ask the sheriff about what Walker had said to him; while she didn't think he would ask her anything she couldn't—one way or the other—answer, in front of her parents, there were a number of things she wanted to ask *him* while they had some privacy. But it looked like her chance was already gone. She stood up and let herself out of the office.

Behind her, the sheriff watched her leave, his eyes sharp.

Calliope walked through the sheriff's department, feeling that familiar frisson that always filled the air when strangers were around law officers in their private space. It didn't matter if the visitors were victims or criminals—alleged or convicted; Calliope thought the simple fact was that there were strangers in perhaps the one place that an officer could feel legitimately safe, and it put them on edge. Since starting work with Josh she'd experienced—and caused—that discomfort many times. She located the deputy that Jim Fletcher had pointed out (the youngest in the room) and repeated his message, then continued toward her parents.

Her father still hadn't turned around when she'd reached them. He was speaking to her mother in the low, steady murmur of half-spoken words and inflection that functions as a kind of impenetrable code between longtime couples. Something inherently stubborn in Calliope's makeup kept her from walking up next to the pair; she stopped, her hands in her pockets, and waited for him to turn around. Her eyes scanned the back of his neck, looking for the scars from the cancer surgery her mother had mentioned, but the collar of his coat was pulled high and tight against his hairline.

Her position meant that she was easily visible to her mother, who had watched first Calliope, then her husband as her daughter had crossed the room. Now, her eyes—troubled in a way that Calliope found perversely comforting—found Calliope's for a moment. She nodded in a particular way and took a half step back from the closed huddle.

Her father turned. Calliope's first instinct—brutally suppressed—was to turn away or close her eyes. From her chair in Jim Fletcher's office, he had looked thin, but she realized now that the jacket had given her a false impression of his remaining bulk. He was rail–thin, gangly, in the way that teenage boys were, with joints that seemed too big for their limbs. His cheekbones and jawline were far more pronounced than she remembered—even the ridge along his temples seemed to press at his skin—and his fair hair had washed out to gray.

"Your mom says you two had a good talk." He reached his arms toward her, an invitation more than embrace.

"Yeah." Calliope stepped into his arms and squeezed almost as tightly as she could with one arm, then squeezed once more, harder. "Where's the rest of you?" she exclaimed. Her voice was muffled by his coat, but he chuckled and stepped back. "Oh, you know; the treatments are a pretty good diet program." He patted his stomach with one long–fingered hand. "I'm putting it back on, though. Twenty—"

"Treatments?" Calliope shot a look at her mother. "What kind of treatments?"

He frowned in turn. "Doesn't matter. They didn't take long, and I'm fine."

"You—"

"Hey," he interrupted. His eyes met hers and matched the stone in his voice. "We're not doing this here. It's not why we're standing in the sheriff's office—we're going to talk about *that*."

Calliope glared at him, feeling a familiar obstinacy seep into her in reaction to his tone. "How about I say *I'm* fine and not to worry about it and not tell *you* anything about what's going on? How's that sound?"

"You two stop." Her mother stepped forward, next to her husband, and gave the sleeve of his coat a soft slap. "No one's been explaining anything to anyone for a long time, and it's mostly my fault, I'm sure, so can we please just . . . stop?" She shared a quick, surprisingly pleading look with Calliope.

Calliope hesitated, her instinctively combative habits wrestling with a real, if newfound, desire to make peace. Finally, she motioned over her shoulder with her head. "Jim's calling someone I know back in the city who can probably straighten everything out."

"The police detective?" Phyllis asked. At her husband's look, she explained. "She's been working with the police on the disappearance of her friend. Partner." She looked back at Calliope. "She works with the police a lot, as part of their business."

That last wasn't anything Calliope had told her, or even implied, but it wasn't really wrong, and it felt good—if more than a little weird—to hear her mother embellishing her accomplishments on the retelling.

"And gets shot," her father said, though low enough that Calliope didn't think anyone else had heard.

"That"—she stepped in closer to him—"that isn't going to help me get out of here faster."

"If—"

"I told Mom; it isn't anything I could get in trouble for," Calliope interrupted. She winced inwardly, not at the falsehood, but at how easy it had become to lie to her family. "But gu— things like *that* automatically mean that reports need to be filed." She indicated the rest of the officers with her hand. "At best, I'd be here filling out paperwork for most of a day. At worst, Jim would make me go back to where it happened and fill out the paperwork *there*." She looked up into her father's eyes. "I don't have that kind of time. Not right now." The real reason she didn't want the gunshot wound mentioned—that the sheriff would ask who had shot her or, worse, might have a good guess—would have bad enough consequences that Calliope tried not to think about it.

"Suppose that's true." The muscles in her father's jaw—far too easy to make out under his taut skin—worked. "Mostly because people getting shot are what police are supposed to take care of."

"Dad, please." Calliope touched her father's sleeve.

The door to the sheriff's office opened, and Calliope turned. The youngest deputy—Dwight—pushed himself out of his chair and headed for the break room's coffee machine. The sheriff watched him go, shook his head a single time, then turned back to Calliope and her parents. "Whyn't you folks come on in?"

"So as I understand it," Fletcher began, once Calliope and her parents were seated, "your partner's dead."

"He's missing." Calliope felt her mother's eyes on her, but her father's gaze stayed on his friend on the other side of the desk.

"Detective Johnson said he was reported dead." The sheriff leaned forward on his blotter. "I'm no expert on it, but that *is* usually how a murder investigation gets started."

"Did he mention the answering machine message?" Calliope said. Her voice sounded high and uneven in her own ears, but no one else in the room seemed to notice.

The sheriff looked at her, his face tired. "He did." His eyes slid to her mother, and he seemed to remember that they weren't alone. He sat up. "It seems that Calliope's partner, who was reported dead, also left a message on their office's answering machine several hours after his alleged remains were found."

"So he's not dead?" her mother asked.

The sheriff blew air through his teeth, his eyebrows raised. "If he isn't, he's been missing more'n a week. Let's say it raises doubt." His eyes flickered back to Calliope. "His wife is flying out to identify the body for sure."

"He's *married*?" This last was to Calliope.

Calliope raised her eyebrows. "We just work together, Mom; we're not—we're friends." She crossed her arms. "I'm just trying to see if I can find him."

"See . . ." Sheriff Fletcher interjected. "That's what I'm trying to figure out. Why would you get involved in looking for him?"

Calliope tilted her head, barely able to contain her instinctive sarcasm. "Well . . . we *do* find people for a living." It was a glib truth that she hoped the others would take at face value. "And I've known him long enough to know where he's likely to be, how and where he grew up. He used to live near Harper's Ferry. First with his parents, then they died, then him and his brother and a great-aunt, then just the two of them for a while after she died, then just him, after he lost his brother."

"Harper's Ferry's nowhere near here, though," the sheriff replied. "If you were coming to visit your folks, that's fine, but if you were in a hurry, this is out of the way."

"On a . . . second message, he told me to talk to my mom." Calliope's face felt hot. "Which I know sounds weird, but I figured there might be some kind of reason."

"Detective Johnson didn't mention that part." The sheriff looked at Phyllis. "Had you two met?"

"No—" Calliope braced herself, caught in an admission she couldn't see a way to avoid. "But he came out here one time." She wanted nothing more than to pull her head down between her shoulders, but she sat straight and kept her eyes on the sheriff. "With me."

Her mother blinked. "You've never brought anyone here."

Calliope looked her way without meeting her eyes. "I

did, Mom. Three years ago." At the confused look from her mother, she added, "I didn't quite make it." Her eyes moved to the floor. "We turned around about ten miles up the road and went back."

The room was silent. Caught in the middle of something unexpected, Jim Fletcher cleared his throat and shifted his pen on the desk.

"Are we that horrible?" Phyllis whispered, her eyes fixed on her own white, intertwined fingers.

"Do you *remember*?" Calliope's voice rose. "Do you even remember the last time?"

"Settle down," her father said, his voice even, his eyes on the far wall behind Jim Fletcher.

"You . . ." Calliope turned in her chair toward him, grounding out some of her growing anger in the abrupt motion. "I'm sorry, Dad, but you weren't there, and the one time you *did* actually talk to me afterward, you told me not to come back. Not to *ever* come back."

"You *don't*—" Her father's eyes hardened, then flickered toward the sheriff. "You don't do that and expect me not to say something."

"What I . . ." Calliope's eyes went to her mother, her chest tight as she started to see the scope of what had happened— what had been done to her family's memory of her. "What did you tell him?"

"Folks," the sheriff said, "I'm not sure this is a talk anyone needs to have in public."

"Christ, Jim, you know everything," her father said. "You're the one who went looking for her."

"He . . ." Calliope felt her head tip as though she'd heard the words wrong—felt the room start to tilt as well, her breath go short as the last ten years of her life rewrote themselves as she watched. "What?" No one would look her in the face.

Finally, the sheriff cleared his throat. He brought his blue eyes up and met Calliope's. "Your mother and you had an argument," he said, his voice even and measured, as though reciting something memorized, "one of several that year." His eyes flickered to her mother, whose head was turned away, the fingers of her clenched fist pressed to her chin. "By some accounts, they occurred almost daily." He cleared his throat, glancing down at his desk for a moment, then back to Calliope. "In this case, your mother was struck . . ."

I'm sorry, a small voice cried in the back of her mind. *I told her I was sorry. I take it back.*

" . . . and you left—"

"I threw her out." Phyllis sounded like she'd been holding her breath. Neither of the men said anything, but the look they exchanged told Calliope that this was the first time they'd heard the words. "I was so"—she squeezed her eyes shut—"I was so *tired* of fighting all the time. It was so *hard.* I just—"

> *"I'm sorry, Calliope."*
>
> *"Mom—"*
>
> *"I should have done this before." She walked out of the kitchen.*
>
> *"Pack, now. Get out of my house."*
>
> *The house was quiet as she pulled the door shut behind her.*

"—gave up." Calliope's voice was barely a whisper, rough with unshed tears. The office rang with silence. "So did I."

No one spoke for over a minute. Finally, the sheriff cleared his throat. "Your parents asked me to try to find you." His eyes went to her father, then back to her. "When your sister got your letter, they decided to let things work out on their own, since you were already well out of the state."

Phyllis let out a laugh that was more than half sob. "That didn't work out so well. Our daughter hates us."

"No." Calliope shook her head, frowning at the sheriff's words more than her mother's. "No, Mom. I just . . . I got scared."

"That—" Her father sat forward in his chair, resting his elbows on his knees, and rubbed at the bridge of his nose with both index fingers. "Your logic makes my head hurt, little girl."

The childhood phrase brought a faint, sad smile to Calliope's lips. "Josh didn't really understand either." She glanced at her parents. "He really wanted to meet you. After we got back home, we—he broke up with me."

Phyllis frowned. "But you started working with him in Sept—"

"It's complicated, Mom," Calliope cut in. "The band wasn't working after he left, so I decided to get into the new business with him. He offered." She sat back in the chair and crossed her arms, feeling defensive. "It's complicated."

"That's a pretty good word for it," the sheriff said. His voice was too loud in the tension of the room, but it served to shift attention away from the revelations of the last few minutes. "The thing is, with a history like that—if you hadn't had about the best alibi you could have, 'complicated' would have turned into 'suspicious' as soon as your partner was reported missing." He looked at his desk, then back up at Calliope. "As it stands, it's just curious as all hell."

Calliope watched Jim Fletcher's face, looking for a sign that she had another enemy to worry about. "You jumping in on the investigation of the case, Sheriff?"

"Calli—" her mother began.

"No." The sheriff raised his hands. "It's a fair question, though I think the answer's pretty obvious." He leaned forward, his elbows resting on his desk, unconsciously mimicking her father, and looked at Calliope. "I've got a badge waving in my face, as you put it, telling me I should give someone a call if I get any word of Miss Calliope Jenkins anywhere in my jurisdiction." He glanced sidelong at Phyllis, but returned his attention to Calliope. "The person you're looking for is an ex-boyfriend, who's now your business partner; which might be a problem except you're only into the company for ten percent, and his ninety percent goes to his wife if he's declared dead, according to Detective Johnson." He sat back in his chair. His eyes were still on Calliope, but rather than meeting her gaze, he seemed to appraise her. "Then Calliope Jenkins shows up at her parents' house, who are friends of mine—and I hope still are after all this—and she's looking a little cat-dragged and a little wild-eyed and"—his lips narrowed—"she's favoring her right side the way someone does when it hurts like merry hell but she doesn't want the sheriff to notice." He leaned forward again, lacing the fingers of his hands together, but leaving them lying on his desk. "I'm not working on *your* case, but I suddenly have a situation dumped in my lap that could turn into a hell of a mess if I just ignore it."

Calliope felt as though the bandage wrap had tightened around her chest again. "What do you want me to tell you, Sheriff Fletcher?" Her voice was soft, not out of any particular self-control or consideration, but simply because she couldn't force any more air out. "I just want to see if I can find my friend. I only came here to see my parents. I wasn't causing any trouble, and I'm still not."

"You have to see—" Fletcher began.

"Everything you said is right," Calliope continued, "and everything I just told you, you already know." She spread her hands, palms up, in her lap. "You called Detective Johnson, and he told you everything he knew, it sounds like. That's all I've got. There's no dark secret or big truth I can pull out to make everything come clear."

"Who shot you?" her father asked.

For several seconds, Calliope continued to look at the sheriff, hoping she'd somehow dropped into one of the surreal dreams that had dogged her since the start of this trip. Jim Fletcher's eyes tracked to her father, then back to her, and he tilted his head slightly. Waiting.

Keeping still simply to contain the frantic, nervous energy in her chest, Calliope turned her head toward her father. "What?"

He didn't return her look. His eyes were on his hands, his thumb rubbing along a callus on the outside edge of his left index finger. "Who shot you?" he repeated, almost talking to himself. "Seems like that's the only big thing we don't know." The corner of his mouth drew up in a humorless smile. "Seems kind of important to me."

"Oh," Calliope replied. She turned back to face the sheriff, though her eyes were focused on nothing in particular. *This is where it ends,* she thought. *I'm not going to find Josh, or . . . anything.* There was a finality—almost release—to the thought. *I lose.*

"Calli—" the sheriff began.

"Walker." Calliope lifted her head, looking him in the eye. She heard a kind of wordless, confused sound from her mother. "Special Agent Walker shot me. In the shoulder. With his service piece."

It was Jim Fletcher's turn for his eyes to go wide. After a few seconds, they resumed their typical hooded expression, and he looked down at the small pile of notes between his hands. "When was this?" His jaw firmed, and he looked back up at Calliope.

"Two days ago." Calliope felt cold—detached from her own body. "In Colorado. Castle Rock."

The sheriff nodded. Sounds from the outer office seeped in to fill the empty space between the room's four occupants. "Guess I need to ask for your personal effects, Calli. For safe-keeping." He glanced up at her, then back at his desk. "Figure you know the deal."

"I do." Calliope pushed herself up out of her chair and dug in her pockets. She felt numb, detached from herself. After everything that she'd gone through, the enormity of what this meant for her—for Josh—was simply too much to process.

"What—" Her mother seemed to choke the word out around her own surprise. She looked at the sheriff, then Calliope, then back to Fletcher. "What are you doing?"

"It's fine, Mom." Calliope dumped her keys onto the sheriff's desk and pulled out her wallet. "That's pretty much every-thing I have on me," she said to Fletcher.

"It's *not* fine." Phyllis turned to her husband.

Her father cleared his throat. "You gonna hand my daughter over to the man that shot her, Jim?"

"Dad—"

"No . . ." The word seemed to come out of the sheriff's mouth reluctantly. He shook his head, looking away from all three of them. "No, I don't suppose I am." His gaze moved back to her father and settled on Calliope. "I *can* still lock her up for a couple days, though."

Calliope blinked, trying to keep up with the sudden shift in the conversation. "What?" Her voice sounded remarkably similar to the way her mother's had only a few seconds ago.

The sheriff leaned back, considering. "Might not be such a bad idea."

"Ex*cuse* me?" Calliope turned to look at her father, but his eyes were still on his hands; it seemed to Calliope that he didn't want to look up and see her face, or the face of his friend. She turned back to the sheriff, whose eyes were also looking away from her and her father; oddly, he was watching her mother, who sat with her arms crossed tightly over her ribs, the fingers of one fist pressed to her mouth. Calliope shook her head and picked up her keys. "No."

"Honey—" her father began.

"Not just no, but *hell* no," she cut in, glaring at Fletcher.

"Your partner's wife comes in to identify the body in the next day or so," the sheriff said. "Figure that you'll be fine if you just stay out of the way until then—let that question get answered." He sat back in the chair. "Unless you promise to stay at your parents' house that long."

"No!" At some level Calliope barely understood—one that might not have even existed a few days ago—she knew that she had to find Josh before Lauren saw the body; that it was, in Vikous's words, the way it worked.

"You didn't have any problem with this when you thought I was turning you over to Walker," Fletcher said. "Now you do, when I'm not? Doesn't make much sense."

"You wanna do your *job*, Jim? That's fine—I understand that." She pushed her chair to the side and stepped away from the desk. "You want to lock me up for safekeeping? Treat me like I need babysitting? *Fuck* you."

"Calliope Jenkins!"

"Oh, *what*, Mom?" Calliope rounded on her mother. "You want to put me in some jammies and get me a pacifier? Because I have a suggestion . . ."

"You'll want to be real careful what you say next," her father murmured. His voice was quiet, but it cut through the room. "That's your mother."

The tone of his voice, so familiar—the sound of dozens of arguments Calliope had lost as a child—cooled her ire only slightly. "What do you—"

"No." Phyllis interrupted, shaking her head. "Calli, they're just . . . you know they're not going to do that." She looked at the two men. "Jim?"

The sheriff shifted in his chair. "Your daughter's already been shot once." He jerked his chin toward the outer door of the department. "Guy that did it's out there, probably not that far away, and he still has his gun. And a badge." Her mother's face pinched with frustration.

"So you're going to—" Calliope shook her head, short and sharp. "You know what? Go ahead." Calliope turned from her mother back to the sheriff. "I changed my mind; I want you to do this."

Fletcher studied her, his own poker expression holding. "I'm not sure I believe you."

"Oh, you can believe me." Calliope bit off her words. "I'll end you."

The sheriff's eyebrows raised slightly. "Really."

"Really." Calliope motioned toward the phone. "You just got off the phone with a cop who vouched for me, and cops don't even *like* me. I live in the most litigious city on the planet, and I chase down alimony dodgers, parole skips, and guys sneaking out on big legal fees for a living. Lawyers fucking *love* me, and I can think of a half–dozen assholes who would sue not only you but the entire department into bankruptcy, for free, even if they *didn't* owe me. It would be fun for them."

Fletcher smiled slightly. "I don't think—"

"And it will take *years*," Calliope drew out the word, letting it soak up some of the anger boiling just beneath the surface. "You'll be going to hearings for so long, it'll feel like a second career." She gestured at the window of the office, ignoring the pain in her shoulder. "Lock me up. Start the nightmare."

Silence poured back into the room. Her mother was looking down at the floor, wearing a peculiar expression Calliope couldn't identify. The sheriff continued to watch Calliope's face, then turned toward her father, who finally looked up at his friend.

"Jesus, Jim," her father said, his voice still pitched low. He coughed lightly, and when he pulled his hand away from his mouth, Calliope saw a wry smile. "I don't think she likes that idea."

The sheriff pursed his lips, shaking his head. "Doesn't sound like it." To Calliope, it seemed he was about to start laughing.

"You . . ." Her mouth worked open and shut several times in exasperation.

Her mother stood up. "All right, that's enough."

"You—" Calliope was still trying to find the words for her next assault on the smirking pair of men.

"Shh." Her mother patted her arm. "Give your father a hug and I'll drive you back to the house." Calliope looked at her mother. Seeing her face, the older woman nodded, her expression a mixture of amusement and annoyance. "Yes, they're being awful. I know. Give your dad a hug."

A half-familiar car was waiting in front of the house when they pulled back into the yard, engine running and plumes of heated exhaust fogging the freezing air around its tail-lights. Her mother clicked her tongue—a mark of disapproval that Calliope thought she might not even know she did. "You should just go in the house and get your things together," she said. "I know it's later than you were hoping."

Calliope gave a halfhearted laugh. "I'm so far beyond the expected time frame, Mom, it hardly matters." She rubbed at her neck. "And I think I should talk to her, anyway."

Her mother's short, sharp laugh had more force behind it than Calliope's, but less amusement. "I'm afraid I'll have to pull you two out of a snowbank."

"I'm not going to get in a fight, Mom." Calliope let her exhaustion seep into her voice. "I'm not twelve."

"No . . ." Phyllis brought the pickup to a stop behind and to the left of the car, shut it off, and swung her door open. "But it's not just you I'm worried about. Don't let her grab your shoulder."

"Sure."

The older woman shut her door and headed toward the front of the house. As she did, the driver's-side door of the car opened and Calliope's sister got out. She leaned forward over the door, mittened hands gripping the top, and said something to her mother—a question—that Calliope couldn't make out. Phyllis didn't turn her head or even look at Sandy, but Calliope heard her give a reply. The words were short and didn't take so long to say that her mother had to slow down or stop on her way to the front door. Sandy's eyes widened at whatever was said—mostly in surprise, it seemed to Calliope. She straightened up, her hands still resting on the top of the car door, and watched their mother stump up the stairs of the house and go inside. Only after the door closed—without a single backward glance from Phyllis—did Sandy turn her attention back to Calliope.

Their eyes met through the slowly frosting front window of the truck and the swirling fog of car exhaust, and Calliope got out of the pickup.

Cold air bit at her face. The snow didn't crunch under her feet as she walked toward her sister; the temperature had dropped to the point where it almost seemed to squeak when stepped on, like Styrofoam. She stuffed her left hand into the pocket of her coat as she went, and let the right hang.

"Hi, Sandy." Calliope supposed she had the right to indigna-tion and anger and a sense of betrayal, but even the thought of mustering that kind of emotion wearied her.

"I guess you took care of the sheriff." Sandy's voice was hard and clipped, driven into a higher register by anger and other emotions that Calliope didn't particularly want to think about. Her job with Josh had given her years of experience deal-ing with people in bad situations who'd been driven to the edge of what they could handle. Her sister's voice—her whole demeanor—was uncomfortably similar. On the one hand, it gave Calliope an idea of what to expect and how to deal with it, but on the other it made the whole thing seem like someone else's problem—not her life, at all.

"There was nothing to take care of," Calliope said. "We visited for a while in his office. Then he called the friendly detectives back home and everything got straightened out."

"Back home." The corner of Sandy's mouth twitched downward. Her face was pale and pinched, her eyes hard, bright and wet. Calliope thought that on some other day, in some other situation, she might have gone to her, offered her a hug and a few whispered words—something to ease her obvious pain. Maybe. Maybe not; she and Sandy hadn't been close for a very long time—Calliope was only now starting to realize just how long it had been bad between them. Regardless, the maybes didn't matter; it was cold and the sun was going down and she'd spent a lot of time in the sheriff's office. "You mean out in the city."

Calliope gave her a short nod, unwilling to let what she was feeling show on her face. "That's my home, yes. I pay a mortgage and everything." She blew air through her teeth and watched the fog spin away from her face, mixed with the exhaust fumes. "I have a job, I have friends, and I know police detectives that tell Jim Fletcher that I'm a great help and a pleasure to work with."

"Nice trick." Sandy's voice shook. "Nice deal you must have made."

Calliope clenched her jaw, then let her instinctive anger go. After the sheriff's office, she simply didn't have the energy for another shouting match. "It's not a trick, Sandy." She pushed her hair out of her face with her right hand, wincing only slightly. "It's a life. I didn't have to call in a favor, and I didn't have to pay anyone off. I just let a friend speak for me." It was strange to refer to Darryl Johnson that way, but it felt right.

"Lucky you." Sandy made a face. "I'm sure you've got a whole city full of friends who think you're just perfect." Her voice was bitter and accusatory. "Living your perfect life with your perfect friends, doing . . . whatever you want."

Confusion furrowed Calliope's brow. "No. I don't. At all."

The laugh Sandy barked out was no kind of laugh at all. She waved her arms to either side. "Well, you never come back here, so it must be pretty. *Fucking.* Perfect!" The word sounded so unfamiliar in her sister's mouth that Calliope almost laughed, but the truth of the emotion behind the words kept her sober. It was hate she heard in her sister's voice, but also pain, and something worse.

"I'm not living some kind of dream," she said, keeping her voice quiet and even. "I'm sorry you think that, but I'm not." She shoved her hands deeper into her pockets. "I'm just living."

"You're playing detective." Sandy sneered. "And before that, you were in a band, which you made me promise never to tell Mom and Dad, 'cause god knows what they would think."

"I know; you were really good about controlling what information they got," Calliope replied. "I figured out which letter you finally showed them." She looked up at Sandy. "Once I was 'well out of the state'? A month of getting to the mailbox before Mom, without her noticing? Must have been exhausting." In her mind's eye, she could see her younger self, hunched over a cheap desk in a cheaper motel in a cruddy little town, writing letter after letter, crying less and less, slowly giving up on her family. Even that only made her sad; the anger was drained out of her. Chances lost. Time wasted. Regrets.

For a moment, Sandy's eyes went wide in shock and shame, then they hardened and went wider still. "Great!" She flung her arms over her head like a cheering sports fan. "Chalk up one more point for Calli California, *Super* Detective. Meanwhile the rest of us are here, at *home*, stuck in old houses, doing the same things we've *always* done, with the same people we've *always* done them with, where nothing ever changes and no one *ever* gets what they want."

"You make it sound like it's my fault that you didn't get to have some other life," Calliope said.

"I got married." Sandy gestured at herself, her chin jutting out. "I had three kids. I didn't get to go running off all over, or move somewhere else, or even *do* something else."

Calliope made a face. "You're absolutely right, Sandy. *You* got married, and *you* had kids. That's your life; you did that instead of something else. If you didn't get to do some other thing you wanted to do, it's because that's what you chose, and it doesn't have anything to do with me." She gestured at her sister. "It wasn't the only option you had."

"I couldn't—"

"You wouldn't," Calliope continued. "I'm sorry if you want to blame me for everything in your life that you didn't get to do, but . . . fuck off." She waved her hand through the fogging air, shoving her sister's sorry protests away like the trash they were, and almost didn't notice the twinge of pain. "Your fantasy about my life works great for you, but it's a little too Lucy Gayheart for me, so no."

"Of *course* it's not your fault," Sandy shouted. "How could it ever be—"

"You grew up," Calliope said. Her voice was calm, but it cut through Sandy's and left wintry silence behind.

"Of course I did! It happens." The angry light in Sandy's eyes dimmed. Her gaze dropped to the snow at their feet. "It just happens."

"Sure, but that doesn't mean—" Calliope looked up at the cloudless, sunset-glowing sky. "It doesn't mean giving everything up." She dropped her head, trying to see her sister's face. "It still doesn't, even now."

"Don't—don't *lecture* me." Sandy's eyes—stony chips of flint, like their father's—came back up to Calliope's. "You always have to try to *fix* everything, even when it's none of your business." Again, she gestured at herself. "I'm stuck here. We're *all* stuck here. I can't leave."

You won't, Calliope thought. *You're afraid. You hate everything that—* Then: "Oh."

Calliope's expression made her sister pause. "What?"

> *He is standing at the very top of the blocky jungle gym. It's his favorite place to stand because he can see so much of the playground and everyone can see him. He's standing at the very top.*
>
> *It's his favorite thing to do. It makes him feel safe. It makes him feel important. He can see Joshua climbing up to him, shouting something. He tries to ignore it, but Josh keeps climbing, keeps getting closer, and finally he can hear him shouting to stop, to let someone else on top.*
>
> *He gets mad. He doesn't want to stop. It's the only thing he has. He reaches out with his foot and shoves, and Josh falls away.*
> *Too far.*
> *Humpty Dumpty.*

Calliope pulled her gaze, gone nowhere in particular in the November sky, back to Sandy. "I . . ." She shook her head. "Just something about the . . . case I'm working on."

"Wonderful. I've got to go." Sandy turned, yanked open the car door, and got inside.

"Sandy—"

"I have kids to feed," her sister snapped. "I have responsibilities, and it's *way* too late to change any of that."

"Then I guess you'll always be mad about it," Calliope replied. Her only answer was a slamming car door. The car pulled past her, sucking its exhaust along with it, and left her alone in the dusk-cold in front of her parents' house. She didn't watch her sister leave; as much as she knew that nothing there was fixed—maybe never would be—she couldn't spare time on Sandy right then, couldn't shake the feeling she was looking at a puzzle to which she might have finally found all the pieces.

Still thinking, she walked up the steps and into the house to say good-bye.

"Now . . ." Her mother walked briskly into the kitchen from the laundry room near the back of the house, carrying Calliope's cleaned sweater and pretending she hadn't been watching her daughters through a window. "I don't want to get you worked up again, but are you *sure* you don't want to stay here?" She raised her hand to forestall Calliope's protest. "If your friend is out there, he'll still be there tomorrow, won't he?"

"He's still in *trouble*, Mom," Calliope explained. "He still needs help, even if he's not dead." Her hesitation before that final word was almost undetectable, even to her. "And no one else is going to help."

"Why—" Phyllis shook her head, sniffing once and blinking her suspiciously wet-bright eyes. "Too many questions." She held out the folded sweater to Calliope, who pressed it gently back toward her.

"Keep it. I'll come back and get it and try to explain everything." Calliope stepped in close and gave her a one-armed hug. "I'm sorry," she murmured.

"I'm sorry," her mother choked out. Calliope realized she was crying. She pulled back. "Mom—"

"You were sixteen," Phyllis blurted out, her face a sudden mask of raw emotion. She raised a trembling hand to cover her mouth.

"I was impossible," Calliope said.

"We were *both* impossible," Phyllis replied, blinking her eyes and turning back to her laundry. "But you're supposed to be, at that age." She sniffed, rubbing tears from her cheek with the heel of her hand. "And I should have been better."

Calliope forced a smile, tears on her cheeks. "Can we agree to let it go for now? Call it a tie." She gave her mother another hug.

Phyllis squeezed back, hard. "I don't think either one of us has ever been very good at settling for a tie," she whispered. "But okay." She stepped back, sniffed once more. "Okay." She glanced at the kitchen window and the violet-to-blue horizon. "Better get going. It's almost dark. Keep that shoulder clean and for godsakes wear a helmet with your friend's motorcycle. Better yet, rent a truck."

Calliope smiled. "I will, Mom."

"Thank you for at least lying to me about it." She smiled with tension-thin lips and walked Calliope to the door. "Are you happy out there?" she asked, the words coming in a rush.

Calliope released the doorknob and stepped back, trying to gather her thoughts. Finally, she nodded. "Yeah. I am."

"Do you have anyone?" At Calliope's look, she shrugged. "You said your partner friend found someone else. I didn't hear you say you did."

Calliope blew out a long breath. "His name is Tom and he teaches music lessons and plays in a band, so yes, I do. Sort of."

"Sort of."

"It's kind of—"

"Complicated. I've heard that word a lot today."

Calliope rocked her head from side to side, trying not to open up another complicated topic. "We kind of got into a fight before I left. I haven't had a chance to talk to him."

Phyllis crossed her arms. "Was the fight about this business with your partner?"

Calliope frowned. "No, it . . ."

She walked out of the kitchen. "Pack your stuff."

She paused. "Maybe? About my coming out here, anyway."

"Do you like him?"

Calliope looked up at the ceiling, trying to find a way to somehow sum up the relationship, and wondering if she could. "He . . ." She looked at her mother. "He gets up in the morning, earlier than he has to, and makes me coffee before I go to work."

"Every day?"

"When he wants to get on my good side."

Phyllis regarded her daughter, her arms still crossed.

Calliope's eyes narrowed slightly. "You don't think I should be doing this."

Her mother shook her head. "I think you need to do what needs doing, but don't . . ." She waved her hand, looking around the room as though searching for the right words. Calliope thought of Gerschon and hid a smile. "Don't stop living to keep a thing from changing. Things change."

"This place doesn't."

Her mother smiled as though remembering a private joke. "Do you think so?" Calliope had no answer and Phyllis opened the door. "Be safe. Come back." Calliope leaned over and gave her a kiss on the cheek.

"Love you," she whispered and stepped through the door.

Her mother watched her from the screen door until she was out to the mailbox and down the road far enough that the trees cut off vision. To Calliope, it seemed that was the way it has always been.

Watch us leave, but figure we'll get back on our own.

The packed snow and gravel of the road stretched out ahead of her between nearly empty fields.

Hope she's right.

J B P D H I A D S O Q I N Y C Y L
H R C Y L D S E E M Y A Y R D S E
H Y M E S E G Z M C R G R S E M Y
F F D C M N I O C E U R E R A Y R
D E A X D O T F B T H A S E H Y M
T I O J M D I L N L H B I V E S E
I R S T Y N I P H R I I T O G Z M
L G C Z E A C E L M O N N L C R G
R J D X W B T U E V Y C S G R S F
Q Y R   F D C

STAGE FIVE

S X T   M N I
S D R   O C E
O K M W S R M J M Y D E S J U R E
X E E T L Q E D F T E S T E R D E
R M A N H T P T M W F P G J A X D
C L O H R U G E O G P H E T O T F
E A C E L M O N N L R J D X B T H
W B T U E V Y C S G Q Y R E A S E
H A R L E Q U I N I S X T E T I O
G L O I F R I E N D S D R A J M D
G O N L O G U I D E O K M W I L N
S R M J M Y D E S J X E E T L H B
L Q E D F T E S T E R M A N I V I
H T P T M W F P G J C L O W R S T
N E G I O H D T U L O H F D Y N I
B O J N M V R W Z O Y W Q J P H R
W R H Y V S I L P J N F C W O K S

18

A DEEP, UNDULATING vibration rolled through the ground and up through Calliope's legs as she walked back to the cornfield. It took her almost a minute to recognize the sound of a dragon laughing.

"It feels like an earthquake out here," she said as she walked up to Vikous where he sat alongside a row of tall, uncut cornstalks, chuckling to himself.

"Mmm. Now you know the secret behind earthquake tremors in the middle of the Great Plains," Vikous said. He looked up and his eyebrows rose. "Someone got a makeover."

Calliope glanced down at herself. The only things that had changed were the flannel shirt and a different coat.

"I wasn't talking about the clothes." Vikous pushed to his feet. "How'd it go?" The tone of his voice made the question anything but casual.

Calliope looked back to the tree-shrouded buildings where yard lights were already coming on. "Good. My sister hates me and switches back and forth between hiding her children from me and blaming me for the fact that she has them, and my mom pulled a Jack Horner on my shoulder, but other than that it was good. Mostly."

Vikous frowned in the growing gloom. "You all right?"

Calliope turned away from the distant lights. "What was the great joke I missed?"

"YOUR GUIDE HAS A FINE TALENT FOR SHAMEFULLY PUERILE HUMOR, CALLIOPE. MORE THAN THAT WE WILL NOT SAY, AS DEFENSE TO OUR REPUTATION."

Calliope smiled into the darkness. "It's good to hear your voice again, Mahkah. I'm lucky to have such a fine traveling companion for the end of my little quest."

"YES," Mahkah replied after an odd hesitation, *"WE ARE SURE IT IS AN HONOR FOR YOU."* There was another short pause. *"SHALL WE FLY TONIGHT, CALLIOPE? TRULY FLY?"*

Something tightened in Calliope's chest even as she felt Vikous grip her arm. "That—that sounds amazing, Mahkah. Please."

The night before, Vikous had explained that the practice of staying close to the ground was useful for camouflage as well as hunting. Dragons paid a price in liberty in order to move virtually undetected.

Until Mahkah leapt into the sky that night, Calliope had had no idea how great a price it had been. The first rush of cold air and speed and distance and motion tore a whoop out of her that could have been heard clearly back at the farm and washed away the stress and worry of the day as though it had never been.

In some ways, it was the same as the night before: the heat from Mahkah's body—more than enough to warm the air around them even as they flew—didn't burn them. The strange texture of the scales, like fine sandpaper and so *un*like the smooth, frictionless skin of a reptile, seemed to cling to them and hold them in place. Even so, Calliope suspected something extra had to be keeping them from falling; in junior high, she'd tried riding one of her uncle's horses bareback after reading *Black Beauty* and had nearly broken her ankle twenty feet from the barn.

But the difference between buzzing along familiar highways at an even height and speed and what she was experiencing now was a continent-sized gap. The ground rushed away from them so quickly it felt as though the whole world had flinched. In five heartbeats, they were looking down at the sparse yard lights of half a hundred farms spread out twenty miles in every direction. The town glowed in the distance; the moving lights of night-bound vehicles crawled like lost insects down the straight paths of invisible roads. The dragon's wings stretched out on either side beyond the distance Calliope could see in the thin starlight. She shrieked with every massive downbeat of Mahkah's wings, gasping and half expecting to die; terrified, and never wanting it to stop. Minutes passed before she could breathe normally.

Almost normally.

"How is this even possible?" she gasped. Her eyes felt stretched as wide as they could go, drinking in everything around her.

Vikous, riding behind her, leaned forward. "Does it matter?"

"It's unreal," Calliope said. "It's a dream."

She felt him shift behind her and imagined his odd shrug. "If I tell you their blood is pure hydrogen, that they're incredibly massive but just about lighter than air, does it matter?"

"Is it true?"

"*Dragons* are true. It doesn't matter if they fly and breathe fire and can eat a town full of people, if they're messengers for god or a symbol of everything lost that you wish you still had. They might be any of those things, or all of 'em, and it still doesn't matter *how* they are. They *are*."

Calliope didn't say anything else, letting the sway of Mahkah's flight carry her thoughts. After a time, she realized that the deep vibration she felt in her chest was the dragon singing. It sounded like a chant. The words, if there were words, were nothing she recognized, but it sounded sad to her, and somehow brave. She began to hum along.

"WOULD YOU SING WITH US, CALLIOPE?"

"Oh!" Calliope started. "I'm sorry, Mahkah, I didn't mean to—"

"WE WOULD BE PLEASED IF YOU DID." There was a certain tension—a waiting—in the dragon's tone.

"I . . . don't know the words," Calliope replied. Her voice should have been too low for even Vikous to hear, but that didn't seem to matter.

"WORDS, WE HAVE FOUND," Mahkah replied, *"ARE NOT WHOLLY IMPORTANT."* The dragon paused, then began the song again.

Calliope listened, then hummed, then sang, and flew through the sky on a dragon. They went on in that way for hours.

It was over all too soon.

<hr>

The grassy hills were quiet and dark when they landed and Calliope slid from the dragon's back.

"Thank you, Mahkah." She spoke to the deeper shadows where the glints of the dragon's scales shone. "You've been a good friend."

"YOU ARE MOST WELCOME, CALLIOPE. OUR TIME SPENT TRAV-

ELING WITH YOU AND THE HARLEQUIN HAS BEEN SURPRIS-
INGLY PLEASANT. THANK YOU FOR SINGING ALONG DURING
THE LAST PART OF OUR JOURNEY. IT WAS . . . VERY KIND." The
great luminous eyes appeared, well above them, blinking once
against the chill, starry sky. *"IF YOU WOULD ENTERTAIN A RE-*
QUEST ON OUR BEHALF?"

Calliope glanced at Vikous. "Absolutely."

"WE WISH TO KNOW THE CONCLUSION OF THIS STORY, IF YOU
WILL," the great voice thrummed out of the ground.

"Oh." Calliope glanced at Vikous, who made a gesture that put
the decision back with her. "We . . . I . . ." She shook her head
to clear it. "You want to wait for us?" She felt odd, granting a
request to a mythical creature that she couldn't quite perceive,
but it wasn't anywhere close to the strangest thing that had
happened to her in the last week.

"IF YOU ARE WILLING."

"Sure. That would be . . ." She hesitated, then said, gravely, "I
would be honored."

"YES."

There was nothing to say in reply. Turning, Calliope walked
into the trees with Vikous, a massive shadow that might have
been a dragon watching them as they went.

"So where are we?" Calliope asked after ten minutes of what
felt very much like aimless wandering.

"Just some old farmland." Vikous nodded to indicate a hill
closer to them whose silhouetted crest was broken by a more
regular, man–made shape. "White was killed up there."

"By Mikey." Calliope's throat felt tight.

Vikous glanced at her as they walked. "By Mikey. White
told you?"

She rocked her head from side to side. "Hints," she said, then swallowed, willing her dry mouth to work. "How do you know this is the place?"

She could feel Vikous's eyes on her. "Quick explanation or complete?"

Calliope thought about the police description of Josh's body. "Quick."

"It's where it would have to have been." Vikous turned his attention back to the hill. "There's a path—used to be a driveway—up ahead. Goes up to the house."

"Not that you're going to get that far," snarled an all too familiar voice from just behind and above them. Calliope spun to face the sound

already too late

heard the gun go off, but didn't see it—was already falling. The ground rushed up and slammed the air out of her body. She saw Vikous already moving in the direction of the voice, then something thick and dank obscured her vision.

Walker got off another shot as Vikous closed in, tearing off his sweatshirt and coat to release his wings. He flexed his legs as he stalked up the slope toward Walker, and his shoes fell away in strips. Walker shot him again. Vikous ignored it, his face stretching into the hint of a smile. Another shot went off as Vikous swatted the gun away and down the slope. His left hand clamped on Walker's throat with the sound of an axe hitting soft wood.

"You've given up a lot to fit in, haven't you, 'Walker'?" Vikous said, grinning through all teeth. Blood, black against his matte white skin, trailed from two dark holes in his chest. "Don't you think it's kind of pathetic you've become exactly like the things you hate the most?" He dragged the man closer to him. "Because *I* do."

"How did you slip the oath, Vikous?" Walker strained against the grip on his throat. He pried at the choking hand, slamming his other fist into Vikous's body. Vikous grimaced and clamped his other hand around Walker's throat as well.

Robbed of his voice, Walker clawed with both of his hands, straining forward. Rather than trying for a mirroring choke-hold, his fingers scrabbled across Vikous's chest until his fingers found purchase in the two bullet holes and dug at the wounds. Vikous's face twisted, his lips drawing back and back in a shark's grimace until he threw Walker away from him, roaring. Walker went with the throw and rolled to his feet a dozen yards away. Vikous eyed him, then tore his gloves away to reveal the claws beneath. "Let's do this right," he murmured.

"Why are you fighting me?" The sharp angles of Walker's face bent into a scowl. "The girl's dead. Even if she weren't, she would fail you, just like the last, and the last, and the *last*." He sneered. "And with this one, you've practically made sure of it. At least my way, we won't lose anything."

"We?" Vikous sneered. "You talk like you're one of us. You're a joke."

"Said the clown." Walker massaged his throat, stepping to the right.

"If we never risk anything, we never *change*. If we never change, we all *die*." Vikous circled the whip–thin man. "Life means risk. Risk means letting them in, to do what they want."

"And letting them do as they choose means we're all dead anyway," Walker barked.

"Choices made by following instructions aren't even choices—they don't mean anything." Vikous wiped blood from his chest and flicked it away. "You know that as well as I do. You don't get to play your new role with *me*." Vikous stretched his arms away from his body in a gesture of harmlessness. "Who am I?"

"A liar by gift." Walker spat on the ground as he circled. "You try to bridge the gap between two worlds that should never touch. You offer hope where there is none. That's why I gave up on doing it the old way. Everything ends."

Vikous's smile returned. "Exactly," he said, and leapt.

Human eyes could never have tracked the speed of the blows exchanged. When the flurry slowed, it found the two locked in another clench. Vikous's body was laced with welts; Walker's clothing hung in bloody tatters. Vikous's smile was, if anything, broader.

"Why are you *fighting* me?" Walker nearly screamed. "You are the guide. It accomplishes nothing."

"I'm not fighting, you moron," Vikous murmured. "I'm stalling." He shoved away from Walker.

"For *what*?"

Gunshots tore the night apart, and Walker dropped to his knees. He twisted toward the sound, and another shot punched through the air, knocking him to the grass.

"Hi," Calliope said, walking up the slope. "Those two were for the holes in Vikous."

Walker sneered. "You can't possibly think it matters if you kill—"

Calliope shot him in the shoulder. Walker grunted as though hit with a tree. "I think I decide what matters right now since I have the fucking gun, *asshole*." She edged toward Walker, the weapon extended, tipped her chin toward him. "That last one was for me."

Walker shook his head like a wet dog and glared up at Calliope. "You don't have the faintest idea what's at stake here."

"I know enough."

Walker sneered. "You'll fail as you think you're winning."

"I am *going* to bring Joshua back, you son of a bitch."

Walker sneered. "Exactly," he said through bloody teeth. Calliope stared at him, shook her head, took a step forward, and kicked him in the face. He dropped to the ground, tried to rise, and went still.

Vikous slumped to the ground. "Kinda wish you'd gotten up there a little faster than—" Calliope whirled, leveling the gun at him. He watched the weapon with an expressionless face. "What are you planning to do with that?"

The gun shook. Calliope's eyes, like those of Gluen's security guard so many days before, were wide enough to show the whites all the way around. *"What are you?"*

Vikous glanced down at himself. Enormous taloned feet gripped the ground. Blood dripped from his clawed fingers. He looked back up at Calliope, a leathery, clown-faced, albino parody of an angel with leathery bat wings, truncated and tattered and pale white under the moonlight, the stuff of forgotten myths and nightmare. "I'm your guide, Calli."

"Don't call me that." The gun didn't move. "What *are* you?"

"I have a hundred names," Vikous said. His voice was calm. "A hundred things that people call my kind, because we don't have a name of our own. We hid it a long, long time ago, and we can't have it back." He looked up at her, his plastic-black eyes shining. "I'd tell you if I could, Calli, but I can't."

"Don't *call* me that!" The barrel of the gun shook.

"Sorry." He sniffed, looking around at the torn ground as though searching for a place to lie down. "Look, shoot me."

Calliope twitched. "What?"

Vikous shrugged, his tattered wings shifting behind him, finally free of their confinement. "Or don't, but you can't waste any more time on this. You have to go, with or without me." He frowned. "You're okay, right?"

Calliope lowered the gun a fraction. "I thought he'd shot me again."

"Yeah, sorry about that. Knocking you down was the only thing I could think of. Did you hurt your shoulder?"

Calliope shook her head. "I'll live, but you're—" She cut herself off. "God, how do you *do* that?"

Vikous blinked, assuming his most innocent expression. "Do what?"

Calliope glared. "Go . . . go put your coat on."

Vikous quirked an eyebrow. "I can move?"

"Yes. Coat. Please." Vikous pushed himself up, grimacing at the ache of the blows he'd taken, hissing through his teeth as the movement pulled at the open wounds high on his chest. Calliope frowned again. "You sure you're all right?"

"Of course I'm not all right; I was shot. Twice. Protecting *you*." Vikous shook his head. "You and your questions."

Calliope tilted her head. "Remember that I still have the gun."

"Good point." He tugged his coat on as best he could, wincing. "Ready for the end of this?"

"I hope so."

"Me too. Can I lean on you?"

She made a face. "You're still dripping blood."

"Right."

Together they walked, still talking, toward the distant house on the hill, oblivious to the dark shadow that moved through the trees behind them.

"I'm kind of surprised you didn't kill him," Vikous said.

Calliope looked at him. "Should I have?" Vikous shrugged and winced. Calliope turned her attention back to the dark path. "I'm tired of death," she said finally. "It seems like this whole thing has been about death, even when it doesn't have anything to do with what's going on. Did I tell you my dad had cancer?"

Vikous shook his head. "Is he all right?"

Calliope made a face. "I *guess* so. It's impossible to tell; he doesn't *look* all right." She looked at Vikous. "But you see what I mean? Joshua died, you died I guess, Mahkah nearly ate us, Dad had surgery and maybe treatments for cancer and no one even *told* me until I showed up at the door with a bullet hole in my shoulder. My sister doesn't want me around her family, like I'm carrying death around with me, and I'm not sure she's wrong."

"It's not you." Vikous adjusted his coat. "This . . . all this right now is just life. One of the things that happens in life is death. That's part of it." He grimaced as he stepped over a tree stump. "Granted, you've got a few more of the exciting parts going on right now than normal."

"Exciting," Calliope deadpanned. "I'm so excited I can barely breathe most of the time."

"I'd say that's my line."

"Give it—"

"Good evening and well done, my dear," called out another voice from the shadow of the house. Calliope recognized it even before the speaker's bulging eyes loomed out of the darkness. Faegos stepped out of the deeper shadow followed by the tall, swathed figure of Kopro. "I believe we have a bargain to conclude," the shrunken man continued. "Something you can provide me, in exchange for something I can provide you."

He gestured, and Joshua White walked out of the shadows.

19

"HEY, CALLI," JOSHUA said.

Calliope's heart contracted, pushing the air out of her in a rush. *Give it time, I was going to say,* she thought. *That's funny.* She stared, her mouth slightly agape, scanning his calm face, eyes that held a hint of sadness or regret . . .

Except that it wasn't him.

Calliope's eyes narrowed. The thin light of the half-moon didn't reflect off his skin. There were odd shadows across his face that she realized were the siding on the house directly behind him.

"You're . . ." she began.

"A ghost, yeah," he finished, making a familiar gesture with both hands that made her heart thump painfully. "A memory might be more accurate, but I'm not really sure." He frowned. "It's hard to concentrate sometimes."

"You're not here?" she asked.

"*I'm* here," Joshua said, "at least for a little while longer. The body's not. That's been lying on a slab in Harper's Ferry for about a week now." His eyes, such as they were, became distant. "They did an autopsy last Monday. Lauren flies in to identify it tomorrow." He looked at the ground. "I think that'll be hard on her."

Calliope watched him, aching with the need to reach out and touch his arm. "You . . . can I . . ." She made a helpless gesture. "Can I help? Is there—"

He shook his head, then: "Can you watch her?" He got a peculiar expression on his face, one that Calliope always associated with lost causes and hopeless battles. "Can you keep an eye on her? I can't."

"Oh, but you *can*, Mister White," Faegos interjected before Calliope could reply. "At least if our intrepid Miss Jenkins has anything to say about it." He was sitting on a rusted bucket near an old rain gutter, his legs carefully folded over each other at the knee. "She likes to have a say in everything that goes on, you know."

"That, I know." Joshua smiled, though his expression when he looked toward Faegos was anything but amused. "Always have to be the hero, don't you, Cal?"

Calliope blinked back tears, or memories, her head bowed. "I should have taken you to meet my folks."

He smiled, looking puzzled. "Where'd that come from?"

She shook her head, sniffing. "I don't know. It's just something I realized. You would have . . . well, my mom would have liked you."

He tilted his head. "You went to see your family?"

"You told me to."

Joshua raised an eyebrow. "Since when has my saying so made any kind of a difference?"

"Since you started leaving me voice mail from beyond the grave." Behind her, Vikous cleared his throat. Calliope ignored him.

"I've picked up a few tricks," Joshua said.

"I guess so."

He took a few steps closer to Calliope and lowered his voice. "How'd it go?" Calliope raised her hand, level to the ground, and wobbled it back and forth. Joshua raised a pale eyebrow in response.

Calliope sighed. "It was okay. Mom and I talked. Dad too. Sandy . . ." She quirked the corner of her mouth downward in a sour expression. "We get along about as well as we ever did, I guess."

Joshua frowned. "You should get that straightened out, with you and your sister." He raised his hand. "And don't tell me it's complicated."

Calliope's eyes narrowed, the old bitterness flaring up so quickly she couldn't stop herself. "More family advice from the guy with no parents and a brother he hasn't seen in fifteen years." Joshua's expression changed—she saw the barriers she'd forced him to build go up, and shame washed over her. "Oh god, I'm sorry."

He shook his head, dismissing the slight but avoiding her eyes. "It's okay."

"It's *not*, you're . . . *god*, I can't believe I said that."

"Hey," Josh said, his voice clear and not at all ghostlike. Calliope looked up at his too-clear face. "It's okay." He smiled, his face full of affection, if not amusement. "It's all okay."

Calliope shook her head. "It's not. You're dead and I'm dredging up ancient history."

"Not that ancient," he said, glancing back at the house. "Anyway, isn't that what you're supposed to do when someone dies?"

"I don't know." She sniffed, her eyes stinging. "I've never had anyone die on me until now."

"Well, trust me, this is normal."

"Said the ghost of my best friend." Her forced laugh caught halfway, choked out by a short sob she smothered with her hand, squeezing her eyes shut, then opening them wide to force the tears away, shaking her head side to side as if she could banish her own grief.

Joshua started to reach out to her, then looked at his hand and lowered it. "Okay, it's not normal, but the ancient-history-dredging part is. Calli, it's all right."

"It is *not*, and quit saying that." She glared at him, her eyes damp. "Someone *killed* you, probably because of me."

He frowned. "How do you figure that, master detective?"

"I've got some sort of quest I'm on and it all started when you . . . when you called." She looked down. "Feels like you died just to get me moving."

"That's a little egocentric, isn't it?"

Calliope looked up. "What?"

"You got my message, right?" He tipped his head. "The one I left with that fat—"

"Gluen," Calliope interjected. "Yeah."

"I *told* you what happened."

"Did you?" Calliope's voice sounded shrill in her own ears. "Because it didn't make much sense to me." Her voice dropped, mimicking his: "I had to do this, Calli . . ."

"Try to fix it." Josh's face was etched with grief of his own. "I made a promise."

"What *happened?*" Calliope demanded, asking the only question she'd really ever wanted answered.

He looked away. "It was a private thing."

"But you called *me.*" Her left hand pressed against the ache in her chest.

"I'm really sorry about that." He looked up into the starry night. "I was making my best play at the end, hoping it would pay off."

Calliope blinked her damp eyes. "Did it?"

Joshua said nothing.

The corners of Calliope's mouth turned down. She searched Joshua's face, desperate for some kind of affirmation. *"Did it?"*

"We still have to see about that, don't we, my dear?" said the dusty voice to her right.

Calliope turned toward Faegos, rubbing at her eyes. "Yeah. Sure. We can fix this. Do your deal."

Joshua turned his attention to the two of them. "What deal?"

"I will be happy to, once you provide your payment." Faegos ignored Joshua's question. "I would like . . ." He wet his lips. "Your companion's name."

Calliope frowned. "Don't jerk me around. You knew that already, the last time we met."

"Oh, goodness me." Faegos sighed, frowning in mock disapproval and leaning to the side to look over Calliope's shoulder. "You really have been shamefully lax in your duties," he said to Vikous, then turned back to Calliope. "I'm not talking about your guide, my poor girl." The thin point of his tongue edged out of his toothless mouth, sliding over his narrow lips. "I'm speaking of your companion. The dragon." His bulging eyes were bright.

"Dragon?" Joshua said.

Calliope blinked. "Mahkah?" Her eyes narrowed in confusion. "What does Mahkah have to do with it?"

Faegos's perfect posture slumped somewhat, his eyes flicking reproachfully toward Vikous. "Your companion has everything to do with 'it', as far as I am concerned. I want you to give me its name."

Calliope frowned. "I just did."

"*Earth and sea*," Faegos shouted, looking to the sky. He closed his protuberant eyes and lowered his chin to his chest. He stayed in that position for several seconds, then looked up. "I apologize for my outburst. I forget that nearly every significant element of this world has carefully avoided your attention."

The trials and wonders of her trip—of which the desiccated garden gnome in front of her knew next to nothing—played through her mind. Calliope's face tightened. "I've done everything I was supposed to do," she growled, her voice a fair match for Vikous's. "If you can't claim your prize after all that, it's not *me* failing."

Faegos hesitated, his bulbous eyes narrow. "Indeed." He clasped his hands over his folded knees and leaned slightly forward. "I want the dragon's *true* name, Calliope, the only one of any significance."

Calliope frowned. "I don't . . ." She glanced at Joshua, whose own eyes were wide and shifting back and forth between her and Faegos. "I don't know it."

Faegos's eyes narrowed as much as was possible, his face pressing forward a scant few inches as he studied Calliope. His head tilted. "Indeed, you do not." He sighed and stood with a nimbleness that belied his frail form. "That is a shame. I believed there was real potential in you."

"But"—Calliope looked from Faegos to Joshua, scrambling desperately for some way to salvage the situation before it spiraled out of her grasp—"you—"

"I think we're both well aware of the limits of our agreement, my dear," Faegos said. "You do not have what I want."

"I—"

"PERHAPS WE CAN BE OF SOME ASSISTANCE IN THAT REGARD," said a voice that thrummed out of the ground.

Calliope jerked toward the sound and the flickering darkness that loomed in that direction. "Mahkah?"

"YOU WILL FORGIVE US OUR INTRUSION. WE HEARD THE SOUNDS OF WEAPONS AND CHOSE TO SEE HOW THE STORY UNFOLDED OURSELVES."

"Excellent." Faegos's toothless mouth stretched in a pleased smile. "All is not lost."

"YOU MAY HAVE OUR NAME IF YOU DESIRE IT, CALLIOPE."

"Calli," Joshua said. "What are you doing?"

"Shut up," Calliope said without turning. Her eyes narrowed as she looked into the half-seen movements of the shadows. "Why?"

Silence greeted her question. Then: *"WE REVILE THE CREATURES THAT CRAWL, LIKE YOU, ACROSS THE SURFACE OF OUR WORLD, BUT THE IRONY OF OUR NATURE IS SUCH THAT WE PROGRESS—WE CHANGE—ONLY BY SHARING OUR EXISTENCE WITH YOU."* Something in the darkness shifted. *"BY KNOWING YOU, WHO SHARES HER SOUL WITH THE WORLD WHEN SHE SINGS, WE HAVE GROWN BEYOND WHAT WE HAD LONG THOUGHT OUR PINNACLE. WE DO NOT FORGET SUCH GIFTS."*

Calliope drew a shaking breath at the dragon's words. The weight of them—the sheer, terrifying *responsibility*—bowed her head until her chin rested on her chest. "Thank you, Mahkah," she murmured, and turned to Vikous; tattered, bloody, and most of all, silent Vikous. He watched her, his black eyes filled with reflected stars. "I know what the true name does, don't I?" she asked.

Vikous nodded. "I suppose you do."

"It is power, my dear girl." Faegos exhaled into the night air, his eyes half lidded. "The power to *know* a thing; to bind it, if desired." He straightened his posture and adjusted his jacket, catching Calliope's expression. "To call it into service, as I imagine you and your guide did."

Calliope shook her head, frowning. "No . . . it wasn't like that." She looked into the darkness. "We got its attention, but we didn't bind it." She hesitated. "We didn't bind you, did we, Mahkah?"

"WE ASSUME THE QUESTION IS RHETORICAL."

Calliope's mouth quirked, glancing at Vikous. "Absolutely." She turned to Faegos. "Why do you want the name?"

Faegos smiled, his lips pressed together. "It is in my nature to suss out the mysteries of the universe. The dragon is one such mystery that lies unknown to me. I would not have it so. I must understand it. I must *know* it."

One of Calliope's eyebrows lowered. "And that's it."

"That, as you say, is 'it'." Faegos folded his hands together.

"You don't have to do this, Calli."

Calliope started. Hearing Joshua's voice was still a shock. She turned to him, her eyes bright. "Oh"—she drew in a long, shaking breath and let it out—"I know." She kept her eyes locked on to Joshua's as she spoke. "Mahkah?"

"WE ARE HERE, CALLIOPE. WE ARE ALWAYS HERE."

"I know," she said, her voice barely above a whisper. "I'm sorry."

"IT IS ALL RIGHT, CALLIOPE. YOUR KIND HAVE ALWAYS HAD

THE POWER TO MAKE OR UNMAKE OURS. AT OTHERS' HANDS, IT WOULD SHAME US, BUT WE WILL GIVE OVER WILLINGLY TO YOU."

"Thank you." She searched the darkness for the shadowy, sinuous bulk behind the dragon's lantern eyes, trying to see some further detail—something she could remember—but her eyes shifted away; her mind wandered.

The first rush of cold air and speed and distance and motion.

Wings stretched out on either side in the thin starlight.

The dragon singing, sad and brave.

"They might be any of those things," she murmured, "or all of them." She raised her voice. "Thank you, Mahkah." She swallowed past a lump in her throat. "But no."

"YOU ARE SURE?"

"What?" Faegos's rasping voice rose in surprise and anger.

"I'm afraid I'm going to have to reject your bargain, Mister Faegos," she said, her voice driven high and shaky by the emotion caught behind it. "The cost is too much for me."

Joshua smiled. That helped.

Faegos snarled. "The cost is irrelevant to you, girl." He leveled a shaking finger in Mahkah's direction. "I want that thing."

"It's not a *thing*." Calliope was looking at Joshua, but heard Vikous's words in her head. "It's a dragon. There are some things that you don't *get* to understand—that you can't *know* without sucking the life out of them." She looked down at Faegos, then away. "Magic things." Her eyes flicked to Vikous. "Hidden things."

Faegos moved—too fast—to stand directly in front of her, his face tilted up at hers. "That's very poetic and noble, but you forget who I *am*, you ridiculous trollop," he hissed. "Do you think this is a *game*?"

She glared down at him, her grief and anger overriding whatever fear she might have felt. "I'm letting my best friend . . ." She shook her head once, sharply. "It's not a game."

Faegos's eyes bulged. "We had an arrangement, and I will have your end of the bargain or you *will* pay a far different price."

Calliope took a step back, remembering Vikous's body lying crumpled in the diner.

The sound of a throat clearing, like a hundred trees falling, broke through Calliope's reply. *"KOPROPHAGOS."*

The tiny man's face jerked toward the sound.

"WE KNOW THAT YOURS HAS BEEN A LONG AND STORIED EXISTENCE. PERHAPS EVEN UNIQUE IN THE HISTORY OF YOUR KIND." Mahkah's voice was a rich, deep burr in the grassy earth, rattling the windows of the old house. *"IT WOULD BE A TRUE SADNESS TO CUT SUCH A THING SHORT, BUT SUCH SADNESS WOULD **PASS**. HAVE A CARE."*

Faegos trembled, clearly torn, looking from the shadows to Calliope. "I should have—" he began, but clamped his mouth shut. His eyes blazed, glowing with an internal light in the darkness.

With that, he was gone.

"Creepy little guy," Joshua said.

Calliope turned back to her friend. "I'm sorry."

"It's all right."

"I just—"

"It's all right."

"I can't . . . it's not . . ." Calliope gestured into the darkness behind her, tears streaming down her face as she looked at Joshua. "You're really dead, right?"

Joshua nodded. Calliope returned the nod automatically, blinking and looking around her. "It's not *fair.*" Her arms hung at her side, unable even to embrace her lost friend. Silent tears ran down her face.

"If it helps, I think you're doing the right thing," Joshua said.

"But you're *dead,*" Calliope forced out.

Joshua gave just the hint of a smile. "It happens. There were even good reasons, I think."

"What reasons?"

He shook his head, his expression troubled. His eyes shifted over Calliope's shoulder. "Hello, Vikous. Good to finally meet you."

"White. You too." Vikous stepped closer to Calliope, his presence a surprising comfort.

"You did a good job. They said you would."

"Did they?" The corners of Vikous's mouth drew down as his eyebrows rose, the very picture—or caricature—of bemused surprise. "Huh."

Joshua smirked, as if the two shared some private joke. His expression, posture—everything about him was just as he always had been, so sharp and immediate the pain in Calliope's chest made her gasp.

But it wasn't him anymore, and never would be. It was a memory.

"So . . ." Joshua turned back to Calliope. "I've got to go."

Calliope blinked. "Oh god, I'm sorry."

"*Stop that.*" Joshua frowned for the first time. "My play paid off." He smiled again, as though hearing his own words for the first time. "I'm proud of you."

"You . . ." Despite herself, Calliope felt the faintest of smiles touch her lips. "What? How—"

Joshua White was gone.

~~~

Calliope felt Vikous's hand on her shoulder. "You ready for the end?"

Breath escaped her lungs in something like a laugh of disbelief. "I think I might be all ended out for the night." It had been two days, she realized, since she had had a real night's sleep.

"It's just this. Then we're done." He gestured to the old house, just beyond where Joshua had been.

She sniffed, wiping at her face. "What's in there?"

"Answers." Vikous watched the front door. "Monsters."

20

INSIDE, IT WAS dark, but Calliope could see light in one of the rooms just off the front hall and continued forward. Her face was reddened and blotchy, but composed; the highs and lows of the night had left her calm, if not wholly at peace. The short hall opened into a living room with a dusty and broken couch in the center, facing a small fireplace.

Dark mold stains streaked the walls, but Calliope could still make out the wallpaper, exactly how Josh had described it to her years ago.

"Your mom put it up on a Sunday afternoon," she murmured, "while you and your brother were in town with your dad." She smiled, sad and distant. "She was so proud of herself that she never took it down or painted over it, even when she realized a few months later that she hated the pattern."

She turned back toward the rest of the house, walking from room to room like someone visiting a museum; hearing her friend's voice, seeing his wild gestures as he told her stories about his childhood.

Finally, she climbed the stairs to the second floor and turned to the room where two brothers had lived until the day their parents had died.

A slim figure faced the moonlit window of the room, looking down at the driveway where Josh had said good-bye. Things unseen gibbered in the shadows, whispering words in children's voices.

Not everyone who disappears is kidnapped, she thought, *and some things are worse than being eaten by a dragon.*

"Hi, Mikey."

"You made him go away," he said, his words echoed by the things within the shadows of the room.

"Not exactly," Calliope said, and the boy turned.

The right side of his face was perfectly normal. The left side was frozen, locked in a permanent scream, the skin a sickly, concrete gray. His left arm was knotted and brutalized, ending in a shredded claw masquerading as a hand. On another night, in another place, Calliope might have recoiled. Gasped. Here, she simply looked.

"He said you would," the thing said. "He thought you'd do better than I did. It was the deal he made. If *you* let him go, I had to let him go." His right eye blinked, and he looked down at the worn floorboards. "'Round his brow encrimsoned laurels waved, And o'er him shrilly shrieked the demon of the grave.'" He looked back at Calliope. "I guess that's me."

The whispers in the walls of the house echoed his words, repeated them, and added in things he had never said, turning them into a kind of jump rope nursery rhyme, but clumsy and uneven, the voices of childlike things that didn't exactly know how to be children.

"I never thought you'd give him up," the boy-thing said. "You must have a lot of friends." He sounded wistful. Envious.

"No." Calliope folded her arms. "I don't."

"Then why did you let him go?" The boy's left brow dropped into a confused frown. The echoes repeated the question. "You could have—"

"Josh is dead." Even as she said it, Calliope felt the words take on the weight of reality for the first time. The whispering voices went utterly silent.

He searched her face with his eyes, one bright and blue, one bloodshot and pale. "You couldn't—" The echoes began again. "Stop it," he shouted, and the sounds cut off.

"I wouldn't." Calliope's response drew his attention back to her. "They wanted something from me that wasn't mine to give." She watched him, seeing all the things she'd been trained to see in the guilty. "But you know that, don't you?" He turned away from her, but she continued. "You did all this once, too."

"I was the last one, before you." He sounded like a child, caught doing something he knew was wrong.

"You gave up your companion." Calliope watched the claw that had been his left hand flex in and out of a fist. "They need people to . . ." She shook her head, still not quite sure how the hidden things worked. "Remember them. Keep them from . . . fading. Whatever. You gave them up."

"Magic goes away." He was talking to the shadows, not Calliope. The words sounded worn out and flat, as though he'd used them many, many times. "It just happens. Piece by piece, it dies. It's not my fault. People die and dreams die and hope dies and magic dies and the world just . . . comes in and covers it up." His jaw clenched. He looked for all the world like a toddler about to throw a fit. "I gave up some of it, but it would have gone out *anyway*. It's not my *fault*."

"What was it?"

He shook his head. "It doesn't matter if I tell you. You can't remember it. No one can. I traded it away and it doesn't exist anymore." His face sagged. "She was so pretty. It was the hardest—"

"What did you *get*?"

He flinched, as though she'd shouted. The glance he gave her was more fear than anything else. "My parents were gone. Josh was—" He cut himself off. The mobile half of his face twisted into a sneer. "I didn't want to be alone anymore." He flung his clawed hand at the crawling shadows of the room, filled with giggling whispers—the sound of a classroom snickering at one child's misfortune. "Jackpot." He turned back to her. "I wanted my mom and dad. I wanted *us*." His voice was an adolescent's on the verge of tears. "Josh kept saying we had to be enough for each other, but we *weren't*. I got a chance to fix it, but it was *worse*. And then Josh came." His one blue eye was shining and wet, the other hard and staring. "I killed him. It was me."

Calliope's heart twisted in her chest, trying to stop. Once. Forever. "I figured that."

The boy-thing looked at her for another few seconds, then looked away. "I don't know why he came."

"You're a liar." Calliope swung the words like a club and felt a sad sort of triumph as Mikey's head jerked back in her direction. The whispers in the shadows hissed. "He came because he found out you weren't gone. He came because he wanted to help, because he promised." She tipped her head, remembering one of Josh's stories. "You put yourself on top of the jungle gym again and waited for him to climb up after you."

"I wanted someone to stay with me," he muttered.

"You wanted Josh."

"Why *not*?" The boy sneered with the side of his face that wasn't locked in a cry of pain. "He came, just like I knew he would. He always had to be so *right* all the time." He flexed his clawed hand. "I couldn't let him go."

"And you couldn't just leave?" she asked. "Go back with him?"

"Like *this*?" He gestured at his face. "With what I did? With what I know?" He shook his head. "I can't leave."

You won't, Calliope thought, feeling a sick kind of recognition. *You're afraid.*

Mikey stared at the ground.

"You knew he'd want to find you if he thought he could. He wanted a family." Her voice was faint, even to her own ears. "That's all he ever really wanted." She looked back up at Mikey and waited until his eyes rose to meet hers. "For the longest time after he told me about you, I thought you were dead." The young man–thing looked away. "The way he said he'd 'lost' you, it always seemed like you'd died, not disappeared." She looked around the room, trying to imagine what it had been like when Josh had been a boy. "He loved you a lot. He used to talk about you all the time."

"But he stopped."

"He stopped," she agreed. "Yeah. You left him with no family—"

His eyes widened. "*You don't—*"

"He had to make a new one," she finished, not even listening to his protest.

"He gave up." The boy's voice was bitter.

"He grew up." Calliope wanted to slap him. "Things change. Everything changes."

"We didn't have to." Mikey's voice was stiff with anger, but behind it Calliope could hear a child's cries of denial. "I didn't."

"You—" She looked around the room. Things both her mother and Vikous had said twined round one another in her mind, sounding very much the same. "Actually, I think you're right, Mikey. That's how you get to a place where you could kill your own brother for company—by never moving." Her eyes traveled over his terror-twisted face, the knotted arm and grasping, clawed hand, seeing it as a whole for the first time. "You really are a monster," she breathed. "More than any of the others."

Tears ran from the boy's one good eye. "So kill me." His eyes drifted down to her coat pocket. "You've got a gun, you can kill me."

The smallest frown creased Calliope's brow at the pleading note in his voice. Her eyes narrowed, searching the half of Mikey's face that was still human. "You . . ." she said, but her voice trailed away, her head tilted, as though she was trying to catch the faintest of sounds. The puzzle-image she'd assembled—which she'd thought complete outside her parents' house—was still missing a piece, and as she stood there, it dropped into place. Her eyes refocused. Hardened. "No."

Despair twisted the boy's face, pulling it into an almost perfect mirror of the frozen left side. "*Why?*" he said.

"You didn't want Josh," she repeated. "You didn't want company."

"What are you talking about?" Mikey pleaded. "Why would I—"

"You wanted someone to kill you." She cut through his protests, her voice flat and hard. "You wanted to end. You wanted
to get away from what you'd done, because you broke everything and you're too"—she shook her head, her mouth
twisting—"*weak* . . . to fix it."

"And you hate me." The boy-thing's voice was shaking.
"Right? You hate me for what I did, for what I am." Tears ran
down the crags of his face. "I'm . . . Why . . ."

Calliope stared into his eyes. "I could lie, and say it's because
Josh loved you, and would want to give you another chance,
but that's not it." She looked on utter despair in his face, and
didn't flinch. "The truth is you killed my friend." She turned
and walked toward the front of the house. "And letting you
live is the worst thing I can do."

The boy screamed as she left, until the echoes in the shadows
drowned him out.

Epilogue

"**THANK YOU FOR** *TRAVELING WITH US A WHILE LONGER, CALLIOPE,*" Mahkah's voice rumbled.

"Thank you for taking me this far," Calliope replied. She stood with Vikous a quarter mile outside the edge of an almost-familiar town.

"*SHOULD YOU EVER COME TO THE HIDDEN LANDS AGAIN, DO NOT FEAR OUR AWESOME PRESENCE.*"

She smiled. "I won't." She glanced at the lightening sky. "You should go, though. It's almost dawn."

"*WE SHALL, BUT WE HAVE ONE MORE GIFT FOR YOU.*"

"What's th—"

And suddenly, she could see the dragon.

"Long week." Vikous walked alongside Calliope, who could only manage a small chuckle in reply. At the edge of the motel parking lot, they both stopped and turned to face the other.

"You did good, Calli," Vikous said.

"Every generation needs a fairy tale." She smiled, and it felt strange and familiar. "I got an amazing one." She narrowed her eyes at Vikous. "You could have told me more."

"Eh." Vikous shrugged. "You knew all the important stuff."

Calliope's eyebrow quirked downward. "Do I see you again?"

Vikous tilted his head, looking away. "If you like."

"How do—"

"You'll know."

Calliope nodded, then stepped forward and put her arms around Vikous as best she could; he grunted.

"Cripes, we've both been shot—"

"Shut up and give me a hug."

They both squeezed as tight as they dared, then released their hold and stepped back. "Okay," Vikous said. "Go on. Move."

"Bossy."

"Hey." He raised a finger once more concealed by his glove. "Trust the guide."

⌁

The key Vikous had given her worked in the motel door's lock. Her Jeep was, miraculously, still outside.

The room was normal. Empty. Calliope walked around the bed and sat down next to the phone. She stared at it for several minutes, then picked up the handset and dialed. Seconds passed before someone answered on the other end of the line.

Calliope straightened, brushing the hair out of her face. "Mom? Hi. It's me." She listened for a second, nodding. "No, yeah, it's okay," she said. "I'm all right."

She turned, leaned against the head of the bed, and looked out of the window of the motel room. The sun was rising. She thought of the dragon. She remembered Josh.

"I'm all right."

Acknowledgments

THERE IS AN order to these things. I owe thanks . . .

. . . to Deanna Knippling, who issued the challenge that started everything.

. . . to Jackie Faulk, who asked that this story be a little different.

. . . to Chris Baty, who built the arena.

. . . to my first readers, Lori, Virg, and Stacy, who found *Hidden Things* in its hidden place, read it as I wrote it, and informed me that I must finish or Face Consequences.

. . . to David C. Hill, who rolled a similarly sized boulder up an equally steep hill and still managed to shout encouragement loudly enough for me to hear.

. . . to Kate Testerman, who asked if she could read it, told me I had to get an agent for it, helped me find one, and married me (in roughly that order).

. . . to Shana Cohen, best of agents, dispenser of unvarnished truth, and mildly amused voice of reason.

. . . to Kate Nintzel, my editor at Harper Voyager and POV Buddha, who said, "I love it, now give me seventy-five more pages," and (eventually) made me glad I did.

. . . to Laurie McGee, my copyeditor and fellow expat Midwesterner, without whom I would look more than a bit silly.

. . . and to my mom, dad, and sister, who made it incredibly difficult to write believably about a dysfunctional, unsupportive family. I love you guys.